J.R.R
UNIVERSITY

Other books by David Bischoff

Philip K. Dick High
Nightworld
The Vampires of Nightworld
Ship of Ghosts, Ship of Dreams
Tripping the Dark Fantastic
H.P. Lovecraft, R.F.D.

J.R.R. TOLKEIN UNIVERSITY

DAVID BISCHOFF

WILDSIDE PRESS
Berkeley Heights, New Jersey

Copyright © 2000 David Bischoff.
All rights reserved.

J.R.R. Tolkein University
An original publication of
Wildside Press
P.O. Box 45
Gillette, NJ 07933-0045

www.wildsidepress.com

FIRST EDITION

To Karl Gebhardt and Steven Jent

Chapter One

On Tuesday I ran an ad in *Daily Variety* that read:

> HUNGRY WRITER looking for Writer's Associate Position. Good typist, computer knowledge, excellent story and dialogue skills. Will work CHEAP, will work GOOD.

Along, of course with my phone number.
No calls.
On Thursday the ad was amended.

> STARVING WRITER IN BARREL looking for Writer's Assistant Job. Excellent typist, computer genius, brilliant story and dialogue skills. Will remember this favor after scrabble to peak of Hollywood Power Echelon!

Same phone number.
That came out Thursday morning.
On Friday I got the call from the elf.

I'm glad my agent never saw the ad, although I did have to eventually tell her about them to explain how I got the job offer she negotiated. She'd have been horrified. Operate from strength, she'd always said. Be positive. Talk about yourself, sell your good points. Be "up." The same old Hollywood blather. Usual line of patter. The old bullshit express.

I had hoped that a healthy dab of black humor might go a long way toward helping my case in the ads. It turned out that Mr. Escutcheon, the fellow who finally answered the ad, didn't know from black humor.

In any case, the part about starving was close enough.

There I was, living in that hovel of a North Hollywood apartment, no job and not a whole bunch of possibilities for a job, wondering why the hell I'd ever come down here from lovely Eugene, Oregon anyway. To be a writer, of course. . . . To make it in show business, to write my name large in letters of sparkling cultural success. I figured the one TV credit to my name would at least open doors far enough to get my foot in. So far, though, no go. Which was why I had the ad in *Daily Variety*.

Beneath the perpetually sunny skies of the Southland, inhaling a heady mix of smog and freeway fumes, dining on tacos and hope, here is the eager young screenplay writer, seeking to scribble his name in the black vacuum of tape or celluloid, clinging to the dream of celebrity and stardom. Of course the fact that I really wanted to be a *writer* in Hollywood is a testimony to the naïveté of the twenty four year old dreamer, stumbling off the I-5 in his limping Toyota Tercel. Smart writers became *producers*.

It's just as well that Mr. Escutcheon knew about as much about the business as I did.

I'd just made myself a peanut butter and banana sandwich and was sitting down in front of my computer to do another page of a speculative television script when the phone rang.

"Harrumph?" I said, incredulous that someone should call the moment I had my mouth crammed with gloppy gunk.

"Pardon me. Is this Ralph 818-234-9867."

It was an adenoidal voice, a little lispy and the way it slurred my Christian name into my phone number made it all sound like a Hugo Gernsback novel of futuristic super science. However, I did recognize the order of phrasing as a direct reading of my ad in yesterday's show business trade newspaper, so I managed to swallow down the mouthful of sandwich with the help of a glug of low-fat milk and was only a little gurgly sounding as I brightly responded: "Yes, that's right. How can I help you?"

"I'm calling in response to your ad in yesterday's *Daily Variety*," (pronounced *dilly var – ee tee*), "yes, and I was hoping that perhaps you have not yet been employed?"

"Gee, I've just been overwhelmed by the offers," I said (not exactly a lie – actually I was overwhelmed by the offers all right. All *zero* of them!). "But I am still available for hire!"

"Excellent, excellent! Tell me now, what is your full name?"

"Ralph Phillips," I said.

"Is that your full name? I need to do some numerology here, you see."

"Uh — well, my middle name is David, so I guess that makes my full name 'Ralph David Phillips.'"

As I as thinking, *numerology?*

"Fine. Now as I am plugging that into my machine, please tell me your critics?"

"Critics? You mean, who's written about my stuff?"

"No, I am so sorry. This accent of mine!" said the man cheerfully. "Credits, I mean."

Not much.

Oh, I'd had plenty of stories in print. Genre fiction magazines, literary quarterlies, things like that. I'd been placing stories since college. Not much money, though, and my big dream was to support myself through my writing. Can't do that at all with fiction — the only real possibility is Los Angeles, and the script mines.

At first, I'd eagerly trotted out my sales to *Ellery Queen* and *Alfred Hitchcock's* and *Chattanoochee Quarterly* to show people in the TV business, but I saw immediately that their eyes would glaze over. Some would ask for 'coverage' of the stories — namely, summaries of the plots, but that was as far as their interest traveled into literary ventures.

However, I had become a fan of one unusual Television show in particular, and this had been my ticket down to Los Angeles and a stab at the world of television and film writing.

I cleared my voice and tendered my solitary credit of industry worth.

"I — uh — I worked on a script for the *Galactic Journey* show."

There was a silence at the other end of the line.

Oh, God, I could hear the objection now.

A *sci-fi* show?

Well, there's not really a way to see if you can do anything with that, Mr. Phillips . . . It's hardly like anything we're doing here. Have you got some kind of spec script for a *police* or *detective* show perhaps. . . ?

I was already mentally rifling through the available things of other kinds of samples I had, when the voice at the other end of the phone broke the silence.

"You wrote for *Galactic Journey!*"

The voice sounded impressed.

"Why, yes I did . . . I mean . . . they liked one of my scripts but they didn't use it, I sold them a story and worked on that . . . I didn't get teleplay credit . . ."

Meantime, I'm kicking myself in the butt. Why are you telling this guy this? Don't denigrate yourself, Ralph — other people will be more than happy to do that *for* you!

"Excellent! That's our favorite show. And you're looking for a job working on a movie?"

A movie? Certainly. Low budget, whatever. . . . I didn't care!

"You mean, like *writing* a movie?"

"Yes! That's exactly the services you offered, is it not?"

"Well, actually what the ad said was a writer's assistant . . ."

"You do not feel you are ready . . ."

"No no! I'm quite qualified, quite ready . . . and happy to work with you on — gee, just about *anything.*"

"Excellent. I'm afraid that we do not have a great deal of money available."

"I'm sure I'm willing to discuss a price satisfactory to both of us."

"Oh, good. Well then . . . a meeting. Yes, I suppose we should have a meeting, should we. 'Take a meeting' is the term that I've heard used, yes. . . ?"

I felt a little queasy about his lack of self-assurance, but then I was hardly Mr. Forceful myself, so I was quite willing to give him the benefit of the doubt. Besides, at least he wasn't handing me a line of doubletalk. He honestly seemed impressed with my credits, albeit meager. Maybe he'd even like my short stories. Perhaps there were miracles in SoCal after all!

"I'd be happy to have a meeting with you, Mr. . . ."

"Escutcheon. Phineas Escutcheon, Esquire."

"Okay, Mr. Escutcheon. Where's your office?" I clicked my pen into readiness to take down the information upon the pad conveniently parked by my phone.

"Yes. Our office is on the corner of Ventura and Laurel Canyon, in Studio City."

He gave me an address, and a phone number. We made an appointment for ten-thirty the next morning.

I went out and celebrated by getting a taco. Deluxe.

Okay, okay, he didn't really *look* like an elf.

Not when I first met him, face to face, anyway. So up front, right here in the narrative, I'll warn you. No pointy ears, yet.

I stopped off for a bracing breakfast at Dupar's, an old coffee/diner establishment on Ventura. Studio City is named after the old Hal Roach Studios which have become the MTM/CBS Studios. The address Phineas Escutcheon, Esq. had given me was for an office building right across the road, with a big sign advertising space for lease. The LA area was absolutely rife with empty office space. The town had been overbuilt, and was now hunkered in the midst of a nasty recession. Offices were going for a song and a dance.

Sipping back the last of my coffee, I glanced across the street, bracing myself for whatever was going to come. Cars were roaring along Ventura in hordes, the Mercedes and BMWs gleaming with fresh polished success. The place had that peculiar SoCal odor of grass and sun and baked palm tree leaves and money. Standing at the corner, though, was a man with a placard reading HUNGRY! WILL WORK FOR FOOD!

I shuddered. It looked damned close to my ad in *Daily Variety.*

You try not to stink of desperation here in Los Angeles, but it's kind of like taking a wallow in a garbage dump and then spritzing on some Right Guard. It's a town of dissatisfaction — somebody's always doing better than you are. Of course, at that time, I would be happy to be doing anything at all, and stretched out before me now was opportunity — albeit uncertain and nebulous.

It was March and still on the cool side of ninety, so I was able to get away with wearing my good sports jacket. I'd polished up my shoes and had on my good slacks and best sunglasses. A nice clean white short-sleeved shirt completed the Ensemble of Hope.

I paid my bill, got the receipt for my taxes, straightened up and drew a wet comb through my recently clipped hair and estimated my looks. Sharp, I thought. Very sharp. A stubby nose poked back at me before bright brown eyes, but that aforementioned eager beaver sharp short cut on my dark locks made me look contemporary and on the mark. My teeth were straight, flossed and clean and ready to take a huge bite out of life.

Thus prepared, my shoe heels clicked across Ventura toward the sparkling office structure.

Up the elevator, to the fourth floor, down a narrow hallway with small offices packed cheek to jowl, smelling of floor wax, a copy machine, and coffee.

I found 425.

That's all it said. "425." No name, no elaborate production sign. The door was slightly ajar and I squeezed through. I'd expected a reception area, but instead all I found was a small office. A small *empty* office at that, with a solitary desk, with a phone and papers scattered across it, a filing cabinet, and a single wooden chair in front of it.

Not knowing what else was appropriate (it *was* precisely ten thirty after all) I sat down on the chair, and tried to look — well, sharp and cool, I suppose.

I waited.

I had a folder with some spec scripts and some Xeroxes of short stories in it. This I casually put on the end of the desk. As I did so, I surreptitiously took in the contents of the desktop. There were several days' copies of the Los Angeles *Times* and *Daily Variety* here and there. A couple of copies of the *Hollywood Reporter* were winged out like airplanes about to take off from a runway. In the center of the desk, by the phone, was a yellow legal pad of paper with a Bic pen on top of it.

I could not prevent my curiosity from making me get up and crane my neck to peer at what was scribbled on the paper.

Whatever it was, it wasn't English.

They looked like runes. Viking runes, stamped out upon the yellow in strange lists.

I heard footsteps coming down the hallway and immediately and speedily reassumed my seat, trying to look totally unfazed. LA cool, LA casual.

The door opened uncertainly and a face peeked in, blinking in the glare of the sunlight coming through the uncurtained windows.

"Hello?"

"Mr. Escutcheon?"

"That's right." My first impression was: hair. My second impression was: *gnarly*.

And I don't mean tubular type gnarly or anything remotely smacking of surfer lingo.

He was thin, with bent shoulders. These shoulders were a launching pad for a head that looked as though it had been concocted by an imaginative artist rather than parents. The nose was long and knobby and hair protruded from it in tufts. His brow was low and swarthy and question marks of eyebrows swirled above the deep-set chocolate eyes. His chin and cheeks were sharp and remarkably smooth and pink for someone so swarthy and hairy. The nest of brown and grey hair hanging from his head obscured his ears. In short, he looked like no producer I'd ever seen before — and I've seen some pretty ugly producers!

"Ralph here!" I said brightly. "Ralph Phillips!" I hopped up and offered my hand. "We had an appointment at ten thirty."

The dark eyes lit and a smile played around suddenly redder lip that broke and showed the whitest, pearliest, straightest set of teeth this side of an ace orthodontist.

"Oh yes, yes. I'm sorry. I was just out getting us some coffee. Would you like some?" He held up a brown bag.

"Thanks. Yes."

He was a lanky sort, encased in a pale blue jacket and jeans. He seemed all skin and bones with not an ounce of fat to him. His anatomy seemed extremely oddly slapped together as though designed by someone with a different set of aesthetics than your normal human sort, but definitely a sense of proportion, if you know what I mean.

With startling grace and dexterity for someone so odd he moved around the desk and took his place at his seat. He smelled of lavender, leather and tobacco and something else I'd smelled before in dreams. Something indefinable, and yet ineffable and not at all unpleasant. Although he looked somewhat grey and old and — well, *gnarly* — there was a sense of ageless youth about his movement and especially his eyes.

"Oh dear, oh dear. I shall never get used to this blasted light! This area is simply just too well lit! You really should do something about that sun here, you know? Although I suppose that's why people started up a film colony here all those years ago. The excellent light for the photography. Hmm. Well, humbug to light right now, eh? Let's make things a little more comfortable." So saying, he went to the windows and drew a set of black drapes that did not look as though they'd come with the office. The effect was to darken the office so much that the man was forced to turn on his desk lamp.

"Phineas Escutcheon! Dr. Phineas Escutcheon. Professor Escutcheon. But Mr. Escutcheon is fine, in fact I almost prefer it," he said, offering me his hand finally. "Welcome to my office. Thank you for coming."

I took his hand and noticed immediately that the backs of his hands were hairy and his fingers were oddly jointed. The handshake was mercifully brief and I was allowed to sit back in my seat.

"Thanks for having me," I said. "I brought alone some of my samples." I laid the contents of the folder out before him. "Along with my resume."

Oops! I immediately realized that I'd opened too quickly with business. Too uptight, man! Not laid *back* enough!

Mr. Escutcheon didn't seem to notice that, nor did he take much note of my scripts or my resume. His eyes, marked warmer and rosier now in the artificial lighting, were looking straight at me as though they were boring through for a peek at my soul.

"Tell me more about *Galactic Journey,*" he requested, his sincere interest giving me reassurance and making me more self-confident about this whole interview. The key word here was sincere: a quantity not often found in Hollywood terms.

I repeated what I had told him and outlined the rest of the story. I found that, under his watchful gaze, I wasn't able to fabricate anything. I told him that although I'd done speculative *Galactic Journey* scripts before (and indeed had them here on the desk for him to examine) I only did the story for the *Galactic Journey* that had aired. The executive producer had decided that I wasn't experienced enough to actually do the script.

Mr. Escutcheon blinked. "But how does one get experience on such things unless one is given a chance?"

"Yes. That's the *Catch 22* of the situation!"

"Catch Twenty Two? I'm afraid I don't follow."

"The name of a funny book that describes a conundrum."

"Oh. Conundrum. That I understand. We have plenty of conundrums where *I* come from. Conundrums and convolutions of a most variegated assortment. And primarily, I must say, economic. Which is precisely why I am here, Mr. Phillips. And why," he shook a friendly finger, "you are here."

"You think I qualify for your project?" I said hopefully.

"We shall see, we shall see. I will tell you something of it, just as soon as I obtain just a little more information from you. Have you ever thought, Mr. Phillips, of writing a script for a fantasy movie?"

I blinked.

Fantasy movie? Why, one of my spec scripts was a fantasy epic, along the lines of *The Lord of the Rings* — well, perhaps more of a mini-epic. It was called *The Bardic Quest*.

I pulled it out and showed it to Mr. Escutcheon. "What a coincidence!" I said.

He smiled knowingly. "Perhaps. Perhaps not." He leaned back in his chair and thumbed through the script for a few minutes, while I was left just twiddling my thumbs. "Hmmm," he said finally. But it was said with a warm smile as he looked at me. "Let me be perfectly honest, Mr. Phillips."

That he did not call me by my first name I thought was promising — for some reason, I'm not quite sure what.

"One of the major reasons we are interested in you is that you are script writer and yet are not a member of the Writers Guild, and therefore can work below minimum. Our company does not have a great deal of capital. However, our project, I believe, has a great deal of potential. We can make a great deal of money here with a very small expenditure — with, of course, the proper talent. Talent such as yours."

"You like my stuff. But how could you have read it so . . ."

"We have our methods. Yes, we are most impressed with you. If you agree to our terms and the your . . . ah, working conditions, I would say that you've got yourself a job."

I couldn't help but leap up, grab that hand again and enthusiastically pump it. "Oh, thank you, thank you! A feature! You can't know . . . I've been looking for this kind of chance . . ." And then I caught myself. A little stunned at my own outpouring of emotion, I sat back down and tried to regroup. How unprofessional, I thought, and yet I could not restrain showing my thrill.

Mr. Escutcheon did not seem at all taken aback by my display. In fact, his eyes fairly twinkled. And why not — talent, youth, and vigor, all in one package . . . and an inexpensive package to boot.

"Be warned, we can only offer five thousand dollars, flat fee, for all your work on the screenplay."

Five thousand dollars! It seemed like a fortune. It would be more than enough for me to survive another few months in Los Angeles — plus, it would not only be experience — it would be a credit. Mr. Escutcheon seemed absolutely truthful about his company's intent to make the picture. If all went well (and I was more than aware of the slips and slides possible in the making of a movie) I'd see my name proudly displayed in bold letters in the credits of a motion picture!

"That would be fine," I said.

"Excellent, Mr. Phillips. I think we have acquired a scenarist!"

A thought intruded on my high spirits. "You know, Mr. Escutcheon, you haven't told me what the story of the project is. And you haven't given me a title!"

"Story? Later, my lad. Title? Let's just call it *Dragon Quest* for now, eh?"

Dragon Quest. That had a really nice ring to it. I liked it.

"Sounds like it's going to be a special effects film, Mr. Escutcheon! Are you going to be able to afford that?"

He gave me the biggest smile yet. "That's where the genius of our whole effort comes in, Mr. Phillips." His eyes fairly glittered. "But I don't have time to give you the details. I think you'll understand as you go along. By the way, a very important part of the deal is your availability to examine locations for shooting, so that you can work them into your script. Can you fit a two week trip into your schedule?"

Fortunately, I hadn't gotten myself a job yet, so I was able to say that yes, I could indeed.

"Excellent. Pack a bag tonight. We leave tomorrow morning. Food and lodging will be taken care of. Here's the contract. Please sign."

It was just a one page double spaced contract stating that I would write (and rewrite, if necessary) a screenplay and perform the functions necessary to get it written. Simple enough. I should have called my agent. I knew that, even then. But I wasn't thinking smart, and I didn't want to lose the deal, so I took up the Bic pen offered and I signed the thing.

"Excellent," said Mr. Escutcheon after sticking it in a briefcase. He pulled another piece of paper out. It proved to be a map.

"Meet me here at nine o'clock tomorrow morning!" He put the map down and tapped a spot that had been Xed in.

"Okay," I said. "But —"

He motioned to shoo me off, his grin still warm, but his eyes straying, unfocused, as his mind leapt on to other pressing matters.

"We'll discuss everything else tomorrow morning, Mr. Phillips!"

Shrugging, still on that high of getting a writing job, I fairly floated down to the elevator.

I often wonder, in retrospect, that if I'd had an inkling of the strange and incredible adventures awaiting me if I wouldn't have just started running away right then, contract be damned.

Probably.

Chapter Two

Huffing and puffing, I scampered down the trail, my travel bag heavy around my neck, the map twisted and dirty in my hand.

According to my watch I was already ten minutes late.

Beyond, the San Fernando Valley stretched out majestically and smoggily to the nether distances, the San Gabriel Mountains bordering the neat rows of streets and houses and blighted trees to the north. Around me stretched the arid brushy canyons and hills of the Santa Monica Mountains.

I was on a walking path in an area called Tree People Park, an area off Mulholland Drive and Coldwater Canyon between fire roads and developed areas in the mountains of Los Angeles.

This, according the specific directions of that X on the map I had been given, was where I was supposed to meet Mr. Escutcheon.

Needless to say, I was baffled. But my more immediate feeling at the time was panic. I was afraid that if I wasn't on time, I'd lose the job. At the very least I'd get off on the wrong foot. I'm an anxious sort — a worrier and a pleaser, and I must say that shuffling along that dusty path that LA morning I was one nervous guy.

Of course, Mr. Escutcheon had been late yesterday so perhaps the times he provided were meant to be approximate. Nonetheless, I'd tried to get here early just in case, and I'd failed. For one thing, the map wasn't the most accurate thing I'd ever seen in my life. I'd gotten used to the Thomas Bros. map of Los Angeles, a highly detailed rendering of all the thousands of roads here. However, the map given me was a penciled version of one mountain trail, with no indication of dips and crests or intersecting trails — and worse, no sense of distance. I felt I'd been wandering in the hills for hours.

According to the map, I was looking for some sort of mound with a cairn on top of it. A cairn is a collection of rocks set in a ceremonial circle — a low rent Stonehenge. What a Celtic convention like a cairn was doing in LA I've no idea, but there was a little drawing of one on the map.

I finally approached a rise in the trail that led straight up to a copse of trees — the only copse of trees within eyeshot. I consulted the map again, and sure enough the cairn was illustrated as being close to that copse of trees. With my last surge of energy, I tackled the hill, pumping up it and through a tangle of brush. At the peak, I emerged into a large clearing which had been obscured from sight all round by the brush and the trees. There, just as promised on the map, was a circle of medium sized rocks, planted in the ground. They were odd looking rocks — they shone now in the sun, filled with crystals and quartz. They didn't give the feeling of pint-sized monoliths like their European cousins, but the way they glittered and the way a pocket of mist was burning off a nearby canyon under the hot eye of the California sun gave a distinctly mystical feel — a strange sensation in the midst of such a mundane, sleazy city as LA. In the middle of the rocks were the remains of a campfire. The smell of charcoal still hung in the air, beside the usual bracing odor of sage. There was another scent to the air — something sharp and briny and odd, and I recognized it as the unclassifiable odor that had clung to Mr. Escutcheon. A mysterious and yet somehow familiar smell of dreams — like something you'd smelled in another life, a life that was somehow more real than this one.

I was immediately relieved. No one was here. I was late, true, but I wasn't *that* late, and chances were that my new employer was simply later than I was. I mean, where could he have gone? Certainly not down the street for a cup of coffee.

Heaving a sigh of relief, I parked the rucksack containing the supplies I thought I might need down on the ground, and I planted my butt on the rock that looked most like a chair. I put my head on my hands and stared off into the smoggy Valley, wondering what I was doing here, though still feeling optimistic and thrilled at the whole prospect of writing a screenplay.

I'd hardly been able to sleep the previous night. Instead I'd reread my two favorite books about screen writing — one by Syd Fields and the other by J. Michael Straczynski — wondering all the time what kind of fantasy project this was. I'd also paid some bills, stopped delivery of the paper and generally prepared myself for a trip, packing and whatnot. Fortunately (or unfortunately, as I often thought) I had practically no social life in LA (i.e. girlfriends) and so I had no one to tell I was leaving for a while.

Now that I'd found myself here successfully, and some of the stress was gone, I took a moment to ponder. And for the first time, a note of doubt crept into my mind. Was this some sort of practical joke? Was a man with a video camera hiding behind one of the bushes, waiting to record some elaborate television hoax, perpetrated upon a gullible young fool who thinks (har har) he's gotten a job (hee hee) as a movie writer (ha ha — knee slapping time at the Polo Lounge!) and was waiting to take a meeting in the middle of *nowhere?*

However, upon reflection, I had to admit that Mr. Escutcheon seemed to be far from an ordinary sort of man — and therefore I couldn't really expect an ordinary meeting place. Besides, he had talked about scouting locations — maybe he thought that this cairn in Tree People Park was a likely and cheap spot to use for a Fantasy film. It had that flavor. In fact, there more I sat there, the creepier the whole thing got.

My hackles rose.

I had the distinct sensation not so much of being watched, but as being someplace remarkably different. There was moisture still on the underside of laurel leaves just beside me and they seemed to winkle and dazzle now in the sunlight against the gloaming of the shadows below with a pixie shimmer.

Yes, there was the distinct feeling of *otherness* about the place, like the cold blow of a phantom breeze in the midst of a warm day.

Suddenly a voice spoke.

Spoke seemingly at my elbow so that the effect was to scare me right out of my precious Rockport walking boots.

"Good morning, Mr. Phillips!"

I stepped back, tilting and windmilling a bit, trying to keep a purchase on my balance. As I did so, I saw that, standing beside me, come from seemingly nowhere, was a man.

I recovered first my balance before keeling over one of the rocks, and then my senses. At first I didn't recognize the man because he was dressed so differently than before and because he was standing between me and the sun and his face was in shadow. But the sunlight limned that telltale wealth of hair, and I was able to make out finally some of the gnarled and decidedly odd features.

Mr. Phineas Escutcheon was dressed in a checkered tweed suit with a matching cap, from which a bright blue and white feather bloomed luxuriantly. He wore a cape of the same material and knickers with thick woolen socks rising up neatly from brightly polished leather boots with shiny buckles. From one of his shoulders dangled a neatly tied leather briefcase. From his mouth dangled an old bent Meerschaum pipe. Those peculiar eyes of his glimmered with amusement at the effect that his appearance had on me.

In fact, he seemed to erupt into existence beside me from no place at all, looking like a mountain traveler from some warped version of Switzerland.

"Do I frighten you, Mr. Phillips?" he asked, a wry smile telling me his true intent was not to chastise but to reduce my alarm.

"I didn't hear you coming up the path. You must walk very quietly."

"I can and I do walk quietly when the need arises. However it was not necessary just then," he said, rather quixotically.

"Well, I was late. I'm sorry." I tapped my Timex. "Had a hard time finding the place."

Mr. Escutcheon gave me a peculiar look. "You will find, Mr. Phillips that we are not a precise folk. Time is merely rather a loose though handy boundary to things. And when measurement of time causes problems though, such should be discarded, hmmm?"

I shrugged. "I guess so."

"Is this being what they call in these parts a 'yes man,' Mr. Phillips?" he said, giving me a faintly scolding look.

I was going to say no, but I decided to be honest. "You are the boss."

"You do not have to please me with your opinions, Mr. Phillips." He took a box of matches with a peculiar label — runic letters it seemed, like those he'd been scribbling on that yellow pad. Struck a match, placed flame to bowl pipe and sucked. The long stream of smoke he blew out roiled along — and then suddenly disappeared, as though swept around some invisible corner. "We need to know what you really think. Opinions will not hurt our egos. We are novices at this sort of thing and we need as much advice as we can get."

His honesty cut through my awkwardness. "Okay." I took a deep breath. "So I guess I should ask first: what are we doing up here if you said we're going to *travel* someplace. And what *is* this place and *where* did that smoke go?"

I was getting a little bit spooked again, and speaking exactly what was on my mind, I found, let loose quite a bit of the tension that was building up. Still and all, that peculiar briny smell, that chill that had nothing to do with temperature was operating now in full force.

Mr. Escutcheon smiled more expansively this time and began "Well, lad you see it's quite simple —"

When suddenly, the most peculiar thing yet occurred.

It started as a rumbling and then the ground began to shake beneath my feet.

"Earthquake!" I said.

Mr. Escutcheon grabbed my arm and squatted down, pulling me lower with him. His eyes darted around, as though looking warily for something. He stuck his pipe in a breast pocket and reached into his jacket pocket and pulled out a soft leather pouch closed by string.

"No," he said, his eyes focusing finally straight ahead of him. "Not an earthquake. Something far more dire — and something I'd hoped to avoid here."

Still shaking, heart hammering, I said, "What?"

Mr. Escutcheon seemed paralyzed, frozen in place, apparently not knowing what to do. . . . or maybe just figuring that out. Meantime his eyes, I noted, were fixed on the remains of the campfire in the middle of the cairn. The quaverings of the ground had resolved into ripples upon the surface of the ground but those ripples, instead of spreading out as though from a rock tossed into a pond, traveled *inward* to meet in the middle of the charred wood. The ground bulged upwards, peaking into the dark and chiseled form of head. A giant head, it broke up out of the ground like an erupting black pimple. Its long hair was a scraggly combination of roots and the soot of the dead fire, but then two goggles of red-veined white — eyes, malevolent and dire eyes — cracked open and stared out directly at us with a balefulness and hatred beyond anything I had yet experienced in this life.

Hollywood special effects could never achieve that furnace of angry evil, nor the realistic immediacy. That the rising form of the body, erupting further now, crackled with an electric shimmer only added to the hysteria of the moment for me.

A dream, I thought. This kind of thing simply doesn't happen. I was a dream, pure and simple — surely!

But all my senses told me it was real. The giant blackened being — a rocky crag of a thing, like a creature formed of stratified rock — smelled of sulfur and blood, and a much more potent version of that briny effluvia I had noted earlier. The ground was still shaking so hard the fillings in my teeth seemed to vibrate. The air had gone chill, digging straight through to lungs and bone. No, this was not only real, I could not doubt that — it had extra facets, additional dimensions of spiritually and beyond that heightened the reality. No dream, no nightmare, this.

This was really happening.

A mouth filled with broken, straggly teeth and obscenely red stringy and flapping tongue opened and the smell of rotting flesh and vegetation and K roiled out, nearly knocking me over.

"Doom!" growled a voice, like a cement mixer, grinding it out. "You were warned.... Now.... Doooooooooooooom!"

Not at all promising, especially as the mammoth shoulders of the beastie broke through and claws began to break through the surface like flashing flowers of death.

My first impulse was to run in the opposite direction, but Mr. Escutcheon grabbed my arm just as soon as I made the merest hint of a motion in that direction.

"No," he said.

I was so shocked by this command — and the vibrant power and authority that now imbued his voice — that I immediately obeyed. He let go of my arm and stuffed his hand into the leather pouch. I had not even noticed that he had opened it. The odd-looking man, now somehow looking a little larger than before, pulled out a handful of some sort of dirt or dust or something and without hesitation, threw it directly into the emerging creature's fiery eyes.

Mid-flight, the stuff turned into vibrant rattling rays and dazzle and they collided with the face like daggers of light, tearing into it.

The creature bellowed. Blinded, he shuddered and shook in the ground.

"Now," said Mr. Escutcheon. "Run. But *this* way!" He pointed in a direction that would take us directly by this demon surely scrabbling his way up and out of Hell itself.

"But it will *get* us!" I cried, horrified.

"Trust me, or surely you will be lost!" said Mr. Escutcheon, and his eyes were alive with sincerity, truth, and perhaps even caring for me.

He pulled me along and I followed.

He'd only taken two steps, and immediately I could see where he meant to exit. Of course, *seeing* does not always spell *believing*, and the sight so surprised me that I stopped in my tracks.

Mr. Escutcheon went behind that same invisible corner in the air into which the smoke had gone. Only as his body slipped into that slit in the air, it *shimmered* like the horizon in the desert does on a hot day. Shimmered and then disappeared, swallowed up by nothingness.

His whole body disappeared.

I panicked.

How could I follow him when I could not *see* him? The very air had enveloped him, tucked him away into somewhere else.

Meantime with a roar my attention was called back to the horrific arrival from Below. I could not help but turn and see that he had not only wiped the troublesome dirt from his eyes, but had pulled a bulbous body and squat, powerful legs up. His body was matted with a thick filthy hair, in which there seemed to be tangled scraps and tatters of dried bones and flesh certainly not his own.

"Hunger!" it snarled. "Engulf!"

Clearly, if it couldn't have Mr. Escutcheon it was more than willing to settle for a lesser tidbit: me. It lifted its foot up for purchase upon the gravelly ground and then started to reach a flashing pointy set of claws toward me.

I felt its hot, fetid breath not only on my neck but all over. And my fear kept me from moving at all.

At that moment, however, I heard my named being called. Automatically, I turned in the direction and as though from instinct survival, stepped forward toward where Mr. Escutcheon had disappeared.

A true leap of faith, I suppose. Or perhaps a true leap of desperation is the more appropriate term.

The beast's arm arced out me, the claws coming in for the snatch. Just before they speared me, though, a hand and arm appeared from nowhere, grasped my shirt, and pulled.

Thus was I pulled from smoggy sunny California through an aperture of blazing darkness and dizzy, vertiginous stars.

Chapter Three

I'm not sure if I actually passed through a field of flashing celestial bodies. It seems highly unlikely that I actually passed through raw space between worlds, the interstitial stuff betwixt universes. However, it certainly felt like it.

I'm not sure if it was my overheated imagination, but it seemed then as though I felt a hot draft of the missed blow from the monster pursuing me. For certain, I felt the pressure of that disembodied hand and arm, pulling me through a slice of eternity, overhanging a very deep section of starry infinity. One moment there was the thrill sense of speed and escape. The next I seemed to slipped through a palpable membrane into an entirely different environment.

And I immediately tripped, staggered and fell flat on my face onto hard and cold damp stone.

I suppose normally I'd have been embarrassed but, truth to tell at that instant, even though the drop was painful, I was merely grateful.

I was aware of bustling activity behind me.

I sat up and looked around.

Two men in robes were busy making busy hand signals above a small crucible above aflame atop a Bunsen burner like arrangement. Mist seemed to waver in a straight line a full seven feet above this, and I could see a glimmer of California sunlight and a dark form quiver amidst the bristle of claws. Indecipherable guttural syllables were urgently muttered and then with a sharp crack a bestial hand, claws attached and reaching for blood, punched through the opening.

"Oh damn!" said a thick voice to my side. Another man stepped past me — I had the distinct impression of lumberjack parameters a streak of steel — and swung a sword. The flashing metal descended with great force and the sharp weapon lopped off the clawed paw at the wrist. The severed thing dropped to floor, writhing. A spurt of dark blood splashed the floor and the limb was pulled back through the rent in the air. And then, as though it were being zipped up by some invisible hand, the tear in space mended. The wavering was gone, and all was smooth and calm once more.

Except my heart and my adrenal system. My blood pulsed furiously and I felt as though my whole body had just been rewired and attached to high voltage. My senses were keen but confused.

Where was I?

"Well, we have a trophy, it would seem," said the big man, taking a rag and wiping his splendid sword free of the noxious juices of the creature that had pursued Mr. Escutcheon and myself. He was at least another half a foot past six tall and his shoulders were broad and symmetrical. His body narrowed to muscular hips and big, tree trunk legs, covered with breeches and a shirt that were, in design and material, not even remotely twentieth century — unless you spent all your time at a Renaissance fair. He wore a doublet and a scabbard and worn leather boots. A grim smile showing vibrant large teeth cracked through a black beard. Grey-green eyes shown with triumph and amusement as they traveled from the now-still giant hand to another part of the room. "But of what?"

I followed his gaze and found myself looking at Mr. Escutcheon, his neat dress slightly askew, his hair disheveled, looking down with disapproval at the clawed paw. "That is precisely why I have retained your services, Mister Toplin. There are forces of evil who would not like me to accomplish what I have set out to do!" His nose flared with indignity and his hand drew up into a determined fist, smacking the palm of his other hand.

The two men in scull caps who had been muttering took out flasks from the folds of their mullioned robes and guzzled. One wiped droplets of sweat from his brow as the other turned off the flame below the crackling smelly crucible. "That was one of the guardians we spoke of before, Mr. Escutcheon," said one. "We warned you. Now there will be ultra-dimensional inquiries into your designs."

"Then so be it!" cried Mr. Escutcheon, pacing. "I will not stand by and allow what is happening to my country!"

"Oh, we agree, sir, and we admire your notions," said the other character, poking now at the severed clawed paw with what appeared to be some kind of combination sextant and slide rule. "However, part of *our* job is to alert you to the dangers." He turned a sallow, beardless face in my direction and his nose twitched, as though there were something vaguely unsavory about me. "A solitary jaunt into another world with our bubble spells hardly causes a ripple. However, once you brought an Outsider into the Circle outside the True Land, the alarms were doubtless rung."

While this discussion was proceeding, calming down a bit, I took the opportunity to look around me and see exactly where I was.

I was in a large dark chamber, lit only by a few torches. The shuddering smoky light revealed stone walls, a high stone ceiling and jointed stone floors. A stone stairway led up to darkness. It was cold and draughty and damp and had the feel of the subterranean. Some sort of dungeon I would surmise . . .

In the center was a large rug, looking of an oriental design and yet clearly something of different patterns. Set out upon this were stacks of old books, amidst piles of obscure equipment of chemical and alchemical nature. Bottles and phials and jars, labeled with that same runic lettering were stacked wily nilly here and there.

In the very center of it all was a table mounted with what appeared to be a stuffed unicorn.

All in all, it looked like a jumble sale for medieval magicians.

"Well, be that as it may," said Mr. Escutcheon, "I have brought an Outsider and he shall be an important competent of my effort. I have given proper study to the process of creating cinema, and the first element vital to preparation is a screenplay. And behold, with me now a young, up and coming screenwriter — Ralph Phillips! Take a bow, Master Ralph."

A nodded and gave a flourished salute, obeying without thinking. I was still not only stunned by recent events, I didn't know what to make of them. However, the screenwriter part got me back enough into my reality line that I at least was able to speak. "Hello. Nice to meet you all. Nice to be here."

From all appearances I'd just crossed over into Twilight Zoneville, the Outer Limit Boulevard, Fantasytown, call it by whatever fantastic appellation you may care to append. However, one important element in all this shifting reality was still the same — and it was the *most* important.

I still had a job, and it was still writing a screenplay.

The big guy grunted and eyed me appraisingly. I wondered if he was sizing up my writing potential or my hero potential — or perhaps just the size of my purse he might cut in some dank alley. He had that kind of larcenous gleam to his eye. "Well, worse comes to worse, we can toss him to the Gullet Gulp as an offering."

Mr. Escutcheon clucked his tongue. "Pay no attention to this scoundrel, Mr. Phillips. As you know, we are operating on a profound budget and he was the best I could afford to hire as guide and protector for our journey. His name is Brank. Brank Toplin of the city of Wapples, to be precise. Brank, welcome our dear and talented guest, Mr. Ralph Phillips."

A large eyebrow tilted and a grin angled up in the opposite direction as Brank Toplin, roguish hero, shouldered his way up to me and presented me the daunting spectacle of a hand the size of a frying pan to shake.

"Welcome to our little enterprise, Mister Phillips and God have mercy on our doomed souls, eh?" he growled, ending with a bark of a laugh.

I allowed his hand to enfold mine and gave the firmest, manliest shake that I could manage. "Pleased to me you, sir. And thanks for hacking off that nasty hand there," I said.

"That's what me and my sword get paid for, eh?" The big man winked at me, patted me across the back so hard I felt as though the breath was knocked from my lungs, and then lumbered over to an oaken table. He picked up a jug and poured a frothy amount of amber stuff into a mug and swallowed a hefty amount down his throat, getting flecks of foam caught in his mouth. Beer, I thought, or ale or whatever — it looked rather inviting and delicious and though I wasn't much of a drinker, I suddenly had a craving for it, if only to calm my nerves.

However, Brank Toplin seemed so intent upon finishing the stuff himself that he did not offer me any.

I'd recovered enough from my astonishment of the events of the past half hour, though, that I was able to turn to Mr. Escutcheon and ask the question that had been forming at the back of my mind and could not finally achieve articulation.

"Where have you brought me?" I said, trying to be polite and a good employee. Nonetheless, I'm afraid that some small amount of resentment and anger gave my words a slight bit more bite than I intended.

A slight smile of apology touched Mr. Escutcheon's mouth. "My home land, dear boy."

"You said nothing about going through some sort of magical portal, much less of being pursued by some kind of monster!"

Fortunately I was able to modulate that in a tone that rendered it merely a statement rather than an accusation. I still, after all, wanted to write a screenplay and get paid for it.

"No. In truth, I did not — the last person I hired balked at the notion entirely and did not work out at all!"

Brank Toplin laughed, shreds of beer foam spitting out from his mouth. *That* fellow! He would not have lasted more than a day on the trail anyway. He shook hands like a willow-thing. Now, I like this young man. I see the stuff of steel in his eyes. In fact, I would dare venture that the lad can quaff a tankard with the best of them. What do you say, fellow?" Even as he spoke, Brank Toplin knelt bellow the table and with one powerful arm hauled a wooden cask out and set upon the table. He ripped the nozzle from one end and amber liquid spouted. He grabbed a large cup, filled it, then refilled his own. Then he put the jug beneath the flowing ale. All rather messy, but he was able to fill everything quickly this way. When the task was down he simply jammed the nozzle back into the side of the cask to save the remainder of the cask.

I watched all this feeling rather ambivalent. On one hand I was thirsty and I could definitely use a beer to unknot the tension that was wound up in my abdomen. On the other, it was an awfully large amount of beer he'd poured and from my take on Mister Toplin, I had to assume that he expected me to drink it all. I looked over to Mr. Escutcheon for some indication of the right course to take, but he seemed busy conferring with the two men in robes who'd been working on that portal spell.

"Here you go, Ralph!" the voice boomed beside me, and I found myself with a wet tankard shoved my chest. I looked down at the overflowing head, by hands wrapping around the vessel despite myself. "Drink up. Grow some hair on your nostrils! Hey, hey!"

I shrugged. Why not? I lifted the tankard up and drank. The beer was dark and rich and though not cold, imbued with a fresh chill. It tasted quite good, and tingled on my palate and slid down my throat with quite a hoopla. The flavor was of mystery and excitement and possibility. I had never tasted magic before, but I swear, that brew had some kind of charm to it. I drank as much as I could without choking and then set the tankard down. My brain felt positively elevated by the effervescence of the drink, which had punched in the alcohol affect to my entire system. I turned to Brank Toplin to thank him, but I think my entire feeling toward the drink was massaged through my eyes.

"Ye like it, lad!" crowed Toplin. "And that's a good sign, upon my halberd, it's a damned good sign."

"It's truly *excellent*," I enthused.

In fact, my spirits were soaring even higher. Suddenly, far from feeling fearful and adrenalized by this weird leap I'd taken into what appeared to be a demented fantasy-adventure, I felt buoyed and excited and overcome with wonder. With the trepidation removed, the whole prospect not just of writing a screenplay but of being in a *different world* was just about the best thing I'd discovered since girls.

Still I had enough wits about me still that I realized that much of this feeling was the drink talking, and so I tried to take that into account.

Still, I liked it, I really did and so when I was able to get over the drink's filling effects with an embarrassing burp, Brank Toplin ripped off a hearty laugh of approval and demanded that we toast each other and 'snort more down hearty.' He picked up his tankard and urged me to take up mine.

Fortunately, the toast was interrupted by Mr. Escutcheon. "Here here! Not right now. Later, before bed, perhaps to help him sleep. But there's much to discuss and I don't think he'll understand or retain much drunk."

Brank let it pass, but he gave me a mischievous wink and clapped me on the back. "There's more where that came from, aye!" he said, with a conspiratorial cuff on my arm. "What say after supper tonight I take you out and show you a drinking establishment that pours the most fabulous glass in town!"

"If Mr. Escutcheon says it's okay," I said.

"Don't worry about it. I'll convince him that, you being an elseworlder, this will be a vital part of your education. If you don't hear from me after supper, though, and you don't get permission from Grumpy — just wander out onto the streets and ask for the location of the Cracked Cask. Everyone knows and they'll be happy to direct you."

There was a warmth and a solidity about the man, a big brotherliness that made me feel safe and welcome. I instantly developed a liking for the man and felt a strange affinity. Maybe it was just the promise of more of that delightful ale, I don't know, but I was definitely looking forward to this coming after-supper, nocturnal activity.

"Now then, Mr. Phillips!" said Mr. Escutcheon, beckoning. "Come over here and let me introduce you to my two technical aides."

I smiled up at my new buddy, Brank Toplin, (probably rather stupidly) and then toddled off to obey my boss.

The two men had somehow removed their robes while Brank and I had been drinking and now stood it simple wool shirts and breeches, sitting at a table with Mr. Escutcheon, both with stumpy looking mugs of what smelled like tea steaming up languorously into their faces.

"Mr. Phillips," said Mr. Escutcheon. "I am sorry that I had to bring you here in this matter and I am sorry also to be so rude as to neglect to immediately introduce you to my colleagues. But they were deep into their enchant mode and were not quite accessible to niceties at that particular moment. This is Thelonius Meistercrow." The taller of the two, a man with a pinched face and nervous eyes allowed me to shake a delicate and long fingered hand soft as baby's skin. "And this," continued Mr. Escutcheon, "is Quenton Quintabulous." The stubbier of the two men had a wider face and deeper, calmer eyes, but I could not help but noticed that his hand was quite different than his counterpart's, being horny and scarred. He, however, was the one who seemed the most interested in me. Where Thelonius Meistercrow's eyes only lighted on me briefly and with some distaste, traveling immediately back to some sort of research he was doing in a thick volume full of rubrics and ornate illustrations, Quenton Quintabulous focused his full attention to me, taking all of me in with an analytical yet not unfriendly look. "Well, you are the scribe, eh? I look forward to reading your literary efforts and of course, to the — er — 'play' that you concoct for our cause."

"Pleased to meet you both!" was the only thing I could come up with.

Filling in the conversation lull, Mr. Escutcheon said, "Mr. Phillips has been a writer for *Galactic Journey!*"

Immediately, I got both men's full attention. "That's our favorite show!" they said in unison.

Mr. Escutcheon could not help but smile. "Thelonius and Quenton are two of the land's best magicians — and it's a truth throughout this world, Mr. Phillips, that the favored leisure time activity of magicians, sorcerers, and necromancers is to watch the American television programs they are able to pull in through their magical antennas."

I quickly answered their fan questions concerning the show and I broke quite a bit of ice by asking questions about their activities. They appreciated the interest, but as soon as the subject was changed, they resumed their serious, dour countenances. "Our country is in dire circumstances and our world seems on a roller coaster toward the Ragnarok described in your Nordic mythology."

Mr. Escutcheon shook his head disapprovingly. "Now don't fill his head with such gloom and doom, gentlemen. We have an immediate problem, which we are going to deal with now, and then, with the resources we obtain, deal with larger problems. Step by step, gentlemen. One task at a time." He patted me on the shoulder approvingly. "Now then, if you'll both excuse us, I have to show Mr. Phillips to his quarters and then tell him exactly the reason for our mission."

With bows, the two magicians went back to their fluttering pages, murmurs and spurts of powders and liquids and susurrations of spells, while Mr. Escutcheon guided me toward the stone steps headed, happily, up.

I was shown to a pleasant room with a fire in the hearth, a chamber pot by a ramshackle bed and a pitcher of water on a side table.

It smelled homey and woody, with quite a bit less of that magical smell, which had been very strong in the underground chamber. I especially admired the patchwork quilt on the bed, which looked extremely warm and cozy.

Mr. Escutcheon then escorted me back to the hall of what he told me was the largest castle in the land, and we picked our way along corridors past huge draperies, tapestries and airy chambers, finally making our way up a circular staircase of what he assured me was the castle's highest tower. Throughout this, he stayed silent and pensive, as though pondering exactly what he was going to say to me.

Finally, feeling quite exercised and not a little short of breath, I pulled my feet up the last of the stairs and walked through the door that Mr. Escutcheon held open for me. I received a blast of colder air in my face, and realized that we were outside, beneath a sky dark and thick with clouds. The top of the tower had several flagpoles with bright flags and banners fluttering in the breeze. Past the battlements I could see the walls of the town, and beyond them fields and clumps of trees and hovels that seemed to stretch up all the way to majestic roll of mountains, complete with peaks capped with snow.

Lightning flicked from thunderheads hanging over the land, and the air had the taste of imminent storm. The flavor of magic crackled in the air out here, but there were other elements mixed in I could not immediately identify. Dark elements, that was all I knew.

"Wow," I said. "What a view! It's beautiful!"

Mr. Escutcheon lifted a curly eyebrow at me. "Do you not recognize a blighted countryside? Oh, of course not — you're from Los Angeles. You're used to it." He directed a well-manicured finger toward the fields. "The crops have died this year. Can you not see the blackened stalks, smell the scent of corruption in the air?"

That was what I smelled — that sour scent. Along with a definite air of melancholy and sadness.

"It happened just this year. Our agrarian economy is almost ruined. Our kingdom is principally living on stored goods and the kindness of our neighbors. Kindness predicated upon distribution of our failing treasury!" He sighed deeply. "Hypotropia. This is my beloved Hypotropia, Ralph Phillips, land of my blood and my bones. This is the land of magic — much of the best and most altruistic of thaumaturgy was developed here. It is the leading light of right philosophy of our world. Our University (at which I, by the way, am a Full Professor) is the best and it has shone its beacon for many centuries. . . . And yet it too is threatened."

"Can't you just plant another crop next year?"

Mr. Escutcheon gave me an odd look. "Were that it were so simple. You see, our land has been cursed — and the magic of the curse consists of a set of spells so intricate that our best wizards have spent years attempting to unwind them."

"Cursed? But by who?"

Mr. Escutcheon looked out over the landscape with a haunted expression. "I mentioned that our University — Hypotropia University — is the greatest in this world. It has been the shining star of education and magical studies and research for centuries. Ours is the study of sorcery complete, however we emphasize the moral and ethical use of the powers involved. Not so our enemy! Not so our academic rivals?"

"Rivals?"

"Yes!" Mr. Escutcheon's hair seemed to bristle at the very notion. "The Thorny League! A collection of colleges devoted to the study of the black in magic, the evil accumulation of power! Before they seemed satisfied to vie merely with our sports teams! Now, however, they seek to ruin us!" He shuddered, as though shaking off the foul, dripping effect on his own soul. "But I will discuss that with you later, Mr. Phillips. Let me get on with hard, cold facts.

"It's really quite simple. Our University needs a few years to untangle and defeat the web of spells cast over our land. However, in the interim, we must find a way to feed ourselves. I, on my own, have figured out a way."

I looked at him. "What? Make a *movie?* But how is a film going to feed the people of your country?"

He was smiling broadly now. "Come! I will show you exactly how — and reveal a little more of who I am and other relevant subjects!"

I followed him down the tower steps, my curiosity whetted even more than before.

Chapter Four

The room was full of movie posters.
Casablanca. High Noon. Little Caesar. Ben Hur.
Singin' in the Rain.

They virtually papered the walls. Upon book shelves, I saw, were large numbers of volumes about the cinema, and upon the massive oaken desk in the corner were movie memorabilia, including what looked like an Oscar.

I looked around this room — lit by the candles that Mr. Escutcheon was lighting quickly — stunned by the incongruity of it all.

"You see, I mentioned that I was a Professor, and this is my academic office. However, I did not mention that I was a professor of Cinema — to wit, Earthly cinema, especially American!"

Yes — except for the lack of electric lighting and the clear medieval characteristics of the chairs the desk and the book shelves, this could very well be the office of an American scholar at some branch of academia.

"Wait a minute, wait a minute," I said. "Something just hit me. It doesn't look like you've got a great deal of technology here."

"That's quite correct. For various mystical purposes, technology hasn't quite caught on."

"You mean it doesn't work?"

"Oh, most certainly it *works*. There'd be no hope for my little project, as you will soon see, if technology didn't work here. However, let us just say that we're more advanced in other areas ... And that is the direction that, for the most part, our knowledge has taken us. However, there are pockets of learning that are quite aware of the technological advances made upon your world."

"I should think so! I mean, my point is, you've got to have technology to get television reception ... and you've got to have technology to project a film ... show it!"

"Precisely. And of course we do — modified to our own methods, of course."

I shook my head, not understanding. "Well, you don't have an electrical system. What, do you have some kind of generator or something."

"Of course. What do you think? That we use an extension cord into your world?" The man seemed awfully amused at the notion. "Well, if the truth be known, I suppose if we could we would. Certainly, we've managed to smuggle enough of your material here and adapted it. Either adapted that or adopted your methodology with our own twists thrown in."

I'm sure I must have given him a quizzical look because he simply nodded and gestured for me to follow him.

He led me out into the hallway and as we negotiated the twists and turns, he spoke, and slowly the outrageousness of his enterprise began to dawn upon me.

"Yes, we academics import things, and it occurred to me at first that we might be able to import food from your world. However, alas, we have not the money. Gold is hard to obtain and there is nothing that our country can sell. And then it occurred to me — there are things that we have in this land and its outlying environs that can be utilized to good value. We have many items that would be considered special effects in your cinema! Why not, I thought, utilize our small amount of resources to make a film! A film with dragons and trolls and ogres and magic unlike anything that has been seen before your world! Why surely such a film, properly distributed and in the right hands, would earn millions of dollars upon Earth. The money could be used to buy supplies, and perhaps even the technology to defeat this famine that plagues or land ... and the rest can be utilized to build up our University. And perhaps even make more films."

This thought had hovered at the edge of my consciousness as soon as I'd entered into the dungeon. Clearly I'd been brought here to scout out location shooting, and the notion of shooting in a fantasy clime would indeed save a great deal of money. But the full extent of Mr. Escutcheon's ambition had not sunk in until he actual began to outline it.

"I'd been entertaining this idea for some time, and even written myself some notes on the subject," he said. "However, it was only the immediate economic need that brought the whole project to a head. Think of it though — even now, in these unfortunate circumstances, it makes me very excited. I suppose any earthly aficionado of the cinema dreams of making films, but that is an achievable dream that happens occasionally. But for a man from another world to make a motion picture... well, it hardly seemed at all probable. However, with the help of my magicians, I was able to operate sufficient time in the Los Angeles area to understand the actual mechanics of film production. A crash course, you understand — but of course I had a great deal of study and books on the subject already under my belt. However, the actual nuts and bolts mechanics, as you've doubtless learned in your efforts, are quite another kettle of fish."

"Yes, they are," was all I could manage to say. And even past my further astonishment, I guess that at least this film project had nobler goals that most. Not only were we talking about a work of popular art here — one made, naturally as all movies are made because of the nature of the finances, to earn money — but something that would feed hungry people, save a whole country. I was filled with admiration.

However, admiration soon gave way to further astonishment at Mr. Escutcheon unlocked a door and beckoned me to enter.

As I strode with trepidation into the darkness, Mr. Escutcheon hit a lever. There was a brief flash of light on one end of the room along with an accompanying clatter and commotion of gears. Flutters and mutters, then suddenly a cone of illumination swept across the room to splash shadows and light upon a screen. Music blared and the opening credits of *The Maltese Falcon* stuttered into view, framed up and proceeded to unspool.

"I though you said you had no electricity!" I said.

"I wish we had!" squeaked a little voice from the other end of the room.

"Hey, pipe down!" growled a deeper tone. "A job's a job!"

"I'm sorry, but I'm completely baffled," I said.

With a wry smile, Mr. Escutcheon lit a lantern, walked up the tilted room aways, and cast the rays upon the most extraordinary contraption. It was a large-framed thing, with two rolls of celluloid moving, and the film running through a series of gears, sprockets, and opticals. However, there its resemblance to an Earthly movie projector ended. For the brilliant light that shone through the frames, bring the movie to life was provided by the tail end of some large and fabulous lightning bug creature, rainbow translucent wings stirring slightly. The mechanical aspect was run by a number of tiny men dressed all in green running with great energy inside a device looking rather like a hamster wheel. They fairly sparkled with spell-induced energy.

"Some sort of animal often works, but pixies are top of the line and give the best picture!" remarked Mr. Escutcheon with pride.

"Hello there!" chirped one of the little men.

"Hello! Good movie!" cried another one. "Sit back, eat some popcorn, enjoy!"

They seemed to be enjoying the attention.

"Who . . . What are you?"

There were chuckles amidst the mechanical whirrings. "You've heard of Jacks-of-the-Green? Just call us Jacks-of-the-Screen!"

General laughter ensued.

"Thank you people, but I only wished to show our guest your excellent work. You may pop back into your burrows now and enjoy your cups and your cards and your pipes."

"Gee, we were hoping to watch the movie!" piped a nasal voice.

"Shuddup! My legs hurt already," snarled another.

"Well, we should save the light. Do give the Brilliance Bug an extra ration tonight for performing so well on such short notice."

The little men scampered from the wheel and, with marvelous industry, bustled all about the magically aided mechanism, closing up shop.

"Sometime soon we will watch our own movie in this little theater, eh?" said Mr. Escutcheon, escorting me from the room.

"Yes," I said. "Right." My brain was buzzing as we walked. "I do have a question though."

"Yes?"

"If technology doesn't work the same way here — then how are you going to get movie cameras to run? Especially if you're going to be filming a lot outside!"

"I have magician technicians working on that right now," said Mr. Escutcheon. "But that really isn't your problem, is it? We didn't bring you here for that, did we? We brought you here to write the screenplay."

"For which I'll need a story."

"Yes indeed. As for that, I think we shall be able to come up with that during our journey tomorrow."

"You mean to tour the possible sights for filming?"

"Yes, amongst other practical tasks." He stopped in mid-stride, spun around and peered at me, scrutinizing. "You aren't having second thoughts are you, fellow. I mean, if you are, please let me know now. We need your full and enthusiastic participation!"

"Oh, of course! But you have to admit, it's all a bit more than I bargained for!"

Mr. Escutcheon grunted. "Yes, that's true. On the other hand, I smell a hit, here. Don't you. You can easily parlay this work into other work . . . it will be the making of your career." He put a hand on my shoulder. "But most importantly you'll be helping aid the survival not just of our country, but of forces of good in this world and keeping them in balance throughout the universes!"

Heady stuff for a guy who only wanted to make his living writing. I admit, I was a bit overwhelmed at the notion of my efforts employed in the battle against Evil.

Then another thought came to me.

"Uhmm, pardon me for asking, but it occurs to me that there if there's a curse on this country, then someone had to have put it there —"

"Yes! I explained. The Thorny League!" said Mr. Escutcheon impatiently.

"In which case, they must be trying to stop us." Something connected, brilliant thinker that I am. "That creature that was after us in the cairn at Tree People Park. Was *it* sent by the Thorny League."

Mr. Escutcheon looked at me in the dim corridor, and for the first time I saw dark mystery in his face. Something slid through his eyes that seemed to veil the beacon of enthusiasm and pure goodness that had shown from them before.

"No," he said. "But as I intimated before, that matter is something that we shall cover at a later time." He shuddered and then clapped his hands as though to break some spell. A pat on my shoulder restored the former good feeling and warmth. "Come, I'm sure you must be famished. You should now wash up and I'll give you some dinner. Then you shall get a good night's sleep and tomorrow." His eyes turned off toward the future and they seemed to fill with light and positive attitude.

I felt better, but nonetheless something nagged in the bag of my mind.

As I'd quickly discovered in Los Angeles, things were not always what they seemed.

Chapter Five

I washed up.

I rested.

I had an excellent dinner of delicious hard cheese, apples, cold mutton, and tea. ("A superior fare to the average received by our nation's citizens this sorry season," Mr. Escutcheon explained. "However, we must keep your strength up for the trek ahead of us")

And then, leaving me a book on the subject of fantasy films, he left me with several candles, bid me good night, and then departed.

I didn't bring up the matter of Brank Toplin, although I had intended to, since I hadn't the faintest idea of where this tavern was he'd invited me to. However, I rather gathered that Mr. Escutcheon would ask me not to go and squander my energy.

I wasn't tired at all, though, and I definitely not only wanted to find out more about this strange city, this odd land, this peculiar if exciting position I'd found myself in — I also had a definite craving for some more of that wonderful ale that the brawny hero had given me earlier.

The question was, how would I find my way there.

Fortunately, one problem was solved. Apparently the language used hereabouts was English — or anyway, that's the way I heard it thanks to a spell or whatever, and I could easily communicate with the locals. Apparently, this particular fantastic alternate world was of the European fairy tale variety. Anglo-Celtic and all that. As much of a culture shock, at least it was somewhere within the arena of my own culture. I didn't do a whole lot of thinking about the reason for the existence of such a world, or the influence it had had upon Earth, or perhaps if in some way it was some sort of mass-psychological off-shoot of medieval times that had lingered, in magical parallel alongside our own. Mostly, I was just happy to have a job, and a chance to make it in the screen writing business. You may not understand, but then again, you've probably never tried to write in Hollywood. You simply don't look a gift horse in the mouth — even if the horse is obviously actually a unicorn.

Too, my mind was on other matters. Meeting up with Brank Toplin, for one thing of course — and the delicious memory of that wonderful brew. I wasn't tired at all, in fact I was absolutely antsy. There was no way that I was going to be able to lie down on that bed, comfortable and warm and downy as it looked and immediately fall asleep. Tossing and turning was all I'd be able to do, and anyway, the book Mr. Escutcheon had given to me I'd already read.

There was the matter of riling my employer by disobeying his instructions and going out onto the streets. I could tell that he wouldn't want me to, so I hadn't even bothered to ask. However, I figured that even if I want out and was caught in the act, I could say that I just wanted to get a little local color and learn more of what lay before me from Mister Toplin. Research, you know, Mr. Escutcheon! I want this screenplay to just teem with life and vigor!

I waited for a few minutes to see if Brank Toplin were going to show up. I wasn't really confident that he would, since he displayed that certain lovable manly quality of being reliable only when he was really pressed to be. Besides, if he had actually gone down to the Cracked Cask and started drinking that delightful beer, I wouldn't doubt at all that he would lose track of time!

After paging through the book, glancing at the hokey pictures from *Wonderful World of the Brothers Grimm*, *Willow* and other fantasy movies (oh how much better *my* film would be, I thought, even though I hadn't the faintest idea of what exactly my film *would* be ... a quest perhaps ... yes, a quest usually worked in fantasy!) I determined that Brank Toplin was not going to show up. So if I was going to get a drink tonight and a good talk, and see something of this town, I'd have to take matters into my own hand.

The door wasn't locked, of course, so it was easy enough to just leave the room, after I'd extinguished all the candles but one. I took the remaining candle and found my wall into the hall. We'd past the castle entrance on the way to Mr. Escutcheon's office, so I pretty much my way.

So, off into the night I went, looking for a party in a fantasy world.

*I*t didn't take me long to get lost.

I found the exit without problem — a large gate through which the citizens were able to pass without any problem from guards and went out into the dark and twisted streets. There, walking along the cobblestones, the smell of burnt meat and baking bread and unwashed bodies assaulting my nostrils, the flash and rumble of the marketplace sprawled in front of me, I was finally able to stop a citizen and make him pause long enough to ask the question I had.

"Pardon me, sir. But could you tell me how I can get to the Cracked Cask?"

He was an older man and he wore a jerkin and a hood and ratty old boots. But at the mention of The Cracked Cask, his eyes previously down turned and melancholic, brightened and looked straight at me. "Aye," he said, through a mouth with not many teeth remaining. He pointed a stubby finger. "Ye just go down Blackburn Alley to Crabtree Mews, then straight across to Appleblossom Way. Then ye duck in at Sally Alley and ye can miss the sign. It's a great big oak cask cleaved in twain with the insides a runnin' out!" All this was accompanied by much flourishing of hands along with appropriate directional hand gestures. "Ye got that, my lad?"

"Yes, I think so!" I said, figuring that I'd be able to tell my way with the help of signage.

"Good fellow!" He patted me on the shoulder. "Then have a drink for me. Finest bitter in town, I say! But then I take it you're a stranger, from your funny lookin' clothing. No matter. Plenty of foreigners go to the Cracked Cask, so you shouldn't feel too much out of place!"

And he toddled off, slunk back into his normal position, hood back over his head.

It was night out, and thought the streets were well lit by a number of torches in the market square. I looked down at my clothing. Yes, I was still wearing my Lee jeans, my Reebok shoes, a red flannel shirt and a Levi's zippered jacket. Perfect traveling clothes, I had thought when I had left that morning for my appointment a world away, and they were . . . by SoCal standards. Here though, they were comfortable but they stuck out like the old sore thumb. Still, Mr. Escutcheon had given me no others and I was bound and determined to get to the Cracked Cask and get Brank Toplin's version of the proceedings along with the promised ample quantity of superior drink!

I struck off in the direction that the kind gentleman had indicated.

I encountered two main problems.

For one, once I was outside the area of commerce, the torches grew further apart and there was precious little other light leaking out the tilted windows and makeshift doors of business establishments and homes.

The other problem was that there were no signage giving names to any of the streets.

As I walked along, taking turns that were more guesses than anything else, the night grew in on me. Fog and smoke were collecting in the air like ghostly capes draping down from the sky and the taller buildings.

I was able to obtain help from a fellow selling chestnuts. He told me that yes indeed this was Appleblossom Mews or whatever, but as soon as it became apparent that I wasn't going to buy any of his wares, he became surly and refused to help me further.

I trudged off nonetheless determined.

And before long, I got myself thoroughly lost.

I find myself walking along narrow, twisting roads overhung with canopies of dark buildings and bridges. Soon it was also apparent that I was no longer in a good portion of town. The streets were strewn with garbage, and it all had a surrealistic tilted and askew look similar to the look of German expressionistic films, only much smellier.

And so I wandered along, looking for a friendly soul to inquire directions of. Yet everyone I saw in this portion looked thin and pale and hungry. . . . and not a little sinister.

I even turned and retraced my steps, but the mist that had fallen made traveling very difficult indeed.

I'd just turned into an alley that turned out to be a dead-ender, when I heard noises behind me.

"Hello there 'mate!"

"Glad you could join us!"

They were grating voices, filled with the broken glass of wickedness. I immediately felt a good deal of alarm.

"This the one."

"That's him, all right?"

A third voice, deeper more commanding. "Well, we know what's to be done with him."

"No, actually we don't."

"Do we kill him?" The voice sounded eager to do so.

"No. Just relieve him of his wits and bring him back with us. The Masters have uses for him. Imagine! A 'Sider, lost over here. The Masters will have much to dissect on this one, yes indeed!"

Relieve him of his wits? Dissect? I didn't like the sounds of those words.

These were apparently no normal thieves.

I knew that just standing around and waiting for them to come for me would do no good. They only hope I had, I figured, was to run hell bent for leather straight through them, opening somehow to break past their number and dash out into the open, where I could either escape or obtain the help of some officer of the law or some noble passerby.

Besides, I had Reeboks on and they didn't.

Impulsively, I lunged toward the forms and the voices, finding an opening in the dimness and ramming through it. I might have made it too, if a hand hadn't stuck out and grabbed me by the crook of the arm.

"Here now! Stop!" the man demanded, but I kept onward, dragging him along with me, fighting to throw myself free of his weight.

However, I was slowed down enough that the other two were able to catch up. I've never fought before, privately or in sports, so I was surprised at how well I did. I punched and I flailed, a surprising number of my blows connecting. Once I even broke free and ran for a space.

However, these were without a doubt expert baddies. My freedom did not last long. In a trice, I was tackled from behind and in two trices the others were upon me.

I had time to yell out, "Help!" and screeched a little bit. And then they started hitting me. They struck me with some sort of saps and I would have been rendered unconscious very quickly except for the way I insisted upon not staying still. At least twice they missed me and hit one of their companions, causing quite a nasty ruckus. Altogether, it was not the silent dispatch they'd probably hoped for, but rather a noisy mêlée.

Which was the reason why what happened happened, I suppose. At least, that was they only reason I could come up with later.

One moment the pain was throbbing through what seemed like my whole body. The next, I seemed on the verge of unconsciousness, the world spinning around me.

Teetering this way, still fending off blows and delivering them when I could, my attackers cursing wickedly, I thought this was it. Soon I'd be a prisoner of vicious dark forces in a strange land. Not a pleasant idea and I suppose that was one of the reasons my adrenaline was spewing on "high" and I was still fighting.

Then, suddenly, a new rhythm of thuds and cracks and groans entered the cacophonic symphony.

One of the bad guys yelped and tripped over me and fell onto the cobblestones, leaking blood from his head. He did not get up. I didn't wait to see what was going on, but with the last ounce of my strength, grabbed a hold of one of my attackers legs and pulled with all my might. He went down as well, his back thudding onto the ground hard. He moaned and started to get up, but from out of the mists a quarterstaff came down, whacking him across the forehead and sending him back down for the count.

I rolled away, trying to get up and trying for the life of me to see who was flinging that quarterstaff. All I could make out was a short my busy figure in brown, leaping about with the energy of a cat.

The last remaining standing man snarled. There was the sound of metal on leather and I could see he was drawing a sword. Apparently they hadn't wanted to kill me, or I'd already be hacked up pieces scattered on the ground.

The man with the sword attacked the other figure, and it looked as though for the kill.

However, the brown figure (and I could not make out any features because of a loose cowl it wore) stepped aside nimbly, did a few gymnastic steps, and slammed its quarterstaff upon the back of the man so hard that he was hurled forward. The figure dodged around swiftly avoiding the awkward aim of the next sword blow and brought the staff down exactly upon the man's wrists.

The weapon clattered down upon the cobblestones.

Without pause, the quarterstaff whipped around, slapping onto the back of the man's neck and slamming him onto the ground. Moaning, he tried to get up but another rip of the quarterstaff put him down for the count.

The figure, shrouded by mist, turned around to face me. I tried to get up, muttering "Thanks!" but something snagged a hold of me and I plunged back down into the deep end of a dark pool.

Chapter Six

I dreamed I was walking.

No, actually it wasn't exactly walking, more like stumbling and it was with the aid of someone supporting me. My dream was streaked with mist and fluttering torch light and bright specks of twinkling pixie dust, hovering above in the alien heavens. It was all quite wonderful, with a Christmas sort of enchantment. A vigorous touch of chill, a shivery touch of the numinous, an almost holy feel to the holly-covered landscape.

And then, right smack dab amidst all this wonder, a cruel darkness blossomed. It grew up like a black weed, a malignant grow of palpable evil shuddering up from somewhere deep and moldy in the ground. It simmered and flittered up before me, its stench like a blot on the landscape, its inky nastiness seeming to leak across to dim the shine to the majestic lights.

Then, from the very middle of this blackness, two red-streaked eyes opened.

And they seemed to glare straight through me.

"You!" A voice gurgled like fiery lava. "You have no business here! Your shall regret your interference!"

And oddly, it was as though I recognized that voice . . .

The specter's appearance in the midst of my dream was so troubling that the whole membrane of the experience was shattered, and I realized that I was no longer in a misty place and it was no longer cold.

I was lying on some sort of couch, and there was a roof over my head.

I also realized that my head, neck, and shoulders hurt quite a bit, and I remembered what had happened to me. Despite my aches, I managed to grope my way to an awkward stoop on the couch and look blearily around me.

The first thing I noticed was a fire in a rickety hearth in the corner of a room. Tiny windows overlooked the total darkness of outside. It was a warm room with a rug and bundle of supplies on a long wooden table, but that wasn't the feature that caught my immediate attention.

It was the books.

On dozens of shelves, lining two of the walls of the room, were books. The place looked like a comfortable piece of library and I realized that the other distinguishing aspect of the place was the smell. It smelled like leather and vellum and paper — a lovely combination of old paper and new paper, with a nice perfume of fresh ink riding above it all.

A voice broke from a dark door at the other end of the room. "Well. So you're awake."

I started and I must have looked over toward the direction the voice came from with alarm, because the voice was immediately calming: "Don't worry yourself. You're in safe hands here. And by all means, don't fall onto the floor."

It was a woman's voice, lovely yet strong, and sure enough, the figure that stepped into the candlelight, cowlless and capeless, was a woman.

She was short, though well built, with a long nose and a sharp chin, and youthful features, barely out of girlhood. Not much older than me, but my reckoning then — but the blue eyes in that candlelight showed a great deal of experience and wisdom.

"You . . . You're the one who saved me from . . . from those men?" I said groggily.

"Me and Quirk." She smiled and I realized that she was really very beautiful.

I rubbed my head gingerly. "I didn't see anyone else. Though I must say you certainly moved fast enough for two!"

She seemed to be immensely pleased with that. "Fortunate for you, eh?" She moved forward lithely and I could see that she held a glass in her hand. "Here, drink this and I think you might feel a lot better."

I took the glass and tilted it back. It was some sort of brandyish concoction, fizzyish with a bitter mediciney taste. I drank it all in a couple of gulps and grimaced. But no sooner than that stuff slipped down my gullet than I began to feel a little calmer and the ache in my muscles, neck and head was relieved somewhat.

"Wow. Thanks. That's great stuff."

"No problem." She walked over to a high-backed chair and sat down, regarding me with an unreadable expression. "Quirk's the name of my staff."

"Your quarterstaff."

"Yes. My quarterstaff. Clearly you're not from around here. Where do you come from?"

I opened my mouth to tell her exactly where I was from, but uncharacteristically I allowed discretion to stop me. I clamped my mouth shut and just stared back at her. "Uhm — I'm sorry. Just from out of town I guess."

I thought I saw a flash of amusement pass across that previously unreadable field — and then again the eyes were dark and blank. "Do you have any idea why those brigands set upon you. Did you lose your money."

"They seemed to want to kidnap me."

She nodded her head. "You know that for sure?"

"They said something about taking me somewhere."

"Those were not normal thieves. They carried the mark of the Dark Universities."

"The Thorny League? You're positive?"

She gestured toward her considerable library. "Does it look like I lack in reference material. And did it seem back there as though I am without experience?"

"No. I didn't mean to insult you. I — I'm just more than a little shaken up, more than a little confused."

She got up, paced a bit, allowing me again to admire her sleek though certainly curvy figure. In fact, she walked as though she had modeling experience. There was a deft self-assurance in her movement and I must admit that as my headache subsided, I found that a normal male response occurring.

I found her extremely attractive.

She must have noticed me staring at her because she immediately stopped her pacing and sat down. She wagged a slim finger at me.

"Let me venture a guess," she said, a slow smile spreading across that sharp though to me increasingly lovely face. "You're in the employ of Professor Phineas Escutcheon, aren't you!"

I'm afraid I didn't have to answer, the surprise on my face did it for me.

"Ah ha. I knew it!" She jumped up, danced about and suddenly she wasn't the hard-bitten sleek and grim street fighter anymore, but rather girlish and joyous. "I *thought* something was afoot! I *knew* the Professor would try something harebrained to help Hypotropia!"

"You know Mr. Escutcheon?"

She sobered up immediately, walked over to a shelf, and drew out a large volume. I recognized it as a textbook concerning the history of American film. "I took his class at University." She plopped the book down. "It was fabulous. Not only the study of an art form, but a study of another world, a fantastic world of strange machines and weird people and wondrous wars and the Wild West and —" She suddenly looked at me as though for the very first time. Her eyes flitted down at me clothes. She smacked herself on the head. "What an idiot I am. Right in front of my nose and I didn't see it! You're from Earth, aren't you? I should have recognized the clothing before! The Prof found a way to import somebody to this world to help us!" A cloud blew over her face, though, as she considered what she was saying. She looked at me closely. "A strange choice, though. What, are you some kind of super wizard or something? But Earth doesn't have any wizards." She scratched her head. "You are quite the puzzle, I must say!" She poked me in the chest. "Well, speak up! Tell me why he brought you here! I'm a citizen! I have the right to know."

I realized that this close I could smell the perspiration and leather on her, mixed with a touch of mint and perfume. I admit, it was rather exciting.

But I'd already told her too much. Although she'd saved my butt, that didn't mean she was necessarily one of the good guys — and I was in alien territory.

"I'm sorry. But I can't tell you."

"Why not!" she demanded imperiously.

"I'm not authorized to tell you!" I shouted back, staring her straight in the eye. "Look, if I had a rank and a serial number I'd give them to you. All I can tell you is my name. Which is Ralph Phillips!"

She clapped her hands. "Very good. An excellent performance. I congratulate you. You are like something out of the movies that Professor Escutcheon shows in that delightfully bizarre theater of his. War movies, yes. World War II. The Germans take the brave American prisoner, but they get no vital secrets from him. You are truly amusing, fellow. Wherever did the Professor find you, hmmm? Somewhere unlikely, no doubt. If Professor Escutcheon is renowned for anything more than his bizarre schemes, it is the fools and losers he chooses to help him augment them!" She spoke quite animatedly, voice rising and falling, mimicking and mocking.

The attack hit me broadside, punching at all my buttons.

"I'm not a fool and I'm not a loser," I said. "I'm a *writer* and I'm going to write the best screenplay ever!"

Her eyes shone victoriously and she smacked the palm of her hand with her fist. "So *that's* it! I wondered what all the activity at the university was. Professor Escutcheon has hired himself a Hollywood writer. He's going to produce a film! He also spoke of that as a silly dream ... What a character! He's actually going to try it!"

I was upset at myself for having let go the goods. But I soon calmed down when it seemed that she was more interested in this information out of curiosity than for any bad intent. "In good cause!" I said defensively. "He intends to use the profits from my world to put this nation back on its feet!"

"Or so he says," replied the girl with great hauteur. "You don't know the mind of Professor Phineas Escutcheon!" She chuckled ruefully. "Or course, neither do I, but I've a little more experience listening to him, anyway, though I don't suppose he'd know me from Adam. Or from Eve, for that matter."

I'd recovered sufficiently at that point to realize that I didn't know my benefactor's name. I ventured to ask.

She raised her eyebrows. Silky thick eyebrows, those, brown and one of her best features, giving proportion to her face and emphasizing the beauty of her eyes.

"Lucinda. Lucinda Macree, actually," she said. Her face contorted and her hand contracted into a fist. "But I swear if you call me 'Lucy,' I'll rip your heart out!"

I confess, she'd been luring my heart by other methods, but I wasn't about to let her know that. Even now I was taken with the intensity and energy wrapped up into this tight little ball of woman. For all the intellectuality she showed with her numerous books, she was extraordinarily physical, both in the athletic and sensual (and, needless to say, for me *sexual*) sense.

"Lucinda. A very feminine name!" I said, with a slight bit of irony in my tone.

My humorous barb seemed to disarm her.

"Yes it is," she said and she curtseyed to me sweetly. "However, I should warn you that some of my comrades call me 'Bash' from time to time."

"After witnessing the way you dealt with my ambushers, I can well see why!"

"Thank you, I think." She looked at me oddly. Then she twirled a straight-backed wood chair around and sat down, tilting it toward me. If she hadn't downed it with such muscularity I'd have said she was flirting with me. "So then, sailor. Just where were you headed when those baddies pounced, hmm?"

I considered this. I'd told her just about everything else. Why shouldn't I tell her that?

"Well to tell you the truth, I was lost. But I was trying to find my way to a place called The Cracked Cask."

She looked at me oddly. "Why in the world were you, a stranger, trying to find your way to a place like that?"

"I didn't exactly get permission from Mr. Escutcheon, if that's what you mean . . . Actually, I'd been invited there by a man named Brank Toplin!"

Those gorgeous eyes went dark again. "Toplin! You don't say. How'd you meet him?"

"He's helping Mr. Escutcheon." I told her about our intended journey, looking for sites and subjects for the movie. I tried to sound like I knew what I was talking about, but I'm sure she knew I was talking through my hat.

This *was* her world, after all, and not mine.

"By the way, I don't suppose you could help me get there," I said. "I very much am looking forward to it."

She looked at me oddly. "Well of course, ninny. You don't think I'd make you a prisoner, do you?" She nodded, almost as though to herself. She winked at me. "Sorry, sweetheart, but I ain't that kind of gal." She swept over and pulled her cloak off a peg. "You feeling up to a little jaunt?"

I rubbed my head. Come to think of it, I realized that I was quite thirsty indeed, and besides some more of that beer I'd had earlier that day would help my rattled condition. I was *more* than ready!

However, I had a thought. "What time is it?"

"You mean, how long were you out of it?"

"I guess so."

"Only a few minutes." She grinned. "The night is yet young and I'm sure that Brank Toplin is still carousing at the Cracked Cask. So why don't we join him?"

I had sudden misgivings. What would Brank Toplin make of my guide? More than that, the handsome lout would take all away all the attention from me. Ah well, there was nothing for it. She was my one hope for getting there, and at the very least she deserved a drink for her efforts — to say nothing of preventing me from getting kidnapped.

"All right."

I zipped up my jacket and, still a little woozy, allowed myself to be helped down the two rickety flights of steps that led to the street. I could have done it easily on my own, but I confess that I enjoyed Lucinda's nearness. Besides, when she went into helper's mode, she wasn't so sarcastic and cutting, but rather sweet and feminine.

"Okay. I think I can take it from here," I said at the doorstep.

We launched ourselves into the dark and the curling fog, and although I could not help but wonder at the strange content of the future that awaited me, I nonetheless was thrilled at my current company!

Chapter Seven

The walk was only perhaps ten minutes long, but it involved a great deal of dodging in and out of alleys, along with a number of twists and turns through the narrow, canted streets. As we walked, I fancied I saw a great number of strange and contorted figures in the whirling fog. Dragons and monsters, trolls and giants, and certainly a ghost or two. But I ascribed it to the beating I'd taken and I certainly didn't let Lucinda know about the fear that I was feeling. In fact, I adopted a bold, self-confident air — which made me look pretty ridiculous the times that I tripped over potholes or the number of pieces of rotting boards lying about willy-nilly in the streets.

So when we reached the Cracked Cask and encountered the mascot chained to the outside, I almost cockily jumped into catastrophe.

The Cracked Cask looked like a dream of the archetypal Victorian English Pub. It was a wide brick building with an oozing thatch-daub roof with beautiful stained glass windows, through which cozy lights glimmered, arousing thoughts of a roaring hearth, toes toasting and much merry-making and good cheer pouring forth. Above the door hung a sign illuminated by a lantern with a colored illustration of a beer cask breaking in two, gushing forth-foamy brew. At the top of the roof, smoke curled from the chimney. Even as we approached, I could smell a wonderful mélange of odors emanating from the place — baking bread, roasting meat, and of course beer. The smell was so strong that I had to wonder if the Cracked Cask didn't brew it on their own premises.

All about the brick sides surged the tides of the fog, and this was the reason I didn't pay much attention to the hulking ball of leathery stuff curled off to one side.

"Here it is!" said Lucinda.

"This is the place, all right!" I said, absolutely thrilled to see it. Brank Toplin was here, and wouldn't he be happy to see me. Probably he'd already drunk all of my beer, — though from the looks and smell of the place, I didn't think they'd be lacking in supply for another round. So happy was I that I broke stride with Lucinda and skipped ahead to the door.

"No!" Lucinda cried out. "Wait!"

But it was too late. I reached out for the doorknob, but did not make the grab successfully.

A roar the like of which I'd never heard in my entire life nearly knocked me off my feet.

The leathery wing unfurling *did* knock me off my feet.

I caught a glimpse of fiery eyes, a flash of sharp teeth, and an outstretch of unsheathed claws. A burning odor suddenly suffused the air, and I thought I glimpsed a flicker of flame, like a Bic lighter suddenly clicking on.

The next thing I knew I was flat on my back, and a large ungainly thing was rearing over me. The fog had broken and by the light of the lantern by the side I could see a dinosaurlike form above me. My first inclination was not to believe my eyes and treat this solidified apparition much as I treated the forms I'd seen in the fog before. But all of my senses screamed its reality, and I when the lizardlike snout snapped less than a yard from my throat, I had to admit that it was real.

"Hypernius!" scolded Lucinda, moving between the creature and me. I noticed that she held in her hand some kind of small bag that she held in front of the thing's nostrils. Its marble eyes suddenly turned soft and liquid and harmless and it snuffled the bag and let loose a gentle sigh.

"You all right, Phillips?" Lucinda asked.

"Wha . . . What *is* it?" I said, slowly and warily moving back and gaining my feet.

"What does it *look* like, you ninny?"

"A dragon," I said, keeping her between it and me. "A small dragon."

"Bingo!" she said. "His name is Hypernius, and he's the bar's mascot. You can't run up the Cracked Cask and you can't run out. Everybody who patronizes this place knows that you have to pay attention to Hypernius." She stroked the thing atop its smooth leathery, hairless head, speaking to it in baby talk. "Did the freaky little forefinger scare snoogums? Hmmm. Bad man! Well, we've set him straight. When he comes out, he'll have a nice treat for you." She scratched it behind its webbed ears and then glared back at me. "Won't you, Phillips!"

"Sure. Be glad to. But I really had no idea . . ."

"Just pat him on the head and I think it will be okay."

I looked at the thing with great hesitation.

"Come on, Phillips. He won't bite!"

"If he does, it looks as though it would be pretty deadly."

"It could be worse. He's a man-bred species. About as domesticated as dragons get. So *do* it, fellow, or he'll probably get really pissed!"

Hesitantly I reached out a hand and put it on top of squarish head. The texture of the grey skin was surprisingly soft and as I stroked it, I swear it emitted an odd kind of *purring* growl. It looked up at me with eminently friendly eyes, and I assumed that, indeed, all was forgiven.

I also noticed that it was tied to the wall by a chain, which fastened to a collar around its neck. By the ring in the wall were bowls, doubtless meant to hold water and food.

Still, I made a mental note to be sure that I brought that treat with me on the way out.

"Bye, Hypy," cooed Lucinda. "We'll see you on the way out."

The dragon nodded as though it understood her words and then it curled back up into a ball beside the wall. I thought I saw wisps of smoke flutter up from its nose.

Lucinda opened the door and impatiently gestured for me to follow. I did so, this time making sure to walk at a slow pace and to the far end of the door away from the bar mascot.

"Amazing what dear Hypernius has done for this place," said Lucinda. "Used to get robbed quite often. Now the thieves tend to stay away. Hypernius can smell 'em, you know. He's got quite a range of talents."

I was about to ask where the dragon was from and get some more details on that startling and fantastic beast, but just then the warmth of the Cracked Cask's interior enveloped me, and the full welcome of the effluvia of sights and sounds and smells grabbed my attention.

The place was filled with people, conversing and singing. Barmaids were bustling about, carrying trays filled with steaming food and dripping pewter jugs of brew. A fire roared in the brick hearth. Men and women — mostly men — lounged around in booths and open tables, garbed in rough medieval style dress. My eyes were slightly stung by the smoke hanging in the air. Tobacco smoke, at first seemingly anachronistic — but then I remembered that I wasn't back in the year 1200, I was still in the twentieth century.

A fantasy pub indeed.

Immediately, I started looking for Brank Toplin. It didn't take long to find him. Actually, I heard his voice first, roaring over top of the crowd above the arguing and the song. He was sitting at a round table with a number of other men, earnestly and loudly discussing some aspect of local politics.

"There he is!" I said to Lucinda, pointing.

"There he is indeed," said Lucinda, and she had a strange look to her as she said it. I was too excited being here to take much note of it, though. I plowed through the people, figuring she would follow and came up alongside Brank Toplin, patiently letting him finish what he had to say before I disturbed him.

"... so I say, throw all the money into the military and let's go out and *trounce* the bastards!"

His words were met with a round of cheers and the successful orator smiled, leaned back in his chair, grabbed his pint of richly golden beer, and rewarded himself.

I tapped him on the shoulder. Still drinking, Brank Toplin turned a lazy eye toward me. He spluttered beer foam down his chin, clopped the glass down to the table, and turned to face me, eyes instantly alive again.

"Well well! Hello pilgrim. What took you so long?"

"You were supposed to come and get me."

"That, all right. I figured you'd find your way. And look at you — here you are!" He stood up and grabbed me and folded me into a manly embrace. He turned to his audience. "Attention, folks! This is my friend, Ralph. He's a writer!"

Slurred greetings of 'Hello Ralph' and 'Jolly good!' floated up from that bilious, partying group.

"Who are they, Brank?" I asked.

"I haven't the faintest! But come, I've reserved a small booth in the back just for the two of us. We will go and have that hearty man to man conversation I promised!"

"I've got company," I said.

"Company?" Brank looked over my shoulder. "I don't see anyone." I spun around. There was no one behind me.

"She was here just a moment ago."

"She? A woman?" I got a jab in the fleshy part of my arm. "You devil, you. So that's what you've been up to!"

A little annoyed, I turned to him. "Actually, what I've been up to is getting lost! I was almost kidnapped by people from the Dark Universities. Lucinda saved me."

That took him back. It also seemed to sober him up considerably. "Dark Uni — How do you know!"

"They confessed as much!"

A troubled look flitted across his face. "You don't say . . . and what was this woman's name . . . Belinda?"

"Lucinda. Lucinda Macree," a voice piped from behind us. We spun around to see her holding a pitcher of beer. "Thought perhaps we could use something not quite so stale as what I'm smelling from this table."

Brank's jaw dropped. "Bash!"

"You two know each other?"

Lucinda smiled. "We've had acquaintance, yes."

Brank shook off his astonishment. "Well. Lucinda. A true surprise seeing you. But then, I shouldn't be all that surprised. I've heard you came to the Cracked Cask. I've even glimpsed you here from time to time. I'm sorry we haven't had time to chat."

"Because I've been sure to *avoid* you, up to now!" said Lucinda. "But come on, this thing's heavy. Let's sit down someplace."

Brank did not act the gentleman and take the pitcher, so I tried to. Lucinda demurred. "In your state, you'll drop it," she snarled.

I was non-plussed. Apparently these two were not on the best of terms. A laundry list of possible reasons went through my head, but I decided not to ask. Best to just see what happened. Brank didn't seem to mind drinking Lucinda's beer, nor did Lucinda mind giving it to Brank to drink. So that was a start.

By this time, all I was really concerned about was getting some of that brew inside of me. I was starting to get my headache again, and I could use a little calm.

I tasted it.

The taste turned into a swallow, and the swallow became a gulp and a larger gulp followed that one.

Half the pint went down smooth and bittersweet as silk. And me, not being that much of drinker!

It was good.

Brank seemed to be happy to take note of how much I was enjoying it.

"There you go! Didn't I tell you that the stuff here is the best!"

"It tastes so fresh!"

"They say they use magic in its making," said Lucinda after a little drink herself. "But actually its just hops, malt, water and barley — and maybe a newt's eye or two, for luck."

I put the pint down. "Newt's eyes?"

"Or was it cat's tongue?"

"Dog's testicles or bat's intestines is what I heard!" said Brank. "Whatever they do, it may as well be magic as far as I'm concerned."

"You're kidding?"

"Nobody has the exact recipe — or everyone would be making it!" laughed Lucinda. "As to the secret ingredient, it's all just idle speculation. Nobody knows for sure."

"Just drink up, lad! There's nothing in it to harm you — long as you don't drink too much, that is!"

By that time, though, my thirst had returned, so I just shrugged and had some more.

By the time I finished the first pint and poured myself some more, Lucinda had drunk a fair share of hers and the atmosphere had warmed and lightened considerably.

I myself found my tongue loosened.

"I'm afraid that I've already told Lucinda why I'm here," I admitted after the first sip from my second pint.

"Have you now," said Brank, seeming to be extremely amused.

"Hope that's okay."

"Well, she saved you from the Dark, then, didn't she. Mr. Escutcheon can't complain about that."

"You really shouldn't have had him bounding about the town alleys on his own Brank! I've always thought you were incredibly irresponsible. But I won't harangue you about it!"

"Mercy yet remains on this world!" said Brank rolling his eyes toward the heavens.

". . . and I won't tell Professor Escutcheon either . . ." She leaned over, smiling slyly. "On two conditions."

"Oh dear. What have I done?" said Brank.

"First, just exactly what's the poop here? Our guest gave me only the merest outline."

Brank raised a rough eyebrow. "How do I know you're in our camp!"

"I *saved* the fellow. What more would you have me do?"

"Buy another pitcher?"

Lucinda chuckled. "You certainly haven't changed, you drunken rogue."

"Better than a roguish drunk, woman. What have you told her then, Ralph?"

"Only what Mr. Escutcheon told me." I quickly and nervously related the barest of details. "But I have to admit, one of the reasons I came here tonight was to find out if I could learn some more from you!"

Brank Toplin nodded. "Aw, there's no harm in it, I suppose." He finished the last of his drink and wiped the foam from his beard with his arm. "Like you said, Ralph, we're heading out tomorrow to scout locations for this film of Phineas' . . . but there's more to it than that."

"Oh?" said Lucinda.

"Really?" I said.

"Yes indeed. Phineas seems to have a couple ideas about the course this film should take, and he wants to try them out."

"Try them out?" I said, confused.

"Yes indeed. We're making a movie about a quest, correct?" said Brank. "And you're going to write it."

"That's what I understood to be the case," I said.

"What kind of quest, though? What kind of adventures happen? And who are the characters. And what fantastic special efforts — ?"

"Effects," I corrected.

"Sorry. What special effects happen to them?"

I didn't need to think about the answer to *that*. "That's the stuff you make up." I tapped my head. "It's the imagination!"

"Imagination, eh?" Brank grinned. "But we're on a tight budget, remember. That's the whole idea . . . We need to shoot reality here, but make up a story around it for the purposes of creating a motion picture."

"Exactly," said Lucinda. "Clever. Reality here is fantasy on the other plane — so why not use it as the backdrop of a story in a film that will doubtless look very very expensive and wondrous.... when it's actually quite *inexpensive.*" She shook her head with respect. "Well, the old Prof. might actually do it! And really rake in the money to boot!"

"Yes, yes, I know all that," I said, laughing. "I told you, that's what Mr. Escutcheon told me. It's very simple!"

"What he probably didn't mention was that we're going to give you the inspiration for the story, oh wondrous Hollywood writer, by actually making the quest first!" A look of great satisfaction appeared on Brank's face. "A quest for quite a marvelous treasure — and perhaps, who knows, the quest itself might ease the problems of our troubled nation!"

"Whatever are you babbling about, Toplin?" said Lucinda crossly.

"Would you believe a trek across the most magical part of this wondrous world?" Brank drank deep of his beer and then smacked his lips with satisfaction. "Would you believe a journey across the Mountains of Mirth?"

"The Mountains of Mir — but what for ... That's madness ... Why?" said Lucinda.

"Why else, my dear. To visit the Dragon Horde of the Quincunx Majestic Order!"

Chapter Eight

"The Dragon Horde!" said Lucinda.

"I think that's what I said."

"Why ... Why that's *suicide!*" Her eyes were wide.

"We want an incredible picture, we have to take incredible measures! That's what Escutcheon says. And I can't say that I blame him. In fact, I think it's a pretty damned good idea!" Another drink, and Toplin clopped his pint glass down with great finality. He folded his arms together and gave a self-satisfied, even smug challenging look to Lucinda.

"Suicide?" I said uneasily. "I guess I've figured out by now that this would be an adventure . . . But I hope to come out of it alive. Dragon Horde? What are you talking about, Lucinda?"

However, they both ignored me. They seemed to be engaged in some kind of glaring battle. I had the distinct feeling of being way out of my depth between these two.

"Wait a minute," said Lucinda. "Wait one hell-blasted minute, Brank Toplin. You used to talk about the Treasure of the Dragon Horde and all the prizes you reckoned were there. It wasn't you who put Professor Escutcheon up to this crazy journey, was it?"

Brank Toplin shrugged. "I might have dropped the idea into his ear once or twice. I told him I was the only hero who'd be willing to take up that kind of valiant effort. However, the Professor is a widely read man. I'm sure he knows far more about those lands than you — or even I, who've actually been through much of them!"

"Yes, but we're talking *book* knowledge — not hard won experience! You can't just waltz through that kind of territory on a quest . . . Much less think about taking a whole film crew!"

"We're *not* taking a whole film crew," countered Brank. "At least not now. And the purpose anyway isn't just research — it's paving the way for the production. Scouting, inspiration, preparation, what have you —" He rubbed his hands together, unable to conceal his glee. "And maybe with a goodly amount of reward for certain noble Protectors."

"Yes, I dare say . . ." Lucinda mulled this over for a moment, tongue producing a comic bulge in her cheeks. A most unfeminine little effect, but one that I found strangely charming. Nonetheless, I was pretty busy coping with this little bombshell dropped in my lap.

"Why did she call the trip suicidal, Brank?" I wanted to know. Some of the effects of the beer were wearing off and I was getting a little nervous, I must say.

"Oh, I admit there are a few hazards along the way. Warring trolls and wicked monsters and gruesome swamps and awesome craggy mountains. And the Dragon Horde are about as likely to eat you as to greet you." He pounded the wood table with his fist. "Nonetheless, you can't go wrong for characters and backdrop for a majestic and exciting movie, and I've got a lot of good friends along the way who tell me that things aren't quite as vicious as they used to be in the olden, golden days, and that the Dragon Horde are getting somewhat kinder and gentler and perhaps are looking for better public relations with other lands. . . . I'm confident that they'll be very open to the whole idea of a film shot in their marvelous realm. I mean, to use a phrase from your own culture — Everybody wants to be in pictures!" He tilted toward me self-consciously. "Pardon me, but I'm not that well versed in things of your world, I'm afraid. I am correct, no? Glamour. Money. Power. Celebrity? It is not so much different here — look at me!"

"Yes, Brank Toplin had always worked hard to achieve the easy life," said Lucinda. "Alas, his basic lazy nature has always held him back."

"You have not seen the best of me!" barked Brank.

"Yes, but I've had my share of the worst."

"Hey! I didn't come here to get into a fight!" I said, holding up my hands. "Settle down you two, please! Let's drink our beers and calm ourselves." I topped off their drinks and then sipped at my own as example. They churlishly drank, eyeing each other balefully. "There, that's better, right? I know it is with me. How do you think *I* feel, hearing that I have definitely bitten off more than I can chew. But I'm taking it like a man!" True, with the help of a belly full of potent bitter — but hey, every little bit helps!

"I'm glad you're taking it so well," said Lucinda. "Maybe I am being a trifle hyperbolic in my estimation."

"You're off in the deep, far as I'm concerned!"

"So it will be a piece of cake. So then I need have no fear in making my next demand!"

"Demand. What are you talking about now, woman?"

"You remember before I said I had *two* conditions for keeping my mouth generally shut about your role in my new friend Ralph's misadventures."

"I thought the conditions had already been met," growled Brank in a surly tone.

"No, they have not. My *second* condition . . . Well, actually, believe it or not, it will be for your benefit, Toplin!"

"Do I have to be grateful?"

She ignored the jibe. "I've been living the bohemian life, lately. I've been writing a book. Well, the book is more or less complete now . . . And I find that I am restless. I could use a little adventure. And yes, maybe I too would like to be in pictures."

She smiled sweetly at me, then turned and changed her aspect to one of scowling demand.

"Uh oh," said Brank, his eyes rolling toward the ceiling. "Heavens help me, I can see what's coming."

"You're going to take *me* on this little warm-up quest of yours, Brank Toplin! That's my second demand!"

At first, Brank seemed more than a little stunned. Finally, however, he was able to squeeze some words out as he goggled with exasperation at the woman.

"As though we weren't going to have enough trouble!"

"You think I can't be of enormous help?" said Lucinda challengingly.

"I think — I *know* from experience — you can be of enormous *hin-*

drance!" bellowed the boozy hero.

"Those were merely personality clashes! I've grown since then, Brank."

"Yes, like a fungus, no doubt!"

"Look, I *know* that area! I've read everything there is to read about it!"

"What good is that if you've never been there!"

"You're going to get me in this expedition and that's that!" she declared flatly and then pushed herself forward as though to meet the opposition fully face to face.

"I won't!"

"You will, or your butt will be in the ringer with Professor Escutcheon!"

"I won't, damn it!" Face red, fists clenched.

"You will!" Face clenched, fists red.

I could see that the conversation was rapidly devolving, so I thought it best if I jumped in and had my say.

"Wait a minute, wait a minute! Don't I get a voice in this?"

"You're just a hireling!" barked Brank, his dander clearly up high.

"True, but so are you!" I said, keeping my tone reasonable. "Besides, Mr. Escutcheon seems to value my opinion."

"Listen to him!" said Lucinda.

"I didn't know you wanted to go with us," I said, turning to her. "Of course, without being specific about Brank's failings, I'll tell him how you saved me. He really should know about the Dark Universities crew."

"True," mused Brank. "Quite true."

"You will simply present your credentials then, Bash."

"You needn't tell him that nickname."

"Lucinda, then. So we'll leave it up to Mr. Escutcheon and make peace the two of you, so that we can enjoy our beer and time together tonight in peace."

Brank grumped, but it wasn't a negative grump so I assumed that the plan was okay with him.

And while it wasn't totally what Lucinda had asked for, she seemed happy enough to take it.

We spent the rest of the next hour drinking two more pitchers of beer.

Afterwards, I made sure that both of these valiant fantasy world heroes walked me home.

By the time they had left me at my room, though, they had both lapsed into sullen silences. I had prodded them before to tell me the details of their past associations, but they'd refused to talk about it.

Despite my questions, in fact, and despite my intentions for guiding the direction of the meeting, I still did not know much about these places were going to.

I still remained mostly in suspense.

"Well, then, Mr. Phillips. Are you ready?" said Dr. Escutcheon.

I wasn't.

I probably never *would* be ready.

I was sitting on top of something like a horse, with something like a hangover shrouding my head. The sun had barely lifted itself beyond the horizon, and I was shivering with the dewy cold, nose pointed toward mystery.

But what could I say?

"Yes sir."

Pad of paper, pens packed into backpack, I was on my way along a most unusual route to becoming a screenwriter. However it was an ambition that I meant to achieve. If it meant having an unlikely adventure along the way, then so be it.

Dr. Escutcheon pointed toward the distant hills, still clogged with morning mist. Just above them you could see craggy snow-capped peaks.

Our party was small, and all on horses. (Not quite totally Earth style horses, with large floppy ears and a little lower slung, but for all intents and purposes certainly horsy enough.) Myself, of course, and Dr. Escutcheon. Brank Toplin and the two court magicians, Thelonius Meistercrow and Quenton Quintabulous. Two pack horses.

And Lucinda.

"It's a *wonderful* morning, isn't it, Brank?" she said, all smiles and without a shred of her former feistiness, just sweet and charming as she breathed deep the sweet morning air and surveyed the land's challenges ahead with bright optimism.

Brank Toplin just grumbled.

When I'd been yanked out of bed two hours before dawn, Lucinda was already at the breakfast table, sharp and awake, talking intensely with Dr. Escutcheon.

"Oh, hello, Ralph!" she said, almost in passing. "I've taken it upon myself to pop by and offer my services to Professor Escutcheon! And can you imagine! He remembers me!"

"Of course I remember you, my dear. You were one of my very best students — I'm just very impressed with how much you've matured in the interim." He cast a stern look my way. "She told me, Mr. Phillips, that she saved you from certain kidnapping by our Opposition. I thought I requested that you sleep!"

I took a look at Thelonius Meistercrow, who'd roused me from my sleep so brusquely, and he just shrugged. "I'm sorry, sir. I couldn't. I had to go out and explore, I'm afraid. Er — Brank Toplin told me about this public house he'd be at and — well, I guess the temptation was too great!"

Fortunately Brank himself stumbled in just then and took some of the heat off of me. He seemed grateful that both Lucinda and I had suppressed his true role in the matter, and he admitted that yes, the woman was damned good with her staff and could juggle a mean sword, too.

After Lucinda's resume on her knowledge of the area and her desire to be in on "your wonderful film project, Professor Escutcheon!" I gave my own testimony while choking some particularly lumpy oatmeal down.

"Hmm. We shall have discuss what this means later!" pronounced Mr. Escutcheon. "However, I must say that since you seem to have a way in dealing with my rival academic factions, it would do well to have you along! Sounds as though, unfortunately, you might well need some strong-armed help, eh Mister Toplin?"

Brank just grunted without a great deal of excitement.

And so, once we packed, we headed out for our adventure — and me, for once wondering if maybe I'd be better back safe and warm in my North Hollywood apartment. However, the glow of the sun on the horizon cheered me immensely and I began to feel faintly human and to look forward to a successful and exciting journey that would net me the material for a fabulous, perhaps award-winning (imagine, me in a tux spangled with pixie dust!) screenplay.

We traveled along a road past a number of farms on the rolling hills and I began to see more of what Dr. Escutcheon was talking about. Everything seemed wilted and stunted. Black and grey were the predominant colors in the fields, and there was the rotten smell of blight over it all. And that brackish spell smell I'd noted before . . . stronger here, *much* stronger.

I commented on this to Quenton Quintabulous, who was the magician closest to me.

"You are quite astute, young master," he said, eyeing me coldly. "But this is a subject that it is not my place to discuss. If you have questions, you should address them to Professor Escutcheon."

"Ah, I see." But it really wasn't necessary to do so. There was something elementally cursed about the land. Even I as an outsider could tell that. And there was also some *secret* implicit in it all, I could tell, that would take some digging to discover . . . certainly more than an idle question to the leader of the group.

The town, with its flag-decked castle, beautifully touched by the rays of the sun and beautifully backgrounded by profoundly fleecy clouds right out of a storybook illustration, was not far behind when Lucinda rode ahead. She cantered up to Dr. Escutcheon and then rode along side of him, leaning over and speaking with him in a low voice.

Dr. Escutcheon nodded, looking quite surprised and even a little excited. "Yes! Yes . . . why, that is an excellent idea, Lucinda. If you can accomplish it, then you've already truly earned your place here amongst us!" He turned to the rest of us. "We're going to take an early break." He eyed me. "I think that our writer could do with a nap, anyway!"

"But we've just gotten going!" complained Brank. "At this rate we won't make any distance today!"

"Lucinda has just come up with a splendid notion that could ensure the success of this journey. And I think it's only fair that we give her a chance to see if she can pull it off!" He turned to her. "Do you think you can do it quickly?"

"Within the time it takes for you to heat cups of coffee and have a nice second breakfast!" stated Lucinda with massive self-confidence.

"Blast. I do not like this! I do not like this at all!" Brank stated in no uncertain terms.

I wasn't certain about what it meant at all. However, Dr. Escutcheon gave the widest grin I'd yet seen him essay — a grin that totally lit up his face and gave me no doubt not only that Lucinda had a worthy plan — but that the being that I'd been hired by was indeed a person of Good.

"I think, Mr. Toplin, that if Lucinda succeeds in her efforts, you will be quite glad!"

Upon that uninformative but positive note, Lucinda was promptly dispatched back toward town, and we selected a copse of trees under which to rest. Thelonius Meistercrow conjured up a quick fire and Quenton Quintabulous cooked a batch of thick coffee. We hadn't gone far, and I wasn't that hungry, however when the magicians produced a bunch of sugary things that looked like donuts coated with bits of dried fruit, I decided that the extra carbohydrates wouldn't hurt. I dunked the confection into my coffee and chewed it slowly as I sat regarding the hills and the mountains ahead of us.

Brank took his coffee off to solitary shadows, there to sulk, but Mr. Escutcheon seemed inordinately cheerful and he took his sitting by me.

We did not talk, however, the strange world that lay ahead of us. Rather, Mr. Escutcheon seemed more interested in discussing my favorite films and what I thought made them work.

Especially plots and characters — We got into a long discussion of exactly what made a primary character sympathetic to the audience. I could see where he was headed, and I approved . . . we were at the very beginning of creating a film that worked, and he was starting with the rudiments. As it happened, I agreed. A film had to have interesting characters involved in a strong, satisfying plot to succeed — Rick in *Casablanca* . . . Annie in *Annie Hall* . . . oh, there were dozens of examples, and we covered only a few.

Finally, though, I said, "Well, clearly our character is going to have to be a hero of some sort."

"Or a normal person who becomes a hero!"

"Or maybe a hero with huge faults who falls and then redeems himself!"

Dr. Escutcheon's eyes gleamed. "Yes, yes. I like that. However, do you not think that is too classical for modern American tastes? That, after all, is the audience we will be selling the film to."

A very good point. And I told him as such.

"Is the audience still mostly young in America?"

"The movie going audience, yes. But there are the videotape watchers — who are older. And all ages of people still go to the movies."

Dr. Escutcheon nodded thoughtfully. "Well, then. Would it be difficult to have a number of characters? Each for a certain group to identify with?"

"Well, look at us! We're on a quest! And we're certainly different characters!"

"But I wonder who's watching," said Dr. Escutcheon. "And I wonder if there is anyone identifying —"

"We're getting a little too cosmic for me!" I said. "Let's just talk characters and story here, first. Clearly you had something in mind. I mean, since you're taking us to the Dragon Horde or whatever. Clearly we're questing for something. But for what?"

"Why, background, scenes, content! Monsters, and creatures of delight and outrage to dazzle the eyes of movie goers." Dr. Escutcheon's eyes twinkled. "And just think! The Dragons themselves. The valleys and chasms and craggy mountaintops. The caverns of gleaming treasure!"

"Yes. I figured as much. So it would be safe to say that we're on a kind of dry run for this movie quest."

"Precisely."

"But what's the goal of the quest? For the hypothetical movie characters, that is. Just treasure?"

"Maybe for one of the characters. Certainly many Americans can identify with that."

Yes. I for one, I was sad to say. "Power. Like the Ring of Power in J.R.R. Tolkien's *Lord of the Rings?*"

"Oh yes, but of course we can't use a ring. We will be accused of plagiarism."

"Oh, you needed worry. Dozens of fantasy writers have already done that!" I laughed. "Maybe not a ring of power, but something powerful nonetheless.... Something that the antagonist wants as well ... the bad guy."

"Yes... Well I suppose there are any number of possibilities in this world's history — although I suppose to you it would all sound like myth and legend... And I dare say there's some exaggeration mixed in with it all."

"Anything appropriate to our project you might know of right off hand?"

"Hmm. I'm afraid I'm going to have to consult with my magicians on that one. And maybe the school's library when we get back. Definitely a possibility — no a *certainty!*" Mr. Escutcheon smiled again. I'd done it as well! I'd made the old guy crack a grin! A real achievement!

He patted me on the shoulder. "Yes, yes, I like the track that our collaboration is taking already! But you must excuse me now. There are matters that I must discuss with the magicians!" There was a sudden explosion. We swiveled around and saw a puff of orange smoke billowing up, shot with crackling lightning bolts. "Oh dear," sighed Mr. Escutcheon. "I dislike it when such occurs."

I saw that the magicians, though a bit sooty in the face, were okay.

"You mean you hate it when that happens!"

"That as well. Pardon me!" He moved away to have his discussion.

I grabbed some more coffee and took my seat again under the tree, studying the horizon as though for some hint of the future. Too much cogitation on this situation would not be good, I knew. Too much rumination wasn't suitable — It was like philosophy, which I never liked to get in *too* deeply. If you looked too closely at things, everything tended to fall apart.

The way I felt now, I didn't want anything to fall apart. Before me was a possibility of achieving all that I had come to California for... In a truly roundabout and peculiar way, true, but it was worth it...

And this peculiar quest could be of value in itself.

But there were other things to consider. This plot for one thing. These characters I was going to have to construct.

At home, my parents would accuse me of daydreaming all the time. "Ralph the DD," my father would say, and that was before the term 'designated driver' came into vogue. What I was doing, of course, was making up stories. I had my own private universes and if I was doing the 'wool-gathering' my mother claimed, it was only so I could place it upon the loom of imagination and create a wondrous cloth. (Well, I thought so anyway.) So as a result, my methods of plotting usually involved staring off at a cloud somewhere and letting my thoughts drift in peculiar directions.

I was doing just that, not accomplishing much but enjoying myself nonetheless, when Lucinda returned with a great deal of hullabaloo and clatter of hooves.

I got up and hurried on over to the campsite, where Dr. Escutcheon was helping her down from her mount.

"Well, my girl!" he said. "How did it go?"

She was positively beaming. "Wonderful!"

"Well! What have you brought! Is this great secret going to be finally revealed?" said Brank rudely. "I see nothing you've brought back!"

"I haven't got it with me," said Lucinda.

Dr. Escutcheon and Lucinda looked at each other . . . And they actually started laughing. This annoyed Brank a great deal, and I must admit it had me wondering quite a bit myself.

"No great mystery!" said Lucinda. "Here he comes now!"

She pointed up to the sky and I looked up immediately.

At first I didn't see anything different. But then I noticed a floating spot, flapping our way.

It was a dragon.

And, unless I was mistaken, its name was Hypernius.

Chapter Nine

*H*ypernius the dragon flapped toward us, and I swear its tail was wagging with pleasure.

Brank Toplin was aghast.

"What . . . What in God's name . . ."

"It's a dragon. Hypernius Dragon, to be precise," said Lucinda, gazing up, clearly filled with pride at her accomplishment.

"A *dragon*. A young dragon at that . . . Whatever are we going to need with a dragon?" He was almost sputtering. Mostly, he looked vexed that this matter had been taken from his hands.

"My goodness," pronounced Thelonius Meistercrow. "An interesting notion . . ."

Quenton Quintabulous nodded. "This shall be an interesting subject indeed."

They both seemed not only appreciative of Lucinda's accomplishment, but of the inordinate *value* of having a dragon along.

I was still in the dark, however, and confessed as much.

"An ally," explained Phineas Escutcheon as the beast landed about twenty yards away and started our way on all fours, its large leather wings contracted and fitting neatly onto its sides. "Not only for our quest — for who can doubt the good of having a dragon for protection... But to deal with the Dragon Horde. We shall be able to gain admission, negotiate, parlay — all without one of our members getting gobbled up! Always that threat, you know. The Dragon Horde can be quite tricky."

With a friendly growly noise and bright jewel-like eyes, Hypernius walked up to Lucinda immediately, who cooed and laughed and clapped and made all kinds of pleasant welcoming noises. She scratched the beast under its webbed, floppy ears and it's eyes rolled, lids fluttering with pleasure. A wisp of smoke curled up from a nostril.

I admit that I was a little frightened. After my experience with the beast in the dark the night before, I suppose I was a little bit dragon-shy, and the sight of the scaly hide, those long sharp teeth and those razor claws unnerved me. However, by daylight, the beauty of the thing was much more apparent and with a friendly gleam in its eyes and its perky, unsuspicious movements it seemed more like a great big puppy dog than some monster crawling out of a darkened nightmare.

I noticed Brank Toplin taking a step back, hand on the hilt of his sword. "I don't care for dragons. You can't really trust them when they're not chained up, you know." He scratched his head. "How'd you get him from the Cracked Cask, anyway?"

"A fortunate coincidence," explained Lucinda. "Just last month I was speaking to the owner, commenting that Hypy here was getting bigger. He agreed and mentioned that sometime this year Hypernius would have to make a pilgrimage to the Dragon Horde for some sort of dragon rite or whatever. He was worried about Hypernius doing it on his own.... I don't know why I didn't think of it earlier, but as we were leaving it just came to me: Since *we* were going to the Dragon Horde, not only could we do Hypy some good.... He'd probably help us a great deal. For the reasons Professor Escutcheon mentioned, and who knows... maybe others!"

"I don't know," said Brank. "I'm still not sure I like this much."

"Like it or lump it, chum. He's going. Now you too make peace." She turned to Hypernius. "Go greet Uncle Brank! Be nice!"

The dragon seemed to understand. It broke from Lucinda's side and slithered on over to Brank, who stood stock still as the dragon's forked tongue waggled out and licked at his hand. A gruff purring sound emanated from its throat. I knew the thing could be quite fierce, but at the moment it seemed as though it just wanted to be friends.

"Go ahead, Toplin. Pet it!"

Hypernius growled. Brank petted it briefly. He turned to the others.

"Your turn, folks," he said nervously and then stepped back. The magicians and Mr. Escutcheon took both approached with some hesitation, but when they actually petted the creature, they untensed. This relieved me somewhat, so when I reached out to stroke Hypernius I did so with less hesitation.

The skin under the ears was not scaly, surprisingly smooth soft and warm. A kind of musky smell surrounded the lizardlike creature, but it was not unpleasant. I stroked the dragon in the exact way that I'd seen the others do, but apparently it was used to pleasure by now. Instead of rolling its eyes, it looked directly at me. The eyes were brilliantly green, except for flecks of chocolate brown, and they seemed to *shift*. They blinked, and the dragon canted its head, staring at me in a most intelligent way as though to say "Who the *heck* are you?"

It opened its fanged mouth, but instead of a growl or a groan, a tiny inquiring *squeak* emerged.

For a moment, I felt as though I were immersed in a dense bank of clouds, gleaming with gemlike stars. There were other forms there past the skein of the fog, but more than that I felt the sensation of *company* in an instinctive way.

The entire bubble burst as a hand fell heavy upon my shoulder. I was back on the ground again, staring at Hypernius the dragon, and the dragon was staring back at me, just a friendly dragon again, its eyes purely emerald green, no sign of those brown flecks anymore.

The pressure was still on my shoulder. I turned around and found myself face to face with Lucinda again, looking at me in a strange way.

"Ralph? Ralph, are you all right?"

"Yes . . . Yes . . . I think so. . . . I had . . . like this *fugue* . . ." I told her about the sensation of being *elsewhere*.

The magicians were approaching and she turned and looked at them as though for answers.

"Most curious . . . most curious indeed!" Thelonius Meistercrow said.

"Did you sense the shift on the astral-spatial plane, colleague?" asked Quenton Quintabulous.

"Was that what it was?" The magician worked his shoulders and stretched. "I thought it was my early morning rheumatism acting up."

Mister Escutcheon came up and stroked the dragon again. "Some sort of communication here, gentlemen?"

"Something distinctly magical . . ."

"Eminently psychic."

These judgments pronounced, the two magicians turned to me and gazed upon me in an entirely different way. "And yet from an eminently mundane sort of plane . . ."

"How curious. . . ."

"What's going on?" I said.

"That's what we should like to know," said Mister Escutcheon. "Did I miss something?" said Lucinda, clearly not wanting to be out of the picture.

Thelonius and Quenton conferred amongst one another briefly in mutters and then swung around to give their opinion. "It would appear that our writer here has some sort of dragon bond, of all things."

Brank Toplin, still staying well away, barked a laugh. "Dragon bond! Sounds kind of *dirty!*"

"The only thing dirty around here," snapped Lucinda, "Is your filthy mind!"

"What Bash," shot back Brank. "Are you an expert in dirty minds?"

"I know one when I see one . . . Small as it seems to be."

"People, people! We've barely started our journey and already we are fighting!"

I wanted to tell him he'd better get used to it — there was definitely an abrasive edge to the relationship between the two — but I was far too involved in the strange thing that had just happened to me.

"Dragon bond? What does that mean?"

"Perhaps it would be best to set the matter aside and explore it later," murmured Thelonius Meistercrow.

"Yes, now that we are assembled we should get on with our journey," agreed Quenton Quintabulous, gently, as though treading on eggshells.

Mister Escutcheon was looking at me in a decidedly odd way. "What it means is that we shall have to explore this further, and we most certainly will. However, we've spent enough time here and if we're going make any progress at all today, we'd best be heading off.

"And I say 'Aye' to that!" agreed Brank whole-heartedly. "Is this creature here going to trot along . . . or are we going to have to worry about dragon droppings from above?"

Lucinda laughed. *"You* might have to worry."

We mounted our horses again and headed for the mysterious horizon, a young dragon playfully flapping overhead.

B efore very long we were in the foothills of the steeper mountains, and I could detect a wildness settling down over the land. The trees were larger and denser, the trail narrower, and a palpable sense of dark dread hung over everything. That smell was there, too . . . that smell of dark magic that cursed this land, like a veritable barricade flung around this country.

For lunch Brank just distributed some bread and cheese and water amongst us, and we kept on riding, quietly. I had plenty of time to wonder what the hell I was doing here, and why I'd ever agreed to go ahead with this crazy journey. But for every fear that popped up before me, I had both rational and emotional answers. Too, despite the fears and doubts that the *feeling* of this journey was bringing up in me, and the strength of my resolve to become a successful screenwriter ably battling them down, nonetheless there were other things bubbling up inside of me, caused by these strange climes.

First, there was the sense of thrill and wonder at this marvelously strange world. It was the sense I'd had when first I'd been read fairy tails. It was the sense I'd had when I'd first embarked on my pre-adolescent and adolescent love for fantasy and science fiction. There was a touch of *otherness* about the place, the taste of *faerie*.

Second, I had a growing awareness that this just wasn't some quest for background for a motion picture I was on. It all had the flavor of a soul quest, a Jungian search for identity and individuation. This, even though I didn't understand really these depth psychology terms, much less the symbolic and archetypal reasons for drinking bitter in the *Cracked Cask* last night.

Third — scary and creepy as this part of the journey was getting, the straight truth was all of this was a hell of a lot of fun!

Here I was, moving through a strange enchanted forest, a dragon flittering over my head, surrounded by an elfish cinema scholar and would-be movie director, slightly demented magicians, a blowhard rogue of a hero and a delightful and attractive woman who I was most taken by.

Concerning Bash — or rather, Lucinda — I must say that a disproportionate amount of my thought was directed her way. She seemed particularly animated and happy today, and looked altogether fetching in her fresh woodsy outfit. All the same, she seemed to have forgotten about my existence and my part in getting her this gig. She seemed far more interested in chatting with her old 'Professor' and making sure that her place in the party was secure.

I somehow resented this, although I felt sure that, with goodness knew how long our trip would last, I'd get my time to talk with her.

A woman hadn't taken my fancy this way for a while. I'd been in Los Angeles for almost a year when I placed those ads, and since I'd never had much money, it seemed, I'd never had much of a social life. Most of the women in LA seemed more interested in what kind of car or what kind of job you had rather than in who you really were inside, and though I'd had a few dates, none of them had gone much of anywhere. I wasn't a bad looking guy and I'd had plenty of girlfriends in high school and college — but I was really striking out in LA Plenty of good-looking guys there, and plenty of success stories. I was just a face in the crowd.

True, I hadn't liked many of the women I'd met. Certainly not as much as I liked Lucinda.

I was really curious about her and wanted to ask Brank about what he knew about her, but he was bringing up the rear behind the magicians, and besides, he seemed to be in a surly, untalkative mood anyway.

A couple of hours before dusk, Mr. Escutcheon asked Lucinda to call down Hypernius. Lucinda beckoned the dragon and the beast flapped down eagerly.

"Do you think you can get him to go and find us a safe place to camp tonight?"

"What do you think, Hypy?" asked Lucinda.

I don't know if it was my imagination, but I fancied I saw those specks of brown in those bright green eyes again. Anyway, the dragon this time seemed to understand exactly what they'd been talking about. It was as though the further into the unknown we headed, the more intelligent it got. Hypernius took wing and was off.

This got me to thinking about what had happened with the dragon earlier that afternoon.

Dragon bond.

What the hell, I thought, did that mean? Some kind of special psychic ability to communicate with a creature I'd previously considered wholly mythological? And yet, it didn't feel like I was actually *communicating* with the dragon itself inasmuch as I was using the dragon as a medium to achieve some sort of mystical vision. All vaguely unnerving and frightening, but only on after thinking about it — the actual experience had been so involving that I hadn't had a chance to be scared.

I figured I'd hear about it more from the magician later — it was something that portended interesting possibilities, to say the least. And it upgraded my opinion of Hypernius — and made the ultimate goal of the quest all the more important.

The Dragon Horde. What strange secrets did it hold? What meaning did it hold for me in particular?

Most important, how could I use it to create the most rip snorting, thrilling fantasy adventure every concocted by the mind of man — utilizing the materials available?

This was going to be the beginning of a Hollywood career, I hoped, that would rival Steven Spielberg's!

The approaching darkness brought a new degree of taintedness to the air — a chill touched everything that made the deepening hues and the encroaching mist and the smells all the deeper and more menacing.

Not a half an hour after he had been dispatched, Hypernius returned. The dragon seemed particularly animated and excited. It even yapped almost like a dog, jumping up and down on the ground and indicating a different direction than we were going.

"He seems to have found a place for us to stay!" said Lucinda. She pointed down a much narrower trail that led through a shallow ravine. "That way!"

Brank's brow furrowed. "What, deeper into Larg's Leviathan Forest? That's madness!"

"Well, you know what's there, hot shot?" challenged the girl.

"No . . . I've never had cause to go there! No reason to. This is an area well known for various lethal beasts that prowl it!"

I didn't like that sound of that, nor did the magicians, but Dr. Escutcheon seemed ready enough to give it a go.

"You think that Hypernius has really found something?"

"I'm sure he understood you," replied Lucinda. She looked over to Hypernius who was hopping impatiently. They stared at each other meaningfully for a moment and then Lucinda turned back to Escutcheon. "Oh yes – it's a place for us to stay that's quite safe – and take it from me, dragons like to sleep in places safe *and* snug!"

"Quite true!" agreed Quenton Quintabulous.

"Often as not caverns, though! And caverns, I think would not be that safe in this kind of area!" added Thelonius Meistercrow.

"I'm sure that, with his ability to guard the Cracked Cask, gentlemen, that Hypernius is more than aware of the presence of danger!"

"True, very true!" said Escutcheon. "And it can't be that far away. Beside, the purposes of this journey is exploration – and thus we may actually be able to find something new." He turned and gestured Hypernius to fly up and lead them. "Go on, our new dragon guide. We may well have a part for you in our picture as well!"

Eagerly the dragon went aloft, keeping just ahead of us so that we could follow him. Ignoring Brank's grumbles, we did just that.

Thus we followed Hypernius along a trail that wound through the forest and dived down into ravines and shallow creeks. I heard strange rustlings in the dimming forest and felt the odd sensation of being *watched* by things, if not malignant then not exactly friendly. However nothing bothered our party and, eventually, just as the sunset, the light in the sky dragging down behind it, we entered a large clearing. This area was bisected by a rough rutted road, and off the opposite side of the road was a building with a smokestack giving off a swirl of smoke that surrounded what appeared to be bright red neon letters.

MOTEL, said the sign.

Chapter Ten

"Well," I said. "So much for a movie backdrop. I mean for a fantasy movie, anyway."

"Well, what *do* you know!" said Brank, his face lighting up at the possibility of a warm place to bunk. "My apologies to you, Hypernius. Though I wish you'd been able to *tell* us what you had in mind."

I shook my head. "Neon? A motel? Isn't this the alternate world equivalent of an anachronism?"

"Actually, 'Motel' is an ancient and magical term for 'resting place,'" said Lucinda. "Besides, you really should learn to expect the unexpected!"

"Yes, I suppose so." And I'd always thought that *motel* was short for *motor hotel.* "But neon? That's definite *technology.* Isn't it, Mister Escutcheon?"

"It has the appearance of technology, my boy. But it most certainly is not. Magicians?" Dr. Escutcheon turned his long hairy face toward his aides.

The protuberant noses of Thelonius and Quenton, magicians extraordinaire, were turned up, sniffing at the air.

"Magic," said Thelonius.

"Without a doubt, magic," added Quenton. "But a most benign sort. I do believe that Hypernius is correct. There is nothing to fear." He rubbed his hands briskly and gazed upward, looking at the darkening of the air, the thickening of the fog that curled through the forest. "Besides, a warm bed would do quite nicely. There are indications of a frosty night ahead."

"Well, I hadn't exactly planned financially for nights of lodging . . ." said Mr. Escutcheon, jingling a pouch hanging from his belt. "But you take these opportunities when they come, mustn't you?"

I for one agreed to that. I didn't really relish shivering by a campfire the whole night. Not that I didn't expect that I'd *have* to, soon and often enough — but if there was a warm place to crash this night, I'd certainly take it.

"Forward then!" said Mister Escutcheon as he led the way.

The place seemed to be a series of thatch roof cabins, sides joined together in a row. The frontmost cabin had a sign dangling above its door – not neon. In the dimness, we couldn't read it, but we could only assume that it said 'Office' or whatever was the local equivalent. Mr. Escutcheon told us to stay outside, that he'd handle the arrangements. He went in and, presently, came out again, accompanied by a dwarf. This dwarf had pointed ears and a thick red nose the color of bruised cherries. He peered at us through thick spectacles and counted us off with a ragged nailed forefinger.

"Well then, I think we can rustle up enough beds, Mr. Escutcheon," the dwarf said, turning back to the professor. "However, I've got plenty of rooms. By the way, name's Lockpin!"

"And we've limited funds, Mister Lockpin."

"Yes. Yes of course! Let me just go and get a few helpers to deal with this, and we're get you squared away in no time." So saying, the dwarf hobbled back into the office.

Brank seemed disconcerted. "Here now. What's this? We're not going to be all squeezed in the same room, are we?"

"I think the rooms are big enough. Besides, we are merely going to sleep. We'd have the same room under the sky. Far less expensive, I assure you, this way – and we *are* working within a strict budget!"

"Economics *is* the purpose of our quest, ultimately!" Quenton chimed in.

"Fine with me," said Lucinda. "Just as long as I'm on the opposite end of the room from the Whiner here."

Brank bristled at that, but he'd been brought to rights and could say no more on that subject. "What about the horses? And we're not going to let this dragon sleep with us, are we?"

"No. I'm sure the horses and Hypernius would much prefer the stables, right behind the motel!" Escutcheon said. "And you'll be happy to know also that I've splurged and bought us a hot meal, which we may eat in the room before we sleep."

I admit, I was ready for both. This morning's early rising and the prospect of another one tomorrow made me bone weary. All I needed to do was to stuff some food into me, find a reasonably warm not-necessarily-comfortable place to lie down, and I'd be out like a light.

The innkeeper summoned another dwarf who looked very much like he did and together they dragged canvas cots and assembled them into the cottage/motel room nearest the edge of the forest. When questioned about this, the innkeeper assured Mister Escutcheon that this was the largest room available and best suited to accommodate us all. "You'll even have space to move about in this one!"

Meanwhile, we tethered the horses in the stable behind the motel, where we also fed and watered them under Brank's instruction. I noticed that Lucinda seemed to disagree on some of his methods, but wisely held her tongue this time. I suspect she wanted a peaceful evening too.

Mister Lockpin also had a chicken stew on sale at a quite reasonable price, so Mister Escutcheon bought dinner for us to preserve our stores. The dwarfish innkeeper also has some ale for sale, but our leader turned down the offer.

"What! We need something moist to wash the dinner down!" objected Brank.

"We'll drink water, just as we would have on the road!" stated Escutcheon, bluntly.

"Why drink water when we can have something more nourishing!" said Brank. He went ahead and bought himself a heady mug of brew. I was quite happy with the water, myself.

We ate quickly, and then found our cots with the help of lanterns that came with the room. There was little conversation as we prepared for bed, since we were all very tired.

"Hypernius seems happy enough with his stall," commented Mr. Escutcheon.

"That's right," said Lucinda. "I don't think that dragon particularly care for extremely closed in places."

"Good for their lungs, a little draught!" Quenton Quintabulous agreed. The magician was off in the corner with his colleague, performing some kind of divination with what looked like an odd combination of cards, dice, bones, and feathers. With all the throwing and bouncing about of the materials, it looked like a very weird version of jacks.

"Hmmm," said Thelonius, scratching his balding pate. "All looks a little bit opaque."

"Positive, though, don't you think?" said the other magician.

"Oh yes. Yes, perhaps . . . Still. . . . Well, perhaps tomorrow the readings will be better."

I noticed that Lucinda and Brank made sure they selected cots on the far end of the bed. Brank built a nice fire in the hearth provided at one end, so by the time I was actually pulling the blankets up and settling my head into the rough but clean pillow, what with that, the lantern and our body warmth the place had warmed up nicely.

My last image before sleep claimed me was of Brank, hunkered down by the crackling fire, sipping at his stein of ale and staring into the flames. I thought I smelled the sweet but bitter scent of the ale, and then was asleep.

I dreamed.

I dreamed I was flying.

On wings of leather, I flew above vast spaces, through cold clouds and misty airways I flew, above fields and rivers and mountains, alive with flight and joyous with the smell of freedom in my nostrils. And now I was cozy and comfortable in a dark hideaway, deep beneath a mountain, amongst rustlings and familiar tastes and sensations.

Elviron, called a voice. *Elviron!*

And I felt an intimation, as happens sometimes in dreams, of a vastness of scope and time unimaginable to normal consciousness. Also of memories, teeming memories beyond my ability to comprehend. When I awoke, quite suddenly, it was as though somebody had poked me in the back with a hard stick.

I started, pushing myself up from my pillow and looking around. The fire was now just a few slowly glowing coals, hissing in the hearth, shedding practically no light onto the humped, sleeping forms on the cots. One of the men was snoring softly and it was a familiar comforting sound of company. Yet I felt a terrible uneasiness, and something more.

A kind of calling.

A voice from deep within me, calling from outside. It didn't seem as though I had much choice. . . . I had to answer that voice. I had to respond to the beckoning. It was almost as though I was *pulled* from my bed by other forces. It felt as though I was under my own volition, but in retrospect there were other over-riding factors involved.

For some reason, I felt compelled to go out to the stables.

I rose cautiously, so as not to wake others, and I walked slowly to the door, which I opened and closed with equal quiet. There was a full moon up — and it was a bluish tinge, larger than the moon I was used to, with not as many craters, much smoother like a great big cue ball hanging in the sky. My breath misted as I advanced across the ground toward the stables. I had not brought a lantern and I did not need one. That bright moon lit my path quite well.

From outside the stables I heard stirrings within. Without hesitation, I walked inside. I was met with the barny smells of straw and hay and manure. A strip of moonlight was flung out from a window upon the folded up form of Hypernius the dragon. The beast's head was raised, and its eyes glowed lambently, even though they were outside of the moonlight.

"Hypernius," I said, almost reverently.

It hissed and rose up on all fours, its wings spreading out, not like it was about to fly — but almost as though in some kind of ceremony.

Slowly, still not know what I was doing, I approached the dragon without fear, but also without control. It opened its mouth, showing its fangs in the moonlight, but it did not seem to offer any kind of harm. Only promise. It made a soft mewling sound and then bowed its head before me, almost contritely.

I leaned forward, stretched out my hand and touched the dragon's head . . .

And fell into the moiling heat of its eyes.

Chapter Eleven

I tumbled into a blankness, there past the lights of the Dragon Hypernius' eyes.

And from there it burst forth into a very strange vision, which can only be related in the form of narrative.

And so I attempt that here.

*H*is name is Ricknow. Doctor Martinus Ricknow, complete with a train of degrees of dizzy number and catalogue.

All from various colleges of that vast and complex body known as Basiliska to some . . .

And the Dark University to others.

Now, he wobbles from his huge library, his black scholastic robes dragging along upon the ground, his hawklike face sullen and deep in concentration. He places the tome upon his desk and opens it. Dust plumes down like the ghost of a waterfall and he wipes it and blows it away. A long, slender finger strokes down the page, past ancient illuminated letters. Thick candles slowly drip wax nearby.

He is old, this man — his wrinkles have wrinkles and dewlaps hang pendulous from his chin. But there is something stubbornly alive in his eyes, and not lights of life, but of a dark determination.

He finds what he needs, scribbles something out onto a pad with a quill pen dipped in black ink. Then, slowly, methodically, he treads back to his sitting room, where he pulls upon a pleated cloth chain. In the distance comes the muted chiming of a bell, echoing through sepulcher stillness.

The man, this Doctor Martinus Ricknow, sits himself in a high backed wing-armed chair, and placed wizened fingers up to his chin, closing his old eyes, contemplating, considering, meditating.

Eventually, three men, much younger, march in. They have the look of scholars, yes, but there is also the aspect of warriors to them — broad shoulders, proud jutting chins, sharp eyes.

They salute their leader.

"Ah — thank you for coming today, my friends."

"We come in shame, sirrah," stated one in a deep and resonant voice. "We come in failure. The men assigned to appropriate the stranger from Earth Associative Prime had been thwarted."

"Yes, yes, I know. But I rather expected that," despite his age, the man's voice, an assured tenor, is strong and commanding. "This makes things all the more interesting, hmmm? No, that's not why you have an audience now." He cleared his throat and leaned forward. "The mission which Escutcheon —" The name produced a curled snarl. "— undertakes is prelude to disaster for our plane. Escutcheon —" (acid this time) "— has already brought down the academic standards of this world alarmingly. Success of his project can only be of more harm. And of course it will counteract the curse with which we have sought to crush his foul school and the land which supports it . . . for the myriad reasons we all know."

His turtle-like head swiveled, regarding each of the academic soldiers carefully. There was Dyrk Ryonne of Defense Mathematica. Shalbot Purseblossom of Philosophical Kill Tactics. And, largest and most intense of the Three, Harfield Moregnash, master of the Martial Arts Magica.

"You know what this party seeks."

"They seek to create a monstrous rendering of our world for lesser beings," stated Ryonne with contempt.

"They seek to commit sacrilege upon our order, doubtless misrepresenting us to another world — but more importantly, revealing our existence," stated Purseblossom, holding a fist up and gritting his teeth.

Last to speak was Moregnash — "All true — but the most immediate threat is breach of the Dragon Horde vault."

"Yes indeed. And pray, Doctor Moregnash . . . do you know why that threatens us?"

"The Secret Tomes stored therein."

"Precisely. The Dragons have guarded those books from both us and other academics. We cannot afford the possibility of those Tomes falling into another University's hands — especially the University whose termination we seek."

"Do you believe this is what Escutcheon seeks?"

"I *know* that he is aware of the Tome's existence. I suspect that it is not a primary purpose in his head to achieve that goal. After all, legend is littered with tragic tales of the demise of heroes and academicians alike who have sought to gain access to those Tomes — alas, those of Basiliska University as well. However, if Escutcheon gains the opportunity on this trip or upon his filming trip — you can best believe that he will seize it. To our certain misfortune."

The three warrior-academicians nodded sagely.

"So. You must dispatch your forces and yourselves immediately to prevent this."

"You wish the villains to be destroyed, Master Ricknow?"

"Only if absolutely necessary. I would prefer them to be apprehended. Especially Escutcheon, for there is much that we can squeeze from that twisted brain of his, hmmm?"

The minions agreed.

"Excellent. We shall maintain communications henceforward by the usual means . . . And be sure that I shall be observing your progress through sources mystical."

"Of course, master. We encourage your counsel always," said Ryonne.

"Tell us, though," requested Moregnash. "If we have the possibility — should we obtain those Tomes of which you speak?"

"It would be very dangerous — but if even one is brought before me — I can assure you that your dreams will be realized!" said Ricknow, leaning forward, a grim smile pricking up the corners of his lips. "Gold — power — - women — but most importantly —"

The stolid faces of the academicians could not help but twitch a bit at this news.

"Yes, that is correct —" He leaned forward and breathed the word as though it were the most delicious and juicy word in creation. "Tenure!"

The men leaned forward, their faces perturbed masks of lust. One swallowed visibly, one licked his lips, one had to work to control his breathing.

One whispered the word again, tenderly. "Tenure."

"Yes! And all that word portends! And imagine the additional power the Tomes will provide our University! I don't think you can, because it is surely *beyond* imagining!"

He let a pregnant silence descend for a time.

"Now then, my heroes! My men of great knowledge, might, and certainly intelligence. Proceed onward with your task. We shall remain in communication, then — by the usual means."

They bowed briefly and then were gone in a flurry of capes and an faint odor of excited perspiration.

Doctor Ricknow waited a moment, and then nodded to himself.

The hawks had been freed. Soon it would be seen how the victims fared.

Doctor Martinus Ricknow set off for a portion of the room. At a bookcase, he pulled a large volume out, but instead of opening and reading it, he put his hand through the space it had occupied, deep into the recesses of the case and there pulled a concealed lever.

A door of books swung open before him.

Turning around once again to make sure that no one had seen him, he trudged forward and lit a lantern. The light blossomed therein, revealing a small room. In one side of the room were knobs and controls. Doctor Martinus Ricknow played with these controls, nudging veneers and clicking switches.

A number of things happened.

First, a panel slid back. Then a humming sound began and a strange protrusion, a misty membrane-something ballooned inward, wavering the air. This cleared, though the effect was a magnification of what lay within.

A box sat upon a cabinet. And upon this box was some kind of mechanism —

They looked very much like a large, state of the art television set topped by a VCR.

In fact, they were.

From another shelf, the Doctor took a cartridge and stepped forward. He stepped forward through the membrane and it shivered with sparkling energy for a moment. He hit a button on the machine atop the television set. Lights glowed. He pushed the cartridge through a slot, observed that everything was correct and then stepped back to the other control panel. He punched a button and the tube of the television flickered to life.

In the middle of the room was a thickly stuffed chair, fronted by a stool.

Doctor Martinus Ricknow settled his old bones back in the chair, and relaxed.

Images began to flicker upon the color television set.

Sound swelled softly from the speaker: snappy music.

"Ah!" said the Doctor, settling back into his chair, relaxing into a mystical and magical meditation.

Upon the screen began a Warner Brothers' *Looney Tunes* cartoon.

Featuring Bugs Bunny and Daffy Duck.

"What's up, Doc?" piped the cartoon.

"What indeed?" said Doctor Ricknow, as he settled his smile back into comfort.

*T*here was more.

I could feel more there — visionary impulses that I could not interpret.

I could feel more burgeoning through even then, but it was suddenly all cut off, this Dragon-contact transmission, by a loud noise that was not a part of it, nor a part of the stable.

I realized abruptly that I was sitting in front of a very alarmed dragon. It was snapping its mouth open and closed and flapping its taut wings noisily, eyes wide and wild.

I thought I heard a word:

TROUBLE

Though it was a concept rather than an actual sounding in my head.

I immediately realized that the sound was coming from the motel. More specifically, from the *side* of the motel, which meant from the cottage where my companions were sleeping.

Clearly, they were *not* sleeping now.

"Hypernius," I said, still groggy and disoriented from whatever had just happened between us. "What's going on?"

But the link — this apparent *dragonbond* that had been whispered of — was no longer in effect. The only thing I had now before me was a lizard like thing with bat wings, claws, and fangs that was suddenly much more frightening than it had been when I'd been much closer. Hypernius looked tremendously perturbed, but made no motion to leave the stables.

I dragged my senses out of deep freeze and hurled myself toward where my companions were, with hardly a thought for my own safety. I'd been proved with no weapons, but there was a pitchfork leaning against the side of the stable wall. I grabbed this and ran down to the cottage.

The commotion became louder, but there were no lights. The moon was still up, though, full and shining. I ran around the side and up to the door and was almost flattened by a burly, hairy form hurling back, screeching, blood spraying from a severed arm.

It roared and I could see that it was some sort of monstrous gorilla sort of creature, only clothed. In its remaining hand it still held a dagger and this flashed in the moonlight as it got up and started back toward the door.

However, with a blast of light and a puff of smoke and the sound of thunder, another creature was propelled backwards. In windmilled back and ran into its fellow, and both crashed down onto the ground, growling and snarling.

Through a veil of smoke, Brank hurled.

After him came Lucinda — or rather, Bash, for that name seems much more appropriate for her fighting mode. Fighting modes they were indeed both in then, for they both had their swords out and they pounced upon the fallen creatures with great quickness and fury. Both of the attacking things had their daggers still up, though, and though they seemed bestial they were talented enough and intelligent — they easily fended off the initial blows of their attackers. They got up quickly enough, too, and suddenly Bash and Brank had their hands full, fending off lightning-quick lunges of those deadly looking daggers. Clack and clank, clank and clack — the creatures were ferocious, snarling out their blood lust.

Quenton Quintabulous staggered through the door, looking as though he was trying to cast a spell — but something fell from his hand onto the ground, and he was forced to his knees, rummaging around for it. Thelonius Meistercrow, unaware of his colleague's bent position, bumbled out, preparing to perform something magical — but tripped over his fellow and tumbled to the ground. Something fell from his hand and exploded right behind Bash, startling her so much that the creature fighting her was able to knock the sword from her hand.

It drove in for the kill.

I don't know what happened, but it seemed as though something elemental took me over. I drove forward with the pitchfork and slammed into the creatures back before its dagger could drive into it target: Bash's chest.

It howled with pain as the tines dug in. The sword was deflected. It roared around instinctively to face me, pulling the pitchfork from my grasp.

Closer up I could see that though its body looked like a gorilla's, its face was far uglier than anything simian. It had a bat's face, with pointed ears and ugly snout and sharp nasty rodent teeth. A nasty-looking thing indeed, far from human. Blood and foam ran down its mouth and it smelled like rotting meat.

I backpedaled to get away, but its fierce keening roar seemed to root me with terror as it lunged forward.

But before it reached me, there was a loud thunk and tearing sound, and the bloody end of a sword rammed through the middle of its chest. It looked down, baffled, at this new part of it body — and then with a gush of blood out its nostrils and mouth, keeled over, spasming.

Behind it was Bash.

"Thanks," I said.

"No. Thank *you*." She leaned over and with a grunt, yanked her sword from the downed monster.

She turned to where Brank was clashing with his own monster. The creature took time to glance over at its fallen comrade. It took one look at Bash and her bloody sword, then caught Brank's sword by the shaft. With one might heave, it pushed the big man backwards so that he really had to work not to topple onto his rear . . .

And then with a speed that belied its size, it ran off into the night.

"Coward! Villain! Monster!" cried Bash, and she ran off on the hills of the thing.

"Lucinda! Don't be foolish . . ." Brank said. "Let the bastard go!"

But it was only when she saw that the chase was hopeless that the woman turned back across the road, harrumphing as she strode. "Drat! I would have had that monster as well — that would be no surprise . . . But I do admit to one surprise, Brank. You called me by my real name!"

"Never!" said Brank. "Nothing of the sort!"

"You called me Lucinda!"

"Why would I call you by *that* frilly name! You act like a 'Bash' and you talk like a 'Bash' — and to me, you always will *be* a 'Bash!'"

"Could we stop with this nonsense?" I objected. "Just what's going on? And where is Mister Escutcheon? Is he okay?"

"No, I'm not, but I'm healthy enough, I suppose!" The fellow himself was at the door of the cottage, looking ragged and bedraggled. There was a small cut on his forehead and a stream of blood trailed down one side of his face. "Looks as though you bagged one of the beasts though." He walked over and bent over the thing, sniffing, then holding his nose with disgust. "Any idea what we have here, Brank!"

Brank was about to say something, but Bash beat him to the punch.

"It's a Wilderamth!" she said.

"Nasty brutes," said Brank. "From the Northern Mountains. Brutal customers all right. I've mostly seen them in the South working as mercenaries in armies —"

"Or in service of the Dark University," added Lucinda.

"Damn it — Just so. That's about what I was going to say."

Escutcheon poked the thing with his toe and sniffed.

"Rum, foul business —" He looked over to the rental office. "And I, for one, would like to know how they knew we were. Here. Come, magicians." Thelonius and Quenton were picking themselves up stiffly. "We have some question to ask our Dwarfish Innkeeper."

Chapter Twelve

"I really don't know *how* they got here!" said the Innkeeper. He let the light of his lantern shine down on the sprawled, still body of the creature. A pool of blood had collected now and it shone back at us, not red, but black as an oil slick. "I tell you I know nothing about it!"

"Definite magic!" said Thelonius.

"A summoning! Smells like a summoning, most certainly!" said Quenton, muffled, his hands folded around his mouth and nose. Little lights glimmered within his cupped hands like trapped fireflies.

The dwarf peered up. "I deny it! I deny it emphatically!" He turned around and made to run off, but was grabbed by the scruff of the neck by Brank and brought back into the conversation.

"You know all right, you little worm. I *knew* there was something wrong with this place —" He looked directly at Lucinda, his words barbed directly towards her. "It smelled bad to me from the first, but you would not mark me."

"If these things were on our tail, they would have caught up with us somewhere," said Lucinda. "You can disabuse yourself of the notion that our journey is being ignored. Witness the reason I was involved — they set upon Ralph here in town. Certainly they know we're on the journey, and clearly would like to stop us."

"Lucinda is right. It's well we brought another warrior along — -" He nodded over toward me. "And it appears we have another that we hadn't known about. Your efforts are appreciated, Mr. Phillips."

"That's right, they *certainly* are!" thundered Brank. "We should give the lad a sword. I'll teach him how to use it!" He turned to the dwarf. "I'm sure you have a sword lying somewhere hereabouts, dwarf."

"Why would I have a sword," muttered the Innkeeper. "And kindly unhand me. You cannot prove my involvement in this unfortunate incident. Have I not suffered enough? And the room is no doubt wrecked, and who is out of pocket for *that?*"

"Do not change the subject, Innkeeper," said Lucinda, and if there was any doubt in my mind of why she'd been dubbed 'Bash' it was now gone. "Dwarves always keep a horde of stuff, and often as not you can find a sword in it. Now our leader here, Professor Escutcheon, is a calm, good man not prone to violence or vengeance. But this big goon here and myself . . ." He cocked a thumb back toward Brank, who leered evilly showing the biggest set of human teeth I'd ever in my life. ". . . we've been known to accidentally on purpose *kill* people for less than you've done . . ."

"But I haven't . . ."

"And all you've got to do is to let us have that sword you've got squirreled away and we might just let you go with no more than a cuffed ear."

Mister Escutcheon cleared his throat meaningfully. "Well, I believe I will go back and consult with my magicians on a few matters."

The two warriors leaned over the dwarf innkeeper menacingly.

"Well, in truth, come to think of it, I *might* be able to find something in my closet!"

Brank and Bash hurried the dwarf back to his office to accomplish just that.

I was tired.

We rode out the next day and I was tired as before I'd gone to sleep the night before. But by my side I now had a sword in sheath, a very handsome sword, more of which later, and in truth it made me feel safer even though I really wasn't trained in its use. As far as weapons go, I might better have brought that pitchfork along with me.

Since the attack had been in the middle of the night, we'd lost some sleep. After the innkeeper had reluctantly found a sword for me, Mr. Escutcheon elected to spend the rest of the night in the same room, albeit with guard shifts. Brank, Bash — and myself, since I was now a weapons carrier. So I did an hour of that and got precious little sleep otherwise.

We set off early as well. All added up to heavy lids on me. I hadn't even been able to tell Mister Escutcheon what had happened with the dragon. Nor had he asked what I'd been doing outside. Doubtless he assumed that I'd been answering a call of nature in the woods. Fortunately for them and me.

We traveled on through a mountain pass, resolved not to stop at any more motels any more, and kept a careful watch for anyone following. The trail led along a number of hills and ridges from which we were able to view the land for miles around — but we saw no one following.

The scenery was quite majestic. Snow-topped mountains. Green valleys. Pristine rushing brooks. Blooming flowers of seemingly magical species I'd never seen before. The mountains seemed to have a bracing, enchanted feel — like a miniature Switzerland painted with fairy dust — and the fresh breeze help keep me more alert than I might have been.

Hypernius swooped amongst the peaks and played in the fields, but always gave us sign every half hour or so that he was still following. Hypernius also apparently saw no danger, for the creature seemed extremely happy and carefree. And why not, after spending so much time cooped up by a bar, sniffing out robbers and bad eggs and sniffing in alcoholic fumes.

We ate bread and cheese again on horseback. And it wasn't until dusk that we made camp, in a valley by a stream of fresh water, in which we all immediately slaked our thirsts.

Brank built a fire and I settled by it, ready for sleep. But I realized that I'd better let Mister Escutcheon know about my strange contact with Hypernius, and the stranger vision that I had experienced. There had never been the right time along the way that day to sidle up alongside him and let explain. It wasn't really the kind of story I cared to talk about amongst the entire group.

Now, the magicians were off by the brook, fumbling with some magic or another, while Brank and Lucinda were off in the brush, collecting firewood, bickering loudly as usual. Mister Escutcheon was sitting on a log, working on some sort of journal or checklist or some other sort of writing task. All alone. The perfect time to approach him.

"Mister Escutcheon . . . or Professor, rather."

"Mister is quite suitable and since you're used to it, by all means continue using it," he said amenably.

"Last night — well, the reason I was outside when those . . . those things attacked — I was in the stables . . . sort of well, *communicating* with Hypernius."

He looked over to where Hypernius was busy making himself a nestlike resting place for the night. "Indeed." He did not look particularly surprised.

"Yes. And I had a very confusing vision. Something that is of extreme importance. I probably should have mentioned it earlier, but I didn't know how. . . . And I needed to talk to you alone."

"Understandable. And an intelligent decision. Visions are not necessary always best made totally public." He seemed a little bit distracted, tapping his pencil on the pad before him, not entirely with the conversation and a little bit patronizing and condescending. "What was this vision about. . . ?"

"Have you heard the name . . ." I dredged it up from my memory. "Dr. Martinus Ricknow.

Immediately, he ceased his jotting and looked up at me. "How —"

He eyed me with increased interest and incredulity.

"I saw him . . . he was plotting . . . against us . . ."

"Of course he's plotting against us . . . me, rather. Damn his eyes! He *always* is." Mr. Escutcheon puffed and snuffed, his feathers clearly ruffled. "But why didn't you tell me this vision *sooner.*"

"I explained . . . I suppose I should have . . ."

"Never mind, never mind . . . please communicate the essence of the experience."

I related what I had seen, heard, felt, through the medium of my 'dragon-bond.'

"And this is why I wasn't totally sure it wasn't an absurd dream, sir. What was one the television was . . . well, a Bugs Bunny and Daffy Duck cartoon. I assume with your knowledgeability in cinema you're familiar with Warner Bros. cartoons. . . ."

"Yes, yes, of course." He said irritably, brushing off the subject. "The kind of cartoons is not what concerns me. You say he was watching them on a *television set* though? Utilizing a *VCR!*"

"Yes, and I thought that rather extremely odd myself . . . I mean, after what you said about technology not working here."

"Precisely. But what you saw you saw . . . it has meaning . . . Some sort of bubble into another world perhaps. . . . An envelope of altered reality to allow this kind of thing to happen. Extraordinary!"

"Yes . . . but do you think that the attack had something to do with the orders . . ."

"Hmmm. Perhaps, perhaps not. The question is, was that vision — and I *do* think it is an accurate vision — was a flashback into the past. . . . Or something was happening even as you experienced."

"Whatever, it would appear that those men have been dispatched to deal with us and stop us. And what he said about those Tomes . . ."

"Aye. Just so. Perhaps we *will* get more out of this trip than simply a screenplay, actors, extras, and a scouting of the scenery." He seemed thoughtful. "Still and all, many a man has gone after those Tomes."

"You've heard of them, then?"

"Oh yes, and you can bet that Thelonius and Quenton over there would *love* to get their mitts on them. Which is actually why I'm glad you waited to talk to me alone. You'll keep this between us."

"Not tell Brank or Lucinda?"

"No, definitely not them. They are certainly trustworthy, and hale-met companions . . . But there can be no doubt that they've got fortune-seeking deep in their blood. No reason to get them overly excited, eh?"

"No. No of course not . . . but what else did the vision mean . . ."

Mr. Escutcheon patted me on the shoulder. "It means, my friend, that my instincts run deeper than I thought. There is much more to you than initially met my eyes — or my mind, for that matter." He reached over and put his hand on my shoulder and I felt a warmth between us, a relationship that I had not felt before. "So then. Have you had any more thoughts on the screenplay amidst all this?"

"No," I said bluntly. "But I've got plenty of raw material to assimilate!"

"So you do, lad. So you do!"

"In my dreams, maybe." I sighed wearily. "And I hope they're not far away."

"Not far at all. We'll eat something and then bed down. And tonight you'll not be disturbed for guard duty. I'll do that myself if need be, though I suspect our two warring champions —" He looked over to the woods and a stream of heated invective murmured through the leaves as though to underscore his point. "— will be suitable, and maybe a magician or so."

"Thank you."

"But I wonder — would you mind if I get you up just a few minutes before the rest — and I think a late rising tomorrow is in order anyway — so that I might get you to attempt another little — ah — *connection* with Hypernius."

I shivered at the thought. "I don't know — It was a pretty wrenching experience."

"Yes, I understand. But if we are being followed in some way, and we are in danger — we should use all the tools of divination at our disposal." He pointed over at the busy magicians. "They're not being terribly successful. Your vision last night had a great deal more information than they've provided."

"But you *knew* who your enemy was before — You know a great deal about the Basilika or the Dark University or whatever it is — don't you? And you knew that they had agents trying to stop you from what you were attempting."

"Yes, but that doesn't mean I know the details. And I certainly didn't know that Ricknow was watching Looney Tunes on a VCR, did I." He gave me a steady, penetrating look.

I had to nod. "I'm sorry. Of course you're right. I just — I'm just not looking forward to repeating the experience. I keep on thinking that if I'm watching that horrid man — he might suddenly spin around and *see* me."

"Hmmm. No, visions don't work like that."

"But can't the observed detect the observer? You always feel somebody looking at you."

"Not in this case . . . at least not to my knowledge."

I straightened. "Okay. I'll do it."

"And perhaps you can incorporate this into the screenplay!"

I smiled. "That has already crossed my mind."

Eventually, Brank and Lucinda returned with armloads of wood and, with surprising agreement, built a very excellent and warm campfire. For some reason the valley in which we stayed was warmer than where we'd been last night, so it wasn't as cold as it might have been. I took the bedroll that had been provided me, laid it out by the fire, and once within its softness almost immediately conked out.

Fortunately, I had no dreams.

The waking dreams I'd been experiencing lately were more than sufficient for my subconscious, I suppose.

I awoke as a hand touched my shoulder.

Groggily I stirred, the charcoal smell of the dead campfire in my nose. I looked up and I saw Mr. Escutcheon, crouched down beside me.

"I've got the lookout. Can I spare a couple of minutes of your time?"

What could I say? Go away and maybe come back in ten? I forced myself up and awake and put on my boots and coat and staggered after the man.

He patted Brank's massive shoulders. "Wake up, my friend. Give the others a few minutes more rest. Mr. Phillips and I will be back momentarily."

He didn't tell Brank where we were going, and Brank didn't ask. The big man just grunted and stirred, looking through bleary eyes over at where Lucinda lay sleeping and then smiling, seeming to anticipate a few minutes of peace on his own to enjoy.

Mr. Escutcheon guided me back to where Hypernius had made his sleeping nest. The creature seemed to be just a ball of grey, a strange article of leather furniture. With great respect and care, Mr. Escutcheon leaned over and tapped one of the furled wings.

"Pardon us, Hypernius," he said softly.

A dragon's eye peered up through cloak of bony wing. He squinted comically at the sudden onrush of light and shaded himself groggily.

"Hello, Hypernius," I said, partly warily and yet partly honestly glad to see the beast.

That eye swiveled over to me and immediately lighted up. Happy noises graveled from its throat and the wings whipped off. The face became quite animated with expression as the dragon hopped up on clawed legs and leaned toward me. A rough, wet tongue slipped out from between its teeth and sloppily licked the side of my face. I felt more in presence of some happy dog than a fearsome dragon.

"It would appear that Hypernius has grown fond of you. That is quite excellent. Dragons are a good judges of character. My instinctive trust for you was well placed."

The tongue rasped against my face unpleasantly. Without disposable razors, my beard was growing and the combination of dragon tongue and stubble wasn't wonderful. Hypernius didn't seem to notice though. He gave me another wet slobber and then sat back on his haunches, gazing at me with an unreadable but benign expression, lights of liking a dance in those mysterious eyes.

"Uhm — Yes, I suppose so."

"I had not known that dragon-bonds extended into emotional areas. I thought it was a matter entirely of domination and psychic affinity."

"Maybe he just likes the way I smell — even without a bath for two days."

"Hmm. And not likely to get one for a few more. Have to take a few hardship for your calling." He adjusted his spectacles and gazed directly at the dragon. "Now Hypernius — a most peculiar thing happened to you two last night. Apparently, there was a beckoning, a vision . . . . and a subsequent notice to our friend here about our danger. Could you give us some more information on the subject?"

The dragon canted his head, eyes sparkling with intelligence. It opened its mouth and a number of odd squeaking groaned came out. It moved back, its tail swinging in articulate patterns, and then it swayed its head languorously back and forth, a mewling and guttural croaking in its throat like distant thunder.

It then looked at us expectantly.

Mr. Escutcheon scratched his head. "Did you get anything at all out of that?"

I shook my head.

"Well, then, Hypernius. I hope you won't mind if Mr. Phillips attempts another bond with you. We'd like to get some more information if we could."

The dragon hopped forward almost eagerly, though I don't know if it wasn't more for a nice ear scratching than a visionary bond. I gave him the scratching all right, and the beast seemed to be in absolute heaven to get it, but when I started trying to repeat what had happened the night before I must admit I got a little upset.

"What's wrong?" asked Mr. Escutcheon.

"You know, I can't say it was an enjoyable experience and I'm just working myself up to it." Although I hadn't intended it, I dare say there was considerable pique in my voice at Mr. Escutcheon's impatience.

Surprisingly, he backed down immediately.

"Very well. No problem. Take your time. I apologize."

Nonetheless, he scrutinized the proceedings with intense interest, and I felt a little uncomfortable with elfish eyes trained on the back of my neck as I tried to link up mentally with a scaly, though increasingly lovable dragon.

I touched it, I looked into those amazing eyes, I concentrated, I did everything exactly as I had before.

Nothing.

"Well?" whispered Mr. Escutcheon, unable to contain himself.

I ignored him and concentrated harder.

Hypernius made an inquiring whimper and that rough tongue came out and licked me again. It was as though the beast were asking me, "Is that enough of this game? Can we play another one now?"

I sighed and scratched the dragon behind his ears. "I'm not linking up this time, I'm afraid."

"Not the faintest intimation?"

"No. I'm getting zero."

"Bad luck!" said Mr. Escutcheon. "Bad luck indeed!"

Secretly I was relieved. Frankly, even though Hypernius seemed to be warming considerably toward me, I didn't cherish the idea of being constantly glued to a fantasy-relation of a winged dinosaur, performing Cassandra-like for a would be elfin movie producer. Just like back in Hollywood, there *were* certain limits to which I would not go.

"Maybe we can try it in a day or two."

"This evening when we camp." Mr. Escutcheon said in staccato, so I guess there wasn't really any rejoinder. However, maybe I could get out of it somehow. Something about the whole business troubled me deeply — something I'd experienced within that vision that echoed with a premonition.

A *bad* premonition.

Hypernius was just as happy to eat his breakfast along with us, greeting Lucinda happily when she woke up and growling faintly at Brank when he jostled back from his ablutions in the woods.

Then he took to the air joyfully and soared over us, guide and protector.

We packed up speedily and headed out once more to thread our way through the mountains.

*S*urprisingly, the path we cut through mountains was well-smoothed by other travelers and the range itself was narrow. So by afternoon we were in view of a vast plain, and by late afternoon we were on a road.

"Look," said Brank. "We have a choice. We can make camp out here in the open tonight. Or, if we ride just another couple of hours and into dark, we will reach a small village I know of. I have a trusted friend who has a barn we can use." He sniffed a bit and shook his head. "I smell storm on this breeze, and I suppose we'd just as soon we'd have a roof over our heads, eh?"

"As long as we can trust your friend," said Escutcheon.

"No reason not to — I've fought with him before in battles and we're good friends."

"Our magic indeed portends rain," agreed Quenton Quintabulous.

"Perhaps even with hail," added Thelonius Meistercrow, consulting some many-armed contraption that looked more scientific than magical — at least to me.

"A roof would be a good idea, then," said Lucinda. "I'm particularly concerned about Hypernius. Dragons don't care to get rained on, and he might just decide to seek dryer company."

"Well, we certainly need that dragon, there's no question about *that*," said Escutcheon, scratching his hairy gnarled, pointed ears. "Very well. Brank has certainly been the most wary of us all on this journey. We will go with his opinion on the matter." He shook his head. "Besides, I have no liking for being rained on."

We traveled onward through a sparse forest, and night dropped down tightly with a darkness of coming clouds and a rush of winds from the west.

On the other side of the forest was the village that Brank had promised. An idyllic oasis of civilization — like something from a storybook. Gingerbread cottages. Cobblestone streets. Chimney pots puffing sweet wood smoke. A dreamy river cutting languidly through the center, spanned by two perfectly kept bridges.

The promise of warm hearth fires showing through stained glass windows.

There were hardly any pedestrians afoot and they hardly gave us any notice as we passed through the streets. Brank's promised farmhouse and barn were on the other side of the town, hardly any distance at all, and there were obviously lanterns lit in the farmhouse. Brank jumped off his horse, skipped over to the porch of the house and rapped at the door.

And the creature that answered was the strangest that I'd seen so far in my stay in this world.

Chapter Thirteen

It was a funny animal.

Not that it was a comedian or anything, as far as I knew — or even that it had a sense of humor.

It was just a well, *funny animal.*

"Brank! Brank you old bastard you! What are you doing in Mollop?" Mollop was the name of the village. "Haven't seen you for the longest times. And what's this motley bunch of tired travelers you've got with you? I didn't realize it was All Saints' Day. I don't have any candy!"

I was surprised that this world apparently had a Halloween too, but then I shouldn't have been — there were plenty of other intersections of peoples and cultures.

But a *funny animal?*

"Hurbal! Greetings! Glad you were in. These are my companions on Quest!" He ticked us off one by one. "What with a storm coming up and being in your neighborhood, I thought you might loan us your barn for the night."

The creature called Hurbal shrugged. "I don't see why not. But you look hungry. I don't have room for you all at my table, but if you go on around back to the barn and make yourselves comfortable. I'll see what the missus can rustle up in the way of chow."

"A wonderful host to the last," said Brank to the travelers. "Too bad he's useless with a sword and can't handle his drink!"

Our new host bellowed with mirth. "Bah! I'll show you, you pile of troll leavings! Get on back there with you!"

A funny animal.

As in funny animal comics. Like Hobbes in *Calvin and Hobbes*, or all the characters in *Pogo*. Recognizably an animal and yet drawn in a stylized way that was, well, *funny.*

The creature that Brank called Hurbal was a bear. But he looked more like Yogi Bear than any normal bear that I'd ever seen. Only a Yogi Bear without the flabby midsection and a pronounced chest and shoulder musculature. And a Yogi Bear in breeches and belt and shirt and a face that actually looked rather handsome in a cartoon bear.

Seeing a cartoon in three dimensions, with the exaggerated colors and angles was a little startling, so I must say that I had nothing much to say during the initial interchange. However, the others seemed to take it all in stride.

Finally, on the way back to the barn, I was able to choke it out: "What . . . who . . . How . . . What sort of creature is *that?*"

"Oh, that's right," said Lucinda. "I suppose he does look rather astonishing to you, Ralph, since intelligent creatures tend to be of the same species where you come from."

"He's . . . he's a funny animal!" I said. "Like from a cartoon!"

"Yes, Mr. Phillips," intoned Mr. Escutcheon. "To you perhaps. But who is to say what came first . . . Perhaps cartoonists, on some deep subconscious level, were inspired by creatures like Hurbal!"

It was almost too much for me to assimilate, so I had no response.

"What's the big deal?" said Brank as we reached a large and pleasant-looking barn. He unclamped one of the latches and swung back the big door. "Hurbal comes from the land of Nodken, way to the south. Creatures like him are just animals who became intelligent, that's all. Good folks, damned interesting — and for my money, a lot more worthwhile than most humans — or for that matter magicians or elves . . . beg pardon to present company!"

It was an overwhelming thought.

Apparently what they were saying was that the minds of cartoonists took little trips to this strange land of Nodken for inspiration. I wondered what minds visited the other areas and what *that* produced. From the looks of it so far, it apparently produced fantasy trilogies.

A lantern hung near the entrance. Brank lit it, and we went into the barn. It was dry and pleasant, with the prerequisite stack of hay and animals mooing and neighing in their stalls. *Serious* animals, fortunately.

We started to prepare for sleep, threw down our bed sacks — only making sure we had plenty of straw for support. For some reason, I wasn't feeling particularly tired. Maybe it was the feeling of safety at being within a clearly civilized area. I felt curious and adventurous rather than weary and afraid. The idea of a entire *land* of funny animals was an aspect of this world that I found incredibly intriguing — and the rather Jungian subconscious ties between this world and my own was something I needed to investigate further.

Before long, Hurbal joined us, carrying a cast iron pot filled to the brim with savory stew.

"Just so happens the missus had some of this stuff on hand. I'll go back and get some plates and utensils and bread. You have to excuse my wife — she and Brank are not on the best of relations."

"What! She still thinks I'm a bad influence on you?" demanded Brank.

"I'm afraid so . . . Perhaps it's because that's the truth of it. You *are* a bad influence on me. Still, she's a hospitable enough lady — and she'll have you in our barn. 'That's where that rogue *belongs!*'"

"Sounds like you've got a perceptive wife!" said Lucinda, laughing. "Can we meet her for breakfast if we lock Brank in the outhouse?"

Hurbal apparently thought that notion was quite amusing. He chuckled and bent over to pet Hypernius. "I'm afraid she doesn't fancy dragons either. But we'll see what we can work out."

He came back as promised with the eating utensils and plates and we supped famously on the delicious meat and vegetable stew. I couldn't quite place the spices and herbs contained in the stuff — but my palate seemed to recognize tastiness.

Although I'd hopped that maybe the food would make me groggy, it just made me more restless and more curious.

So when the time came when we all turned in I could not go to sleep. And so when the hand descended on my shoulder a few minutes later, I was just as ready for trouble as it was ready for me.

A whisper.
"Ralph?"

Brank's voice. I recognized it immediately. It was almost as though I'd anticipated it, *hoped* for it.

"Yes."

"I've roused Hurbal. His wife was right. I *am* a bad influence on him. We're going down to the local public house for a drink. Want to come along?"

Needless to say, I did indeed want.

"You're going to have to be quiet. We don't want to wake anybody up."

I had a troubled thought. "Who's going to stand the first watch, then?"

An immediate sigh and a feminine voice. "I guess that'll be me."

"Lucinda? You were the last . . ."

"We struck a deal!" said Brank. I could imagine his grin even in the dark.

"Boys will be boys. Bring me back a canteen of brew, will you?" I found a container thrust in my hand. "And please do me a *big* favor and don't get into trouble."

Once past the barn, I spoke in a more regular voice. "Was that like making a deal with the Devil?"

"Not far from it, fellow. But it will be worth it — just you wait and see."

I was bursting with curiosity about what concession Brank had given Lucinda, but figured the warrior would be more forthcoming with a few drinks in him.

Hurbal was waiting for us on the road, well outside his farmhouse. "She's out for the night. Time to roam, my friend. Good to see you. Let's got knock off a few heads — but atop beers this time, eh?"

He sounded normal enough, but I still couldn't *quite* deal with idea of spending a few hours drinking beer with a funny animal.

I was determined that I wasn't going to make the same mistake I'd made the first night here in this world. No, tonight I was going to just drink a couple of beers and that was all. I'd just nurse them, and keep a sober head about me.

But it certainly looked like my companions had no such intention.

I could tell they were old drinking buddies from the time they'd made their first exchanges. I hadn't expected them to immediately go and dive in the stuff at the first opportunity. Fortunate for me, I thought then, not only because I happened to be restless, but because I figured I could use the excursion to obtain some local color, to say nothing of local liquid.

And I still wanted to know more about what a real live *funny animal* was like, up close.

His full name, it turned out, was Hurbal Infrees, and he led us down a lane that ran along the river and then branched off into a clump of buildings. The name of the public house was the Purple Ploughman, and it was situated right along side of the river so that it had a patio on the riverside. Apparently this was not in use now, although I wasn't certain why not. Lanterns would certainly have lit it well enough. Perhaps the night air was a bit too chill. In any event, the patio was closed — but the pub itself was quite open. It was brighter and airier than the Cracked Cask had been, and there was no dragon guarding the door.

Nor was it so crowded as the Cracked Cask: The few people sitting at tables or standing at the bar looked like farmers and trades people relaxing after a hard day's work. Skittles and darts were being played off to one side. A fire was in the hearth, adding that delicious wood-smoke smell to the odor of draught bitter and fresh baked pies. It had a much healthier feel to it than the furtive old Cask, and the natives barely paid attention as a stranger strolled in alongside a cartoonish bear. Apparently, the people of this world took not only dwarves and dragons in stride, but funny animals as well.

"Here you go," said Hurbal, showing us to a table in a corner, fairly close to the warmth of the fire. "Have a sit and I'll get pints of the best. Will that do?"

"If it's on you?"

"I have a tab here, gentlemen. Have whatever you like!"

"How about a saucy wench?" proclaimed Brank.

"Only sauce here, fellow, no wenches. Let's put a cap on the anarchy this evening, all right? The wife is likely to kick the lot of you out of the barn and into the yet non-existent rain."

As he went off to get our drinks, a rumble of thunder reminded us that rain was due. However, it hadn't been a far walk and I didn't mind the risk of getting a little wet outside if I knew for sure I'd get a little wet inside.

"Country beer!" exclaimed Brank, patting his abdomen. "There's nothing like it!"

"You like it better than the stuff at the Cask?" I asked.

"I said nothing of the sort. I just said there's nothing like it. Maybe I'll have a little of the scrumpy too. Tasty stuff, but deadly. I'd give you maybe a sip. You didn't seem to take too well to the jars of beer you drank at the Cask."

"Too true. I'm limiting myself to two drinks tonight. Just call me the designated walker."

"I'm afraid I don't follow."

"Cultural differences. Never mind. Tell me, though, while we've a minute alone. Just what *is* it between you and Lucinda?"

"You mean Bash? You mean how we don't get along?"

"Exactly. Until tonight you've been at each other's throats . . . and you didn't want her on this little quest, that's for sure, even though she's proven to be an extremely useful companion. Why?"

Brank was silent and suddenly sullen.

"And I'm dying to know what you offered her to take the watch so that we could take this little jaunt."

"That will come out in its own time," said Brank. "As for our differences — well, as you might surmise, we've journeyed together before."

"I gathered that much."

"Hmmm. The usual quest. Hidden treasure. Old map. An ancient dwarf jewel mine was the prize. Never found it, of course. Half these sort of treasure trips find absolutely nothing — but let's just say, we got along *too* well on the trip."

An odd quirk of jealousy fluttered in my stomach. "Romance?"

"Nothing so elegant."

"Ah."

"Well, our personality differences became known by the end of the trip and we were arguing a bit, but I wanted to patch it up. But when no dwarf treasures showed up — well, one morning dear young Bash and another younger swain just up and galloped off before the rest of the party was even up." Brank sighed. "Well, no real harm done. We weren't in particularly dangerous territory. To tell the truth, I was about to give her the boot myself — damned witch beat me to it!"

He said it in a hearty, manly voice, but I was looking at his eyes and they betrayed real hurt. The dump wasn't just a blow to his ego — it might just have possibly broken his heart, and he was covering it up with bluster. I recognized the symptoms too well — I'd gone through the very same kind of thing at least twice, once in college and once after, and it wasn't fun. I wondered if the guy still carried a torch for 'Bash' — and I really couldn't blame him if he did.

"Ah. I suspected you had feelings for her!"

"What! That tomboy? If I ever did, they're gone and good riddance to them!" said Brank, defenses back up. "Best thing that ever happened to me. You take a fall and you get back up — you get back up *stronger*. If anyone's carrying the torch it's her — why do you think the little she-devil's tagging along with us, hmm?" He tapped his chest self-importantly. "Waiting for the chance to hook up with Brank the Crank again!"

I opened my mouth to disagree, but I thought better of it. Besides, if I talked too much on this subject, I might actually get to learn what "Brank the Crank" meant, and in the context of his relationship with Lucinda, I didn't particularly care to.

"That must be it," I said. "Can't really blame her, though, can you?"

I'd said the precisely correct thing: I saw that immediately. His face lost its sadness, and good cheer blazed from it. "Blasted right, Ralph! So let's drink and look forward to an absolutely splendid future!"

"Yes, let's do!"

I didn't let on that I had an interest in Lucinda. That would be impolitic.

We were fortunately interrupted by Hurbal, returning with a huge pitcher of beer in one hand and what looked like *quart* sized glasses in the other.

"We're in luck. We've a special tonight." Brank pulled out coins, but Hurbal shook his head. "That's all right. You buy the next shout."

Shout? An Australian term for round of drinks. I looked down bemused as furry Hurbal filled up my huge glass. He'd bought it, and I was obligated to drink it — such, I gathered, was the way amongst drinking men and I was loathe to go against custom.

I sipped and to my dismay it was about double the strength of the city brew. Oh well, I thought, maybe if they weren't looking I could spill a little under the table.

We set to drinking and joking and laughing. I must admit that I forgot to drink sparingly. Before long I was a little tipsy and having a marvelous time. In the corner a fiddler had struck up, playing lovely airs and folk songs, a few of which some of the pub crowd sang along to. Hurbal proved to splendid company, full of stories and good cheer. He didn't prod too deeply into what we were doing headed Dragon Horde's way in the company of a small dragon, and I'm sure that Brank appreciated that. I know I did. I confess that I never thought I'd find a *funny animal* good company, but after a full quart or so of that potent beer, I felt as though we were fast friends of long standing.

When Hurbal went back to the bar to fill up that terrible container again, I leaned over to Brank and half-seriously suggested that I should write Hurbal into the movie.

"Yes! A splendid idea!" the big man said.

"We'll have to check with Mr. Escutcheon first," I said.

"Bah! If nothing else, just a minor character! Marvelous! This will be wonderful!"

"But does he even know what movies are?"

"Hmm. I don't know."

"We'd have to explain."

"Don't know if I'm really up to that." The broad shoulders shrugged. "Oh well, write him a part anyway. We'll cast him if we can."

I wondered vaguely if Hurbal Infrees on film would look like an animated character. As he approached, I tried to imagine the way lights and celluloid would capture him.

Nope. He'd be far too three-dimensional.

And very odd.

I discarded the topic altogether, and managed to also abstain from drinking too much of the brew that was poured into my glass. The other two, however, drank just as heartily as before, without growing effect.

Not only did I have a funny animal across the table from me, I soon had a *drunken* funny animal, weaving and bobbing and singing and babbling, all in a curiously human manner, albeit extremely *tilted*.

Brank kept himself pretty straight, though, and I confined myself to the smallest of sips.

So, fortunately or unfortunately we were only a slightly squished when the three men walked through the door.

Chapter Fourteen

"Oh my God!"

"Getting religious, eh?" said Hurbal.

"Which God are you talking about, lad!" said Brank. "We've got plenty to choose from in this world."

"It's them!"

The three men were wearing traveling clothes and feathered hats. Halberds and sheaths stuck out jauntily from their apparel as they sauntered through the door. They looked around casually and then moved to the bar to order a drink.

At first I hoped I was mistaken, but the more I examined those sleek, angular self-satisfied faces, the more sure I was. I scooched down into my chair as though to hide myself from them, though of course they'd never actually *seen* me.

It was the three men in the vision I'd had.

Dyrk Ryonne. Shalbot Purseblossom. Harfield Moregnash.

The three men who'd been dispatched by Dr. Martinus Ricknow to terminate our quest.

"Them? What are you talking about, lad?" said Hurbal Infrees. He followed my gaze. "What . . . those three travelers who just stepped in. Nothing unusual about that. Travelers stop in here every once in a while. The place encourages it. Good business."

"They don't mean us well."

"Of course not. Northerners, from the look of them. Rum lot. Plotting some kind of bad deal down here . . . but what are you going to do about them? Take their money for now, fairly and squarely is all, through trade and what not. Hate to be on the wrong end of *those* swords! Sharp and damned quick. University swords, most like. *Dark* University."

That got Brank's notice. "Bunch of snobs, that lot! Those are the guys that Escutcheon says would like to scuttle things for us. You say you think those are villains over there, Ralph?"

"Think. I *know* they are!" I told him about the vision.

Brank laughed. "Just because of some *dream?*"

"It was real . . . I mean, it might as well been."

"And those are the specific men who were sent off to do us in."

"Yes!" I said emphatically.

Brank mulled that over for a moment.

"Well then," he said finally getting up and staring blearily ahead. "There's only one solution, then! I'll just have to go over and *ask* them. Hurbal, would you be my second!"

"Gladly."

"Wait a minute. Those guys are vicious. And what about those swords?"

Hurbal patted his own. "I never said that they were better than mine —"

"But you've been drinking, guys!" I objected.

"Just makes us better!" said Brank. "Right Hurbal?"

"You bet."

I immediately regretted that I'd mentioned my concerns. I should have kept it to myself, should have realized that it would be a challenge to Brank's manhood — and maybe Hurbal's funny animalhood — to ascertain just was what these guys wanted.

Chances were they were truly *looking* for a fight. In which case, from all I could tell, we were in *big* trouble. I hadn't the faintest doubt that these were those men, and so it was my drinking buddies who were really at a disadvantage.

I had to do something, and do it fast.

I shot up from my chair and ran toward the bar, easily outdistancing the lumbering drinkers.

"Message!" I cried. "Message from Doctor Martinus Ricknow!"

The men were just getting their drinks and were in the midst of downing the first portion. Surprised, they swung around, spilling some of their beer at me in the process. They gaped at me.

"Message?" said one.

"What?" said another.

By a table was a chair. "This chair — it's been booby-trapped! Run! Escape!"

Of course they didn't, but my ploy gave me time to grab hold of the chair and make it look as though I was tossing it away, for their protection. However, instead of doing so, at the last possible minute I swung it as hard as I could, crashing it against the head and shoulders of the nearest of the Dark University minions.

To say that they were surprised goes without saying. I am not a violent looking guy at the fiercest of times, and I made sure that as I'd approached them I looked a positively simpering milquetoast. The man I had just brained was more than merely surprised — he tumbled immediately into unconsciousness as he tumbled hard against his neighbor, knocking him down as well. Only one of the men was left standing, and I jumped on him before he could do anything, delivering a solid blow with my fist into his face and drawing blood from his nose.

However, these were not inexperienced fighters. The man I hit shook me off easily with a deft move, and the conscious middle man was already getting up, making to draw his sword.

"He's gone mad!" cried Brank.

"Oh well," said Hurbal. "Let's join him!" With a quickness surprising for someone who'd put away the beer he had, the strange-looking bear dropkicked the man against the bar. Any consciousness remaining to him was promptly removed by those fierce paws cracking against his head. The man wilted down, collapsing on the floor.

I was in trouble though. The man whose nose I'd bloodied — Shalbot Purseblossom, as I recollect — had his sword out in a trice and was raising it handily to skewer me, eyes wide and furious.

I'd distracted his attention sufficiently, though, and even as I scrambled to get out of the way of his sword point, Shalbot Purseblossom was not so lucky with Brank's.

A sword the size of Brank's is not designed to stick people with, it's made to *hack*. Nonetheless, Brank drove it directly through Purseblossom's chest, pinning him to the bar.

The blood was copious.

Brank frowned down at him. The action had completely sobered him. "What have you wrought, fellow? We'll be kicked out of this tavern for sure!"

"No!" said the barkeep, a burly sort with a bushy mustache, looking alarmed but relieved. "I recognize the clothing of these men. They are from the Dark Lands and certainly they intended no good here. In fact, they even asked if we'd seen strangers — and they described you, sir!"

Brank looked at me oddly as he helped me up. "You have more and more talents than I was aware of, fellow. It would seem you did the right thing ... though how you pulled it from your hat I haven't the faintest." He turned to Hurbal. "What should we do? Finish them off?"

"Logical choice, but hardly proper form, don't you think? No, let's just send them back on their way with the body of their companion and tell them they're not fooling with just anybody!"

"Shouldn't we question them first?" I said. "Hopefully relieved of their weapons and tied up!"

"I've a back room," said the barkeep. "But please — don't mess it up too much. Oh — and could you unpin that the dead gentlemen and take the corpse too. Don't know how I'll ever get that blood out of here. This kind of thing hardly *ever* happens here."

I was glad I wasn't stuck with the job. It was Brank's sword and he knew his way around it, so he attended to the surgical niceties. Me, I was put in charge of the man I'd smashed the chair over, and I had my hands full, in all senses. He wasn't a small man — Harfield Moregnash, if my recollection was correct — and he was dead weight, out cold. Dragging him took all my attention, but I did it as quickly as possible, to avoid the rest of the bloodier details of the job.

The rest of the room settled back to drinking and talking as though the incident had never occurred. Apparently, this *wasn't* anything unusual. But then, this was also a world of greater violence — and paradoxical peace — than my own. Simpler in some ways, and yet more complex in others.

It was just a darkened dining hall from the looks of it, with tables and chairs stacked up to either side. The barkeep was good enough to light a lantern. I placed Moregnash in the center of the room and pulled over a chair to tie him up against. The barkeep provided some rope.

Hurbal the bear dragged in Dyrk Ryonne, and then Brank pulled the dead man as well. We tied the living ones into a chair and then Hurbal went and got a pail of cold water, which we hurtled over their heads.

They both gasped and choked and spluttered awake.

"Maybe I'd better go and get Mister Escutcheon," I said. "He'll want to be in on this, I'm sure."

"All in good time, all in good time," said Brank. "We'd better see who exactly we have here before we go and make further idiots of ourselves. Besides . . ." He nodded toward the deceased. "I know him, and he's definitely not going to like that."

Hurbal shrugged. "You go questing, you get into bloody territory. Surely he's aware of that."

"He's the bookish sort. I think he realizes there are many dangers, but he doesn't want killing," said Brank. "I can respect him for that." He nodded down to the dead man. "But if you're right, then we did the only thing that we could." He patted me on the shoulder. "Looks as though you did the right thing, fellow. These men are killers . . . Evil nasty killers. I've seen their type before. And I can smell it on 'em. I doubt if we could have taken 'em on! Not in our conditions."

"Aye, though I'll admit, I'm a good deal more sober now!" allowed Hurbal.

"What . . . What's the meaning of this?" blustered one of the men after blinking his eyes, looking around and down at himself and his bonds.

"Untie us immediately," cried the other after groaning. "Or bear the dire consequences!"

"You'd best do as we ask," said Brank. "Or you'll end up like your friend over there."

The two turned their heads, noted the bloody and perforated condition of their companion, and promptly grew grave and quiet.

"Much better. Now then. Who are you and why are you here?" demanded Hurbal.

"We are travelers."

"Negotiators for a merchant, traveling south."

"Negotiators seldom carry the weapons you carry."

"These roads are dangerous!"

"You look more like assassins to me!" said Brank. "And I understand that you've been looking for one Doctor Phineas Escutcheon."

Despite themselves, their faces flinched.

"Dead on the mark!" pronounced Hurbal. "Well, you haven't found him. But you've found his friends. And we also understand you're the henchman of a very nasty man named Dr. Martinus Ricknow. Would you care to deny that?"

"We have nothing to say."

"You certainly responded to our friend's news of a message from Dr. Martinus Ricknow."

The two men looked at me, and I swear they were trying to bore holes through me with their dark and penetrating eyes. I felt my insides rimed with chill.

"You shall regret this."

"And in dreadful agony while doing so!"

"Hmm. Threats are rather silly when trussed up like you two are. You want to make things easier on yourselves by spilling a few beans our way?" Brank said. "To wit: who exactly are you and what is your mission — and how much does your Doctor Martinus Ricknow know about our quest."

"Guess our names!" said one of the captives, sneering.

"How about Dyrk Ryonne —" I pointed to one. "And Harfield Moregnash." The other.

The both goggled at me but their mouths were clamped securely shut.

"You see — we've got talent here, you pieces of refuse. Real honest supernatural talent . . . And if you don't start yakking, we're going to bring in our heavy guns. Magicians, no, *necromancers* who like nothing better than to torture the truth out of their victims!"

"I rather doubt that," said Harfield. "That's our lot's game!"

"Shut up, you idiot!" said Dyrk.

"No, actually I think our magicians would hurt you — but inadvertently. So you aren't going to give us any information?"

"Yes. You are all as good as damned!"

"Well — that's all very interesting," said Brank. "But it doesn't give us much to work with." He turned to me. "Oh well. There's nothing for it. Run off and fetch old Escutcheon, Ralph. We'll see what the magicians can do. Meantime, while you're gone, maybe we can make these guys a little more talkative." He fitted a fist into a palm and rubbed it enthusiastically. Hurbal looked just as eager, in a bearishly way.

I didn't particularly relish the idea of watching these ruffians work our captives over, so I was happy to be off. However, even as I turned, something happened that stopped me in my tracks.

The dead man got up.

With a creaking, a shudder, and a scraping, the corpse lifted itself off the floor. Its eyes were blank and dull, pure zombies eyes. The gaping hole in its chest still glistened with blood, but jetted the stuff no more. There was a curious stench about it — a metallic smell I recognized as an extremely distasteful version of the smell I'd detected before.

"Guys," I managed to say. "I think we've got problems. Instinctively I backed away.

"Yikes," said Brank. He too backed off, brandishing his sword. "Hurbal, do the dead generally walk around here?"

"No, not usually," said Hurbal backing away as well.

The dead man, pale as a drowned worm, did not seem particularly interested in revenging himself, though. Instead, it thrust one of its clawlike hands into the pockets of its breeches and pulled out a glass vial. Gaining speed, it lifted the vial and then turned its face to face me.

It opened its mouth, however it did not move its lips.

A voice emerged from the hole, as though from a great distance:

"We shall see *you* again — you may be sure!"

And then the dead thing tossed the vial.

End over end, it flipped . . . But not toward us, but the tied up swordsmen. It smashed on the floor by their boots. A lightning-shot cloud moiled up, enveloping the men and the chairs.

The dead man staggered forward like a puppet that had just cut its own strings and was desperately trying to walk, but failing. Its boots clumped and dragged along on the boards and its arms were all akimbo. Not only was I startled by all of this, but also a kind of supernatural fear froze me in place, so I did nothing to halt its progress.

Brank did not seemed so limited. He started toward the zombie and the cloud, raising his sword, but Hurbal grabbed him by the arm and pulled him back.

"No. Not a good idea. This is powerful stuff, and you don't want to get caught in it."

"Damn! But we just can't let them go."

"They are already gone, Brank."

Even as Brank stepped back, the dead man fell into the smoke. As though the fall detonated something, there was an explosion inside — a cracking, bloody-light shot explosion — and the cloud expanded, turning black as burnt flesh. It ballooned up to the ceiling, and then billowed out, dissipating.

And where there had once been two men tied to chairs and where there should have been a body sprawled on them, there was only a large smudge of soot upon the floor.

Blinking, we stared upon this astonishing sight for a long time, aghast.

"What has *happened?*" the barkeep said, his face all screwed up with the stench. "Where did they go?"

"Who knows?" said Brank. "But no place good for us."

"Perhaps you'd be so good to draw a few more drinks for us," said Hurbal. "I confess, I'm far too sober at the moment."

"Do you think they'll return for vengeance?" said the barkeeper, nervously. "There's the smell of grim magic to the air, and that bodes evil."

"No. It's us they were after," said Brank. "When we leave, we take any trouble with us. I promise you." He pulled out a gold coin and gave it to the barkeep. "I hope this will cover the expense of repairs."

"I am only happy to be rid of them," said the barkeep. However he did not return the gold coin. "This should cover the rest of the drinks as well, I think."

"Good." He turned to me. "It's time to be even more useful, Ralph. Go back and quietly fetch Escutcheon. We'll set up food and drink here. There must be a meeting. We must decide what's to be done about this. We've got serious problems."

I didn't even think about having another sip of the stuff myself. I just nodded and departed.

Outside, the night seemed much colder and darker than before. The moon that peered down from clouds of raw black seemed malevolent, and the smell of death and even a touch of hellish sulfur seemed everywhere. Perhaps it was just attached to my clothes, I don't know, but I confess the whole experience spooked me enough that I ran as quickly as I could back to the barn were the rest of the company were sleeping.

Every hoot of an owl I heard, every cracking of a branch were evil spirits after my soul. So when I finally got back, I was in a pretty wretched condition, wishing that Brank or Hurbal had come along with me.

I didn't know what to expect when I got into the barn.

But it wasn't what I found, that was for certain.

Chapter Fifteen

They were up waiting for me.

The lanterns were all on, and they stood, patiently waiting. But nonetheless I could see the fear in their eyes — and I was gratified to see the relief when they saw that I was okay.

Especially in Lucinda's eyes.

"Something has happened," pronounced Mr. Escutcheon. "Something awful."

The magicians looked particularly askew, as though not only had they been woken up from sleep, but then rolled around in the straw. Their hats and their spectacles were dangling precariously, their articles and badges of magics were tangled and off-center. They were, in short, profoundly rumpled. It might have been comical, had not the situation been so serious.

"Is Brank all right?" asked Lucinda.

My heart sank. Maybe she did care about the big goon — I knew it was more than just a professional question from the expression on her face. It clearly mattered to her *a lot* that Brank was still in one piece.

"Oh yes. And Hurbal's fine too. They're down at the tavern getting food and drink ready. They want a meeting . . ." I took a breath, steadied myself. "How . . . how did you know. . . ."

Thelonius Meistercrow shivered and looked at me with a haunted look. "We felt an incredible surge of power — -"

"*Dark* power," added Quenton Quintabulous.

". . . quite *evil* power on the mystical plane. We've kept our senses particularly trained toward this area, but even without antenna up, as it were, I think we'd have felt *this* blast."

"Shook us to our socks."

"Blew mine off, I believe!" Thelonius looked down at boots doubtfully. "Still, we don't know the exact nature of whatever occurred."

"Something nasty! Something extreme!"

"Yes. So what happened?"

I knew that to tell the whole story I'd have to mention how I knew who these men were who had walked into that public house. So I kept it short and incomplete.

"We were attacked by soldiers of the Dark University," I said. "We killed one, and had the others tied down for interrogation. But the dead one got up, threw something down and they all disappeared in a puff of smoke."

"Necromancy indeed!" said Meistercrow.

"Works of the dead. Dark University's expertise, certainly!"

"You should have waited for me," said Mister Escutcheon.

"I believe they wanted to use a methodology of information extraction that you would not approve of," commented Lucinda, nodding knowingly.

"They wanted to get the truth out of them quickly," I said. "Who knew what was going to happen?"

"Well then, they want this meeting . . . but why not here?" said Escutcheon.

"I believe the boys need to be close to their drinks!" said Lucinda, her old sardonic self.

"It was a truly terrible experience!" I said defensively. Suddenly, I felt the need of a drink myself.

"Well, we'll go to them then," said Mr. Escutcheon.

"I confess I feel a mite bit peckish!" said Meistercrow.

"And I could use a nice cool cider!" affirmed Quintabulous.

"Well then, do you think that Hypernius might enjoy a walk?" asked Escutcheon.

"Oh definitely," said Lucinda. "I'm sure it will be like old times. He can just sit outside the back door and we'll slip him drinks and tidbits. Would you like that okay, Hypy?"

The dragon seemed to growl affirmatively. It stretched, unfurled its wings, and began to crawl toward the door.

"Off we go then!" said Lucinda. "You'll have to lead the way, chum!"

"Just one moment," I said. "Mister Escutcheon . . . we need to have a quick word together. Privately."

I took him back to the back of the barn and quickly told him the whole story.

"I see," he said, when I was done. "Well done — you seem to have saved us all. But we shall have to explore this aspect of the matter further. For right now . . . let's just go and have that drink, eh?"

And I was astonished that Mister Escutcheon seemed as interested in that aspect of the meeting as anyone.

"Dr. Martinus Ricknow," pronounced Mr. Escutcheon, after another long swallow of beer.

"Who?" said Hurbal.

Brank grunted. "Yes. You've mentioned the name before. The person you'd hoped you could avoid. The Dark University creep."

"Apparently the man who set those goons upon Ralph in town," said Lucinda.

"And I guess he was the reason we had that little problem at the portal, right?" I added, but Mr. Escutcheon pointedly ignored that last little bit. There were some unexplained elements in all this mix, that was for sure, but I figured it would take a little while for me to get the full picture.

"And don't forget the motel." He cleared his throat, calling for attention. "What I hadn't quite expected, though," said the hairy fellow, "was that Ricknow would bring out his big weaponry!"

"You mean the magic?" said Lucinda.

"That, yes — but more to the point, some of his top men."

"Yes, the ones that Ralph, here, recognized . . ." said Brank, looking at me in a funny way.

"Yet another interesting talent and one that *shall* be explored further. However, what is before us is now is a terrible decision." He paused and looked around at all assembled. "Clearly, Dr. Martinus Ricknow does not wish for us to reach our destination. For whatever reason, he is willing to throw much against us. I was not aware of the strength of his determination. Ours is not a warrior party. We are a questing party, after specific goals. We were aware of possible hardships. However, this relentless pursuit by our adversary can possibly be the death of us all.

"What I wish to discuss now is the possibility of turning back."

"Turning back?" said Brank.

"How boring!" said Lucinda.

"You are clearly not aware of the full power of the Dark University!" said Thelonius Meistercrow.

"And if they should apprehend me . . . I mean, us . . . Woe is the day. Torture is too gentle a word for what would happen!" added Quenton Quintabulous. "In short, it would be no sin to return to our base, regroup and try some other plan!"

"Wait a minute, wait a minute," I said. "We're just scouting for movie locations. What, this Dark University doesn't want you to make a *movie?*"

"You are unaware of the deep and abiding rivalries of Academia?" said Mr. Escutcheon. "Surely you have similar problems back on your world!"

"Yes, but I don't think swords are used. And wars are not declared . . .

well, not precisely."

"Ah, as I thought. Then perhaps you *do* understand."

He really had a good point. If some departments I knew of had magic and soldiers I suspect they *would* attack one another with them, instead of just wielding money and reputations and football teams.

"Okay, okay, point taken. But you know, it's not like all this has been easy for me, and while I'm not thrilled about doing any more adventuring, I'm doing my best. I know enough about the film business to know that if you don't soldier on, you end up in a morass of intention without a bit of momentum." I paused and trying to muster determination in my voice, I said, "I really want to make this film."

"Yes, so do we," said Quenton.

"Certainly it would be the salvation of our economy and rid the curse of our oppressor, in one way or the other. But if we're having these problems now . . . Imagine the difficulties that Dr. Martinus Ricknow can cause us with a film crew and actors and such!" said Thelonius.

"Wasn't that factored in before?"

"It was . . ." said Escutcheon. He sighed wearily. "However, there is more going on here than I have admitted . . . And perhaps I should confess now . . . My own personal ambition to make a film perhaps has played to much a part here. But now that we are so seriously threatened — I wonder if the risk is worth it. Perhaps we should just give up and return . . . You, Mr. Phillips, can go back to the pursuit of your chosen profession and at least be alive."

He looked quite grave and quite serious then, did Mr. Escutcheon, and I could tell that he meant every word he said. Apparently, this direct confrontation with the full power of this academic evil had made him realize fully our weaknesses.

Alive. I focused on that word, *alive,* and I realized suddenly that for all the fear I'd felt and all the insecurity and terror, I'd never felt so *alive* before.

Certainly a lot more alive than when I'd been sucking in smog and hustling in the hellish canyons and bizarre motorways of Los Angeles.

"Well, sir," I said firmly. "I can't speak for the others, but as for myself, I can certainly say I'd like to go on."

"Aye — count me in on that!" said Brank. "This is becoming more fun than I thought."

"You know where I stand, Doctor Escutcheon," said Lucinda. "I asked to come. I'm in this no matter what! I too share your enthusiasm for making a film . . . just for its own sake. And you . . . this is your dream. You shouldn't back down now!"

Mr. Escutcheon smiled grimly and nodded. "That is true . . . it is my dream. But I do not wish my dream to cause tragedy. However, I too would like to go on and I am gratified that you agree. Apparently only my magicians would like to go back."

"You do not understand!" said Quenton.

"There is serious and dire necromancy afoot!" said Thelonius.

"We do not know if we've anywhere near the amount of magical knowledge to deal with it should it be unleashed upon us!"

"There are risks, true," said Lucinda, rising up and putting her hands on their shoulders. "But just think of the glory, the power and the knowledge that you'd gain. And my goodness, the *experience!* Why, that alone would make you into superior magicians. To say nothing of better men."

"True," allowed Thelonius. "Very true."

"And besides," she said to the other. "You may well have a bit of a hard time getting back home without a couple of swords and a dragon to protect you!"

Quenton Quintabulous clearly had not considered this. He looked over to Thelonius and they seemed to confer with their eyes, appraising each other's ability for defense during such a journey. "It is true," he said finally. "We *have* proved to be an excellent defensive team."

"Indeed," bellowed Brank. "We've defeated the bastards at every turn ... And they have had the advantages. Now that we are on guard, we shall make a truly formidable team. And perhaps Hurbal here would like to join our company, making us even stronger."

"I'm afraid my wife would rather kill me herself than allow me that ..." said the creature. "Though in truth I would rather relish an adventure."

"We can discuss that in the morning," said Mister Escutcheon. "But I take it that we are all decided again."

"Yes!" said Lucinda, with a gleam of triumph in her eyes. "We're off again to the Dragon Horde. And just think ... now we've got even more to work with in the film!"

True. Too true. My mind was teeming.

"Then let us drink again to our success!"

Mister Escutcheon seemed only too happy to join the toast.

W e slept late the next morning, and when we awoke, Brank and Lucinda went over to Hurbal's house to try and talk Hurbal into coming along — and his wife to agree to allow him to venture forth. I didn't particularly envy them the task, but it did leave me alone with Mr. Escutcheon.

"I think we should try again."

I knew what he meant but I said nothing.

"I realize it wasn't a pleasant experience ... but you clearly saved us and bought us time with your knowledge last night. I think you may be able to do so again," he said somberly.

Of course, I had to agree, but that didn't mean I had to like it. "All right. Is Hypernius around?"

"Yes, he's over in the corner. I made sure he got a good breakfast this morning, so he should be in a proper mood."

"I haven't had *my* breakfast," I said.

He gave me a hunk of bread and some milk. "I think it's best to utilize this particular moment that we have presented to us."

"Why not just be honest with everyone. I mean, Brank knows that something's up from the way that I identified those villains. And the others know that I have some kind of talent . . . Why not specify?"

Mr. Escutcheon nodded his head, his eyes veiled mysteriously. "I have my reasons."

I sighed. "All right, all right. There's no guarantee it's going to work, though."

"Of course not. But we must try."

After I crammed the bread into my mouth and then washed it down with the milk, I got up and wearily plodded toward the dragon. I must say, I could have used a cup of coffee. Or even tea. I never knew before how much I need caffeine to get me up in the morning. Still, the milk and bread had a revitalizing effect and by the time I got to Hypernius, I was actually feeling sort of human.

The dragon still was very much a dragon, though, and it was peering out of the barn door toward where the mist was coming off the trees upon the distant plain and the blob of the golden sun was rising up off the horizon, burning off the moisture.

It turned to me and gave me a very clear and calm expression as though to say, "Oh hello, Ralph. I think I'm actually ready today."

"Looks like it's going to be a nice day. Why don't we go out under that apple tree there, and give it a try."

"Come on, Hypernius. We've work to do."

And the dragon obediently slithered out after us, shaking its webbed wings against the fresh air.

I knelt before the beast again, and this time it almost seemed as though it were all a part of some kind of religious rite. My hands studied the leather brow of the dragon, and my eyes met its eyes again — and this time, they seemed to open up into that color of communication again, and I found myself falling again into them.

"It's working!" I said. "It's working!"

I felt myself falling through a swirling tunnel of clouds, with something indistinct but solid at the end.

"Excellent! Excellent!"

But his voice was fading.

"What do you want me to do?" I said.

Fainter: "Find out more. Find out his plans. You will not be disturbed, I promise..."

But then it wasn't just a fall, it was a plummet.

And the indistinct things at the end of the tunnel turned into glaring bloodshot eyes.

I lost consciousness.

Chapter Sixteen

It was as though I'd been lowered into a deep well, and then the rope had been cut and I'd plunged into darkness. I don't remember any impact, but when I woke up I felt as though I'd been through a pretty devastating one.

I just lay there for a moment in dimness, as though groping my way out of particularly groggy sleep. I didn't know who I was, I didn't know *where* I was, and I felt a free-floating anxiety that was indescribable.

I just closed my eyes and tried to collect my wits.

"I'm alive," I told myself. "I am... alive and that is all that matters." It somehow seemed very important to establish that and to just lay there and concentrate on identity. I had no memory and no sense of a future. I only *existed* — that's all I knew and what I had to cling to.

There was pain, but it slowly dissipated into a kind of generalize ache that I could deal with.

"Ralph," I thought. "My name is Ralph."

And from that starting point, my identity rushed back to me. For a moment, I thought maybe I'd been to some wild LA party the night before, slept over instead of driving home and was now suffering the consequences. But although I ached, it didn't take me long to realize that the pain wasn't of the hangover variety. And slowly, as I came to,

I noticed I could see better.

I was in some sort of cage.

All around me were bars, and the bars were draped over with a cover.

Prison? A cage? What was I doing behind bars? Had I been in some sort of auto-accident — Was I in jail? If so, this was most certainly the weirdest jail I'd ever been in!

But then the memories began to seep back. Mister Escutcheon. Lucinda. Brank ... And a dragon. A dragon who I was supposed to be in some kind of mind link-up with.

"Hypernius!" I said out loud. "Hypernius, where am I?"

I was no longer in the town of Mollop, that was for sure. I'd been transported somewhere, seemed.

"Hypernius?"

There was no answer.

Groaning, I lift myself off the floor. The strange thing was that it seemed a very easy thing to do — and my groans were not my normal groans. My body felt weird ... different. I lifted up a hand to look at it — and saw that it, and the attached arm were covered with a thick coat of hair. I could not distinguish the color in that dimness, but I knew it was definitely *hair!*

I panicked. I leaped to my feet. I put my hands to my face. My palms were hairless and quite sensitive. They touched my face and traveled down to my neck.

Hair. Fine, smooth hair, short ... but definitely hair. No question about it.

What was going on? Had a hair-growth spell been cast upon me? I knew that was a definite possibility, here on this very strange world of fantasies made real. But it was more than just the hair. I just *felt* different. And my exploring hands bore out this suspicion.

I wore no clothes, they told me ... but I wasn't naked.

I was *covered* with hair.

It was all too much. I cried out, and the sound that emerged from my mouth was not me at all. It was the shriek of some kind of animal.

It frightened me so much that I clamped my mouth shut immediately. I walked forward, pacing, and realized that my arms were leaning onto the ground and there was a balancing weight to my rear. I spun around and caught a glimpse of something behind me. I jumped and screeched that alien sound again and twitched my rear spasmodically, and again that something it glimpsed swung around into view.

It was a tail.

A long, hairy tail that leaped and quivered and shot around as though it had a life of its own. And yet, even in the dimness I could tell that it was attached my rear end — and I most certainly could *feel* it behind me.

The horror and surprise were so great that I froze. I had no other previous experience to call on to compare this with. Back home, of course, you generally never got changed into an animal...

From the prehensile tail, the fur and the other aspects of my change, I could only conclude I was some sort of monkey. However, not being at all certain of what varieties of animals there were on this world, I hardly had the vaguest what *type* of monkey.

I collapsed on the floor, stunned. Quite possibly I was still making noise, because I felt like crying. Lost, alone in a strange world — and turned into some kind of *monkey*.

However I had I gotten here? I'd just been safely in the company of my friends. *How had this happened?*

Suddenly, the cover of the bars was lifted. Light flowed in, dazzling me. I scampered back, and brought my hand (paw?) up to cut the glare and give my eyes time to adjust.

"Good morning!" said a familiar yet chilling voice.

I looked up still shading my eyes.

There was a giant peering down at me through the bars, grinning. I started and scrambled back a bit, a screech coming out unbidden from my mouth.

"There there, little pet. I'm not going to hurt you — not if you behave," said the giant. As I looked up, he looked familiar — and then I realized exactly who he was.

The man in the vision I had, and the vision I'd been seeking. Dr. Martinus Ricknow!

"You!" I said — and I could not recognize my own voice. It was reedy and high — but certainly nothing that had sounded like me before.

"Recognize me, do you?" said the man, his robes swishing as he walked away, hands clasped behind his back. He spun around, pointing at me. "Your snooping has been cut short a little this time, eh, interloper?"

I could see that I was in the room where first I had seen this man — the study/library, crammed with books, models and oddments of magic. We were its only occupants now — save for a very odd *presence*, a very peculiar feeling of someone else there, watching us. It sent a shiver up my spine — a shiver that my present situation did not really need. I felt on the edge of nervous collapse. Before I had been detached, removed from the scene somehow — now all its sights and sounds and smells and feeling whirled in on me with ferocious immediacy, quite overwhelming.

"I don't know what you mean?"

"You don't think that after you helped destroy one of my most valued men, a truly distinguished soldier in every sense, I explored the situation thoroughly. You doubt the efficacy of my magic to ferret out intrusions — even in the past? Oh no! I knew it was you — a psychic projection, somehow come to spy!" He approached, waggling that finger as though chiding some naughty schoolboy. "Oh no! Do you think that I did not expect you to come again? And not have a *trap* ready for you?"

"What have you done?"

"Oh, I think it's fairly clear — your soul is trapped in the body of one of the lower primates. A monkey, actually . . . its species is not important. Are you enjoying it . . . Ralph Phillips!"

"You know my name," I said, despite myself. "How . . ."

"Easy enough. You see, once your soul had vacated on its little mission here, and we caught it up . . . It was easy enough to send a substitute soul into your body. Just think . . . A perfect spy! Thus we are able to monitor the progress and adventures of my adversary Professor Escutcheon . . . a viper in his very bosom. Oh, it was brilliant! Absolutely delightfully an accomplishment of genius." The old man skipped about happily, his energy belying his age. "Ho ho, ha ha! What a marvelous turn of events! And so simple!"

"This is horrendous! A crime against humanity!" I declared. "I demand to be returned to my body." I threw myself against the cage and began to rattle the bars.

"Well now, this *is* the Dark University!" said Dr. Ricknow. "We're supposed to specialize in that sort of thing, don't you know." He snapped his fingers and chuckled deep in his throat. "Well now, I'm glad you're awake. We shall leave you there in that cage and let you stew in your juices for a while. And then — maybe we'll let you help us in another matter!"

He turned to go, but I called out after him. "Wait!"

He swiveled around, eyebrow cocked at a jaunty angle. "Yes, your highness."

I took a breath and stepped back from the bars, adopting what I hoped was a non-threatening stance. I knew that I had little chance to obtain any information inside a cage in an empty room. If I was going to have any hope at all, I had to know just what was going on. And the only source was my captor. "I'm sorry."

"You're sorry. You're a sorry *sight*, there's no question about *that!*" Fortunately, the old Doctor seemed disposed to chat. Evidently he had no place to go in any real hurry.

"It's a bit startling . . . I mean, being a man one moment, and a monkey the next. Ever tried it?"

"No, but similar sorts of transformations, certainly, in the my practice of the arcane arts! You get used to it."

"I hope that I don't have to. Be that as it may, Doctor Ricknow — I'm not particularly happy here. Is there something you wish me to do to release me?"

"I'm afraid that it's bit too late for that, friend. You see, we're just keeping you out of trouble here, until things take their course."

"I don't understand . . . why not just kill me. You seem to be quite capable of that."

"My you've become talkative. Hmm. Perhaps we must might be able to obtain some needed information from you —"

"In return for a few answers to *my* question, that could certainly be arranged."

"Fair enough. Beyond your questionable source as bearer of information . . . there are things we need to find out about you. Like how you were able to utilize that dragon to spy upon us. A dragon-bond. It is a rare gift."

"But there is more, isn't there?"

"How perceptive of you! Yes, perhaps there is . . . Oh there's no harm in it . . . You don't seem the suicidal type . . . Frankly, unless your soul is placed in a living creature . . . You actual body will just rot and wither away. Slowly, true, but still it will become of absolutely not use to anyone. So you see, whether we or not we want your life story, your body would be of no use to us if we do not contain your soul."

"I see. But how are you animating me? I mean, surely the magicians will detect something wrong. And even though I've know the others less than a week, they'll be able to detect the personality change!"

"Questions, questions!" said Dr. Ricknow. "I'm the one with the questions for you."

"Very well. I suppose I can do nothing but answer them then, to my best ability."

"Very good. We might just be inspired to actually *feed* you in that case!"

I had to admit, my belly did feel a little empty.

"Tell us about this dragon link of yours! And a little bit more about what you are doing on our world."

I saw no real reason why I should not. After all, I was innocent enough of a great deal of facts, much of what I could impart to Ricknow he probably already knew — and whatever else was clearly the painfully obvious. And as for the dragon link . . . and what had happened with Hypernius. To the truth, I knew absolutely nothing and was hoping that Ricknow might clue *me* in. Certainly his knowledge of things of this world far outspanned mine and if I could keep him rambling then I might have the chance to learn more.

So I told him. Just the basic facts, no real shadings or curlicues. It was really simple enough, I said. I was here to help Mr. Escutcheon put together a film. With myself as scriptwriter. I knew he knew this, and I knew he knew what films were — but to hide that, I started to explain the cinema of my world.

"No need, no need," he said. "But may I ask, if you're just here to write — what are you doing loping around the countryside?"

"Scouting for locations of course. And characters for the film, and a plot."

"But you are headed for the Dragon Horde."

"Yes, but that seems as good a plot for a film as any!"

"No other reason?"

"Well, I suppose that none of the party would be unhappy to find treasure along the way — or at the Dragon Horde itself."

"Hmmm. I suppose not. Well, I must say, you sound truthful enough. But about this Dragon Link . . ."

"Sometimes I just touch Hypernius' head, and stare into his eyes and there's a contact made."

"That's what happened when you came to spy on me the last time?"

"That was unintentional."

"But you admit it was spying!"

"I saw you sending off those three men to waylay us. That is how I recognized them at the tavern."

"What else did you hear and see?"

I thought it best not to stay off the subject of those hidden tomes at the Dragon Horde. So instead I steered him in another, unexpected direction.

"I saw you watching Warner Brothers cartoons on your video machine!" I chattered at him. This time it was my turn to waggle my finger.

The result was not what I had intended at all. He went into a fury, a tantrum. With more energy than I thought his old bones could contain he hurled himself at the cage and started shaking it. The metal clanged and rang and I banged about inside the container. Finally my tail wound round one of the far bars and my hands gripped others instinctively. I was quite quick and agile in my new body, it seemed. Frightened, I looked over to him, expecting him to pull the cage down and crash it onto the floor. Instead, I found myself staring at red rimmed, blood shot eyes gazing at me in an entirely new way.

"I should kill you for that!" he said.

"What," I gasped. "Hey, I like cartoons too. Nothing to be ashamed of. You've got good taste! I like Daffy Duck and Bugs Bunny too!"

"You cannot understand —" he began, but then cut himself off. "Did you tell Escutcheon what you saw?"

I knew I was in trouble then, but I had to decide whether or not to lie or to tell the truth. So far he didn't seem to have a good grip on my intelligence (and some times I wondered if *I* did for that matter) so I decided to play it dumb.

"Why should I? What's so special about watching cartoons? Like I said, I do it all the time. Besides, he seemed far to preoccupied just with the idea of you coming after us."

Doctor Ricknow snorted. "He would, wouldn't he?" He let go of the cage. "It is fortunate you are so ignorant of the way things are ... I'm not sure you are stupid, but it hardly seems worth expending my energy over the matter."
   "Does that mean you're sorry for scaring the hell out of me?"
   "Oh, believe me, there are probably far worse things in store for you if you do not cooperate! But not for now ... No, for now, we will just keep you safely tucked away here where you can be of no harm. And so that we can use your true body as we please."
   He'd told me quite a bit by that outburst. What I'd witnessed in that private room was perhaps even more significant that even Mr. Escutcheon had realized. But if he left now, I wouldn't be able to get any more information out of him.
   "You certainly have my tail in a wringer."
   "Indeed we do."
   "I gather, though, that you are interested in the cinema of my world. You know, the reason I'm here — well, it's mostly to get a shot at doing a film. I don't care who its with, or what its about. I just want to be a success. Know what I mean?"
   "I know enough of the city where you are from to understand the sort of person you are, yes." Those bushy eyebrow pricked up with interest. "However, I also know that I cannot necessarily *trust* you."
   "Is there some special plan that *you* have that I can be helpful in —?"
   He seemed most amused by that. "You mean you're interested in helping *me* write a screenplay? How amusing. Well, I shall have to give *that* some thought. I hadn't thought much about exploiting my world for the purposes of entertaining *your* world for money, and I must say the whole notion strikes my funny bone most peculiarly. I shall give it some thought."
   "Perhaps if you gave me some notion of what you were up to I might be able to think about ways to assist," I said. "I don't seem to have a great deal else to do here," I pointed out.
   "Except betray your friend ..." He shook his head, laughing. "I think not, sirrah! I think you are just tapping information from me. Well, perhaps I have information for you. But not now ... No, not now — I have other, more important things to attend to, I think. In the meantime, this should keep your for awhile." He pulled out a small bottle of liquid and a handful of nuts and placed them on the ledge of my cage. "Don't move around too much, or I'm afraid you'll lose them. Ta ta! We shall talk more later ... Though what about, I can't imagine! Ha ha! In the very least, now you'll have *plenty* to write about. Perhaps I shall relent and give you a pen and paper!"
   The academic swept from the chambers, leaving me in a royal funk. I'd done just about everything I could, but I wondered now if I'd done

the right thing. Even if *I* knew I'd done the right thing — in afterthought, it *did* seem rather sleazy. I hoped that Dr. Ricknow had no way of recording what I'd said. I'd be hard pressed to explain it to Mr. Escutcheon.

And I hadn't really gained a thing from the ploy.

I sat and sulked over the matter for a moment, despondent. Eventually I realized that I was both hungry and thirst. I managed to pick up the bottle. The stuff inside was clear and odorless and certainly tasted enough like water for me to try drinking it. It seemed okay, so I drank my fill.

The nuts were easily crackable. I did so and ate the meat, which tasted like a cross between walnuts and cashews. I ate my fill and then sat down and stewed some more, eyes sweeping the library to find some kind of clues or information I could use.

I was doing this for some time, when suddenly I thought a noise. A skittering, a tweaking, a slurred whispering. A slush of echoes, softened by the walls of books.

My attention was caught immediately. I hopped up and trod to the edge of the cage, careful not to make too much noise.

Something, it seemed, something *alive* was in the room.

Cautiously, patiently I waited, peering unobtrusively over the edge of the cage. I wasn't sure what this meant, or that it would be any good — but I felt that surely if I made noise I'd frighten away whatever it was.

There were some moments of silence and I thought maybe whatever it was *had* scampered away.

And then the whiskered face peered around a bookcase, bright eyes peering about.

"All right," said the cat. "Look like the coast is clear!"

And, walking not on all fours but on standing on its hind legs like a man, a cat wearing a bow tie and a jacket and spectacles strode out below me.

Chapter Seventeen

I stood in my perch, staring down with amazement.

I suppose I should not have been so startled. I mean, on a day when one sees a man rise up from the dead and then transport his trussed up companions elsewhere with a puff of smoke, a day when one journeys through the eyes of a dragon into the body of a monkey, a day with a dialogue with a deadly demagogue out for power over a fantasy world, a talking cat should not have been much of a surprise. After all, currently I was a talking monkey. Nonetheless, it is rather shocking to have a cat come creeping out on two legs and launch into speech.

"Come on then," he whispered. "Come on, Sid, and make it snappy! We've not time to lose."

"Okay, okay," another voice answered petulantly. "Just got my tail caught." With a puff of dust, a badger wearing tennis shoes and a football jersey with the number 00 padded up, peering nervously around, whiskers twitching.

The cat looked down at the badger disapprovingly. "If the thing wasn't so heavy, I'd do it myself." He looked down an aisle. "All right. There it is in that corner down there. In the purple. Let's go get it."

"I don't see it," said the badger. "Are you sure? That might be a trapped area. I say, lets go back, have a cup of tea and a cookie and plan this very, very carefully."

The cat whacked the badger lightly on the top of the head. The badger winced, but did nothing.

"We're *not* going to go back empty handed!" declared the cat. "There's important work to be accomplished, and this book holds the key to much of our efforts!"

"Very well, very well," whimpered the badger. "Lead me to it. I'll do my best, I swear I will. Only you have to understand, I'm not like you, I'm not used to this stress, I just get all knotted up —"

Whack! Another swipe of its paw shut the badger up. No mistaking the dominant one here. The poor thing trudged onward behind the cat to be about its task.

"Hello!" I said.

I may as well have lobbed a hand grenade into their midst. They both shot up into the air, did double takes, then scrambled back in the direction they'd come.

"No, please!" I said hastily. "Look over here. There's no way I can harm you! I'm in a cage, and I'm definitely *not* on Doctor Ricknow's side!"

The badger kept on going, but the cat stopped. It peered up at me through its glasses, ascertained that indeed I was in a cage and threatening absolutely no harm and then, in a trice, reached out and grabbed that football jersey. It stretched but it held, and the badger thumped down on its tailed buttocks, quite confused.

"Let me go!" it squeaked.

"Shut up. It's a fellow Speller. Smells new, too."

"Well, I just got here, if that's what you mean. And don't worry about Ricknow. He's gone. Do you think you can help me get out of here? I'm really in a fix."

"No kidding," said the badger. "And so will we be if we stick around."

"No, wait. There's something about this one," said the cat. It sniffed the air. "He's most peculiar. And quite important, I think."

"I don't know if *I'm* important," I said. "But I have friends who are doing something vital and I need to warn them that they're in danger."

"This could be a trap, Purrvis!" squeaked the badger. "Ricknow could have put this guy here to trick us!"

Again those nostrils twitched. "No. The nose knows, Squawker. I smell nothing of Ricknow's work in this monkey here. Strangely enough, what I *do* smell is . . . no. It couldn't be — Earth?"

"Earth! Yes. The United States. Los Angeles! That's where I'm from!" I said, excitedly.

"How could that be?" said the badger called Squawker. "A talking monkey from Earth?"

"You're a talking badger from Lifton!" said the cat. "All the stuff we know that Ricknow is doing with Earth these days, it really should be no surprise."

"Then you'll help me, then?"

"If you'll help us."

"Confound Dr. Ricknow? Save this world from the Dark University?"

"That was my general line of thought."

"Hmm. This is most encouraging. And you say you are from Earth?"

"That's right? I'm a scriptwriter. From Hollywood."

"From *Hollywood!*" Now it was time for Squawker to be impressed. He rather goggled me, his previously squinty eyes suddenly round as marbles. "You mean you make movies and video shows and such."

"I write scripts," I said, not wanting to lie or to get too specific. "Movie scripts, television scripts."

"Get him down, get him down!" the badger insisted. "We've got lots of questions to ask *you*. Lots!"

I wondered how these creatures knew about Earth, and about movies and television. However, more important was getting out of this cage and away from this room – presumably to wherever these folk lived themselves.

My cage dangled from a large chain that was slipped through a metal ring in the ceiling. This chain in turn slipped down one corner of the room, where it was tied to the wall. Although they looked to be just animals, these creatures had marvelous abilities with their limbs and after examining and debating the issue of knots for a very short period of time, they managed to untie and untangle the chain where it was moored.

Unfortunately, they had underestimated the weight of my metal cage.

With a loud clanking, my cage pulled the chain through the ceiling loop, and my would-be saviors found themselves being hoisted up into the air. Purrvis the cat let go; Squawk the badger clung and shut his eyes. The badger shot up toward the ceiling willy-nilly. The cage, with me in it, banged down onto the ground.

There was a great deal of tumult and crashing, and I was bounced around, not unpainfully. Somehow, though, I retained my consciousness, although I did see a few stars scattered here and there.

Actually, it was all just as well, since I didn't really know how the cage was going to be unlocked once I got down. As it happened, the crash had bent two of the bars just enough so that I could slip through.

After staggering through, I scampered over to the cat to thank him. I automatically extended my hand to shake his, but he ignored it. Awkwardly, I withdrew the offer. He was looking up and I followed his gaze.

Squawk the badger still hung from the chain, only inches from the ceiling.

"He's not always this stupid, you know," Purvis said, scratching his head. "A little cowardly, yes . . . Tentative, definitely."

"Help," squeaked Squawk.

"Jump, old chum," said the cat. "The monkey and I will catch you."

"Why doesn't he just climb down the chain?" I asked.

"Him? It would take forever."

"O . . . kay. . . . O . . . kay . . . Here I . . . gooooo."

The badger let go, and fell, holding his nose as though he were jumping into a river.

I held out my arms to aid in this rescue effort, however the cat disdainfully pushed me away and then stepped back from the falling figure himself.

Squawked thumped on the floor, bounced once on his rear, sailed up, and then landed easily on springy legs. He shot an angry look at his associate. "Ouch! Where was my living net?"

"With *that* butt? You did fine, chum. No reason to risk breaking our arms! I knew you'd be okay."

Squawk didn't particularly seem to agree, but simply settled into a quiet sulk, rubbing his tail.

"Well, we've made quite the ruckus, haven't we?" said Purrvis. "Perhaps we'd better go and get that book and then depart before an investigation into the noise arrives!"

"I'd be quite willing to help!" I said.

"I'll go and deal with the door then," Squawk volunteered and was promptly gone.

"Just as well," sniffed the cat. "He probably would have dropped it on my foot anyway. Come on then, friend —"

"Ralph. The name's Ralph," I said.

"Ralph, then. Let's see if we can't grab a hold of that book I need before the universe comes tumbling down over our heads, eh?"

I looked up, wondering if this was some sort of Chicken Littlish pronouncement of imminent doom.

"No, no. I speak metaphorically of the return of Ricknow and his men — Hurry, hurry!"

So I followed him around the bend of library shelves. He quickly ran a claw down a set of volumes, finally stopping on a thick book labeled in Gothic script, YE OLDE TELEVISION REPAIR55. He pulled it halfway and then gestured for some aid. Astonished at the title, still nervous about the possible advent of enemy soldiers and necromancers and such, I assisted the cat heft the volume out. Together we carried it down the aisle.

"Hurry!" called Squawk. "Hurry, I think I hear something!"

Sure enough, faintly though emphatically from outside the door there came the sound of heavy footsteps. A gruff order was delivered.

The volume was heavy indeed and we were only able to increase our speed slightly. "Is this thing absolutely necessary?" I asked, puffing with the exertion.

"Imperative!" said Purvis.

"Okay." I managed to put a little bit more muscle into the task, and when we rounded the corner, I was relieved to see Squawk only a few feet away, holding a door for us. A most peculiar door, it was really a panel cut into the bookshelves with hidden hinges. Beyond was a tunnel that dived into darkness.

Together, Purrvis and I jostled the book through and into the dimness. Quickly, Squawk closed the door behind us — and not a second too soon. Almost instantly afterwards, a commotion of voices and clomping boots rang out in the library. There was much huffing and gruffing and then an exclamation as the fallen cage was noted.

"Oh Gawd —" someone said. "Ricknow is just going to *love* this!"

"Quick — fan out!" Another gruff voice. "Find the bastard! But don't stick him or knock him unduly. We can't kill him!"

Comforting to know, but nonetheless it was nice to be shut up in the dimness, away from that no doubt burly and unruly crew.

I felt a tug on my shirt and a pull on the book I still hefted and I was off again, struggling down the tunnel, a monkey in the company of a clothed badger and a cat, lugging a medieval television repair manual!

Our destination was a ways.

Fortunately, we were able to rest from time to time. Squawk spelled us from time to time, and I was not surprised that Purrvis spent an inordinate percentage of the time unencumbered.

Eventually the tunnel — filled with twists and turns and zigzags — eventually widened and became better lighted. We had, I also noted, descended well below the level we had been on, so I was not surprised to find us in a cavern like hallway. It had the feel of a basement — damp and cool and dim.

"Not too far now," assured Purrvis. "You two are doing absolutely wonderful!"

We turned the corner and what lay beyond so filled me with astonishment that I dropped the book I was carrying. The end fell on Squawk's toe — and he fulfilled the promise of his name.

"Owww!" he cried. "Have a care!"

The corridor widened out into an avenue of little hovels, but this was not what astonished me. Immediately before us in this little town below the surface of the Dark University was a large open shop, with workbenches and tables and chairs. A number of small animals — dogs, squirrels, and such — were busy poring over all manner of odd laboratory arrangements and piles of mechanism.

Upon the nearest worktable sat on old Sylvania color television tube, attached by an umbilical of colored wires to exposed electronic guts.

I suppose that the name on the spine of the book should have prepared me for this, along with what I'd seen in Dr. Ricknow's private office. Still the sight of anthropomorphized animals industriously working on a weird mélange of magic, chemistry, and technology was all a bit too much.

"Over there!" said Purrvis. "That's my workplace," he said, pointing a claw over to where the naked television innards were strewn. "Pick up the book and put it over there, folks. I think that this will do it, just!"

"It's a television set — a television set from Earth," I said. "What's it doing here?"

"Little bit of interdimensional theft, I'm afraid," said Purrvis. "Oh well, it's all in a good cause."

Squawk and I hefted the book onto the indicated bench. I brush my hands of the dust and shook my head.

"That's what I don't get. All this importation of technology into a world that really doesn't have a use for it. Why not just be happy with magic or whatever you use?"

"Ah, now *there*'s the Fifty-Four Thousand Dollar Question."

"Sixty Four."

"Whatever." Purvis jumped up onto the stool and opened the manual. He perused it for a moment in silence through his spectacles, then turned back to peer down at me. "I can see that just as soon as I make the necessary adjustments to my work here, there we are going to have to sit down for some refreshments and have a long chat, hmmm?"

"I'd like that. The sooner the better, as a matter of fact. I need to find a way to get back to my friends. . . . I mean. . . . There's a lot of explanation to do, I guess."

"You do look pretty tired. This will take me some minutes. Perhaps a nap will help. Squawk, let him use your bed."

"*My* bed. Why —"

"Squawk, I'm pulling rank here . . ."

"Oh very well!" The badger turned disgustedly and gestured for me to follow.

"See you in a few — and oh, be careful of the rats!"

"Rats?" I said.

"They're *real* rats," explained Squawk, "And they can be very nasty indeed."

I followed the badger through the strange town beneath the Dark University. We arrived at a small ramshackle hut, and he showed me a disheveled mat inside.

I tried to ask him questions on the way, but the creature was very taciturn.

"Well then, sleep well, and as much as you can," he muttered. "If you'd going to hang around with the likes of us for awhile, you're definitely going to need it."

I lay down and Squawk left. A blur and whirl of thoughts and questions consumed my head, so I thought I'd have trouble sleeping. Although I was out of that dreadful cage and away from the control of that awful Doctor, I still hadn't much of an idea what I was going to next.

Fortunately, my monkey body was more interested in brass tacks than worry and promptly bedded my brain down in slumber.

Chapter Eighteen

"Actually, believe it or not, I'm from Earth as well," said Purrvis. "Here you go — have a biscuit. I do hope your tea is satisfactory!"

My tea was quite satisfactory, hot and sweet and milky. It was just the thing to both wake me up from a groggy state and calm me down from my state of anticipation. I waved away the tray of cookies the bespectacled cat offered me, however. I was far too excited by what he'd just said to actually eat anything.

"You're from Earth?"

"Yes. England. Bristol, to be precise. I was an engineer there." He crunched a cream-filled cookie loudly, chewed thoughtfully. He waved the remaining half of the cookie around, indicating the community. "Like these other folk — and, I presume, like you — I am part of the brain drain."

"Brain drain?"

"Yes. The Dark University brain drain — the reason why we're here in the world." He took off his spectacles, cleaned them with a cloth, and then donned them again. "A most perfidious enterprise, I assure you."

We were sitting in Purrvis' little shack, a much neater, much cozier affair than Squawk's, taking tea. Just the two of us, in comfortable if patched, chairs in a haphazard kind of place. A monkey and a cat in clothing trying to figure this whole thing out. I'd been given some pants and a shirt at my request. I wasn't used to running around in the buff, even if it was amongst a bunch of animals. Just as well — even with my fur, the place down here felt a little damp and chill.

"Let me get this straight," I said. "You mean to tell me — you and all these other animals running about building things and what not — you're all human!"

"Well, I can't exactly say *everyone*. But a goodly number of us are. We're escapees from Doctor Ricknow's labs. Just like you! Only he had us a good deal longer!"

"What did you do for him?"

"We *built* things for him. Technological things. Damned touchy getting the materials, it all being imported in curious ways from Earth. Grabbed you know. And none of this stuff works, of course, unless you either get a bubble or you alter the molecular make-up of this reality. The latter of which is damned dangerous, by the way, and highly unrecommended."

"Wait a minute. A bubble . . ." I remembered what I'd witnessed in Doctor Ricknow's study. "You mean, like somehow stretching the boundaries of Earth's reality so that it comes into *this* reality — in such a way that you can step into it and operate technology!"

"Exactly. You're quite a smart fellow, you are. I can see that you're going to comprehend much of what I have to tell you."

I'd already related bits and pieces of the important aspects of my particular back-story, but now I let the cat have it all, including how I'd experienced the 'balloon' thing first hand. All through the story, he smoked a meerschaum pipe, nodding and encouraging me, asking me a question here and there, and generally understanding must of what I said.

When I was finished, he put his pipe aside, leaned forward, clasped his hands, and cleared his throat.

"Well, Ralph. I know it must have been quite a shock getting transported to a fantasy world . . . but Los Angeles was probably a better place to start with Bristol. Anyway, let me tell you as best I can what I believe is happening, from my point of view."

And thus Purrvis began to tell his story.

*H*e'd worked for a British Engineering company and was thirty-five years of age when it had happened.

He'd woken up in a body of a cat, in the magical chambers of the Dark University much as I had, though not in a cage. The interview with Doctor Ricknow had been brief. "You are now working for me," the man had said. "You will be kept in a decent way, and you will have rewards beyond your wildest dreams."

He was then put in a workshop in the Dark University, along with other animals similarly nabbed from technological backgrounds. There they worked on a number of projects — until, finally, one by one, they escaped and established this strange small colony below the University.

"Why doesn't Ricknow smoke you out?" I asked.

"Oh, he knows something's up — but there were so many recruits, and the organization around here is such a mess, that he's barely tried. We haven't caused any problems — yet."

"And if you're an electrician, why did you need that electronics manual?"

The cat shook its head sorrowfully. "You won't believe this, Ralph, but there's a brand of electronics that we're working on here that involves *magic*. These books indicate that technology on Earth is an offshoot of the ancient magical technology of this world — and our own medieval times. Quite loony, I know — but not as bizarre as what I'm about to tell you."

I had to admit I was all ears.

"Look, I realize that on the face of it, your mission here seemed very cut a dried. What's the term for it in Hollywood? Ah yes, *High Concept*. — But let me tell you, there's a lot more involved in the making of a film on this world than just colorful characters and dragons! And whatever Professor Escutcheon has told you, he wants a great deal more than money out of the patrons on Earth from his great fantasy epic!"

"But with money he can buy supplies for his beleaguered land . . . He can do all sorts of things . . . Maybe even break the curse that's been thrown over it!" I said. "Believe me, I've been there, and I've seen the place . . . it's a mess."

The cat bent over, licking the back of his paw and then smoothed his whiskers thoughtfully. He took off his spectacles and sighed. Then he put them back on and stared at me, his eyes swimming bizarrely in the lens. "This Escutcheon chap really has everyone flummoxed, doesn't he? Except perhaps his magicians. Those magicians would *have* to be in the know on this one."

"What are you talking about? Mr. Escutcheon is very sincere. And I *saw* the place. It's been cursed or something, and they definitely need money and supplies!"

"I don't doubt it, but it's all just a byproduct. And as for Escutcheon — well, being sincere is all very well and I'm quite sure he is — and a far more ethical being that Dr. Ricknow, that's for sure — but he also hasn't told you the whole truth, that's very clear."

"Whole truth? And *you* have the whole truth?" I said doubtfully.

Purrvis chuckled ruefully and settled back in his chair, picking up his tea and taking a sip. "No, can't say that I've got the whole truth. But I've seen enough and figured out enough to give a nicer slice than you seemed to have obtained."

I found my tail curling and uncurling, betraying my nervousness. "All right. Sorry. I'm listening."

"Right." He put the cup and saucer back on the table and leaned forward in a quiet shushed manner as though he were afraid that someone else would hear. "Ever see the bit in *Peter Pan* when the audience has to resurrect Tinkerbell the fairy by *believing* in her?"

"Sure," I said. "And clapping and crowing or whatever. And Peter Pan flies by thinking a happy thought."

"Well, let's not take it quite that far into schmaltz. I'm just trying to make a difficult subject a little easier to assimilate." He tapped his head. "The human mind, the human spirit, the human soul — it's quite something, my friend. A mystery in enigma wrapping paper. I mean, the very fact that this —" He tapped the side of his head "— is just a cat's brain being controlled by the vast powers of a my own true mind. Well, the strangeness just gets deeper. But let's just talk in generalities here. Let's not get too specific." He took a breath and composed himself. "Have you heard the term 'consensus reality,' Ralph?"

"Sure. It's something that's true or real because a large number of people agree that's its true or real."

"Let me try another term on you that I've coined myself — 'consensus *fantasy.*'"

"Okay. That would be something that wasn't real because a number of people agreed it wasn't real."

"Yes. You are following me so far. The power of human minds . . . consensus reality and fantasy . . . However, there are levels of the human mind other than the conscious . . . That has been proven, correct?"

"The subconscious, yes."

"And perhaps even more levels . . . Jung's collective unconscious, say . . ."

"But that's only a tendency toward archetypes and whatever . . ."

"Have you heard of mind fields? That there's real power in the human mind that it *projects*? Actual energy."

"Sure . . . But I don't know where . . ."

"Excellent. Where there is energy there is power, and where there is power that is directed — there is a reaction. A creation. A reflection. Now how many worlds of the imagination are there, Ralph? Just the human imagination."

"Well, there are thousands, of course. . . ."

"Suppose enough people believed in Tinkerbell. . . ."

"I'm not following."

"This world . . . This odd place . . . full of dragons and talking animals and magic . . . and yet real enough to you, correct?"

"Yes."

"Because it's a consensus fantasy that due to the power of the collective human subconscious has become a consensus *reality*. Matter, after all, is only a form of energy. And this matter . . ." He knocked on the arm of his chair . . . "Is the direct result of energy from the mass human mind!"

My own mind struggled to deal with that concept. "Okay, but that's just a theory . . . right? How can you prove it?"

"Come *on*, Ralph! Dragons? Magicians? Loony magic. It doesn't make sense . . . only in books and movies and *imagination* does it make sense. I'm not saying that this world is not real . . . I'm just telling you why it's so *strange* . . . And yes, perhaps even filled with fantasy archetypes . . . clichés. . . . Whatever you want to call them."

I found myself speechless.

"And suppose there were other worlds of the imagination — alternate worlds, alternate universes, whatever — created not by deviated channels of history but by one imagination capturing and controlling the power of imagination in sufficient human minds."

"All right. So maybe the Earth itself is all just a dream in the mind of God. So what?"

"Well, Ralph. Suppose you gave God a little bit of brain washing. A little nudge . . . you could change the world . . . Or maybe create a whole *new* world. That's what I'm saying, my boy. There's power to be tapped in the minds of man . . . vast power to control worlds of consensus fantasy . . . *real* worlds. And that is the ultimate goal of our Professor Escutcheon and Doctor Ricknow — control, power, domination over this world — and who knows, perhaps others."

I shook my head, groping with this immense and overwhelming idea. I wasn't quite sure I could get my comprehension around it. "Wait a minute. Let me see if I've got this straight, Purrvis. You're trying to tell me that Mister Escutcheon's *real* reason to make a movie is for power over this world. But how are people eating popcorn and watching light flickering to THX sound in dark movies theaters going to affect an entire world?"

"If it's a popular film and an intense enough experience for them. And why shouldn't it be? They'll be watching their own vivid dreams! Aren't you listening to me? This entire world was created by human minds. If enough of those minds' attitude toward the dream can be altered, the dream — the consensus fantasy — will be altered as well."

"Altered according to the parameters built into the movie. . . ?" I said stunned.

"Exactly. And dollars to donuts, the Dark University folks are going to get seriously decimated in this movie . . . Which will doubtless spell curtains for them in the consensus fantasy!" Happy with his explanation, Purrvis leaned back into his chair and tamped some shag tobacco into the meerschaum.

"What's wrong with that? You hate these Dark Academics as much as anyone."

Purvis shrugged as he lit his pipe with a match. "True. But there's a balance here now. What's the saying? Absolute power corrupts? Who's to say that Escutcheon's plans for this world are better than the Dark University's in the long run, hmm?" Smoke and sharp sweet odor blossomed. "I shudder at the thought of any world run by an Academic, anyway. Chances are he's a Marxist and will want to deconstruct everything."

"But you've no proof of that."

"No." Purrvis pointed his pipe stem at me. "No, I don't, but just you mark my words. And when you start writing this film, check to see what he wants you to do with the plot."

I was still struggling with the concept. "Are you telling me that there's a whole world modeled on *Casablanca* somewhere? A universe where Darth Vader and Luke Skywalker really exist? A planet where the Three Musketeers are still dueling with Cardinal Richelieu?"

"That's hard to say, but I wouldn't be surprised. Perhaps it's all jumbled up on one world . . . An odd thought, eh?"

"I think there's more than enough oddness just on this world to deal with."

"Doubtless. But I'm glad you're getting my drift."

"But what's with all this balloon business . . . And your own techno-magic efforts."

"Ricknow of course has been trying his own methods to obtain power. As this is the birth place of techno-magic by resurrecting the art and by making this world capable of supporting technology — such as missiles, atom bombs and all that. But you see, there's also a reverse angle on what I said before. I'm certain now that Ricknow believes that by altering this world, he can get control of *our* world. Which is an entirely different and maybe even more dangerous kettle of fish."

"And so you're trying to battle that."

Purrvis nodded. "Precisely."

"Well, whatever Escutcheon truly wants to accomplish, it sounds a lot better than what Ricknow seems to have in store!"

"No question about that. I just wanted to make sure you realized that there's a lot more involved here than just whether children in Escutcheon's kingdom eat gruel or steak."

He wasn't pressing or insisting. Clearly, Purrvis was just presenting me with the situation as he saw it. I had to weigh and decide myself, which I certainly would. Right now, though, I had to figure out how to either get out of here or break the spell that was keeping my soul locked in this cat's body.

I said as much to Purrvis.

"Well now," he said, standing up and clapping his paws together. "We might have just the thing for you."

My tail started flapping with excitement. "You do?"

"Yes, indeed. You just so happen to have stumbled on the right person in the right place. 'Course, there's a little risk involved," he said as afterthought.

"*Anything* has risk involved at this stage of the game!" I said, as I gladly scampered after him.

We went back to the workshops, darkened now. Only a couple workers were still in their places, doing whatever they were doing. One of them was a dog – a beagle, actually, but with the bearing and hands of a man. He seemed to be working on some sort of radio device, and was twirling a dial with resulting wave-band squeak as Purrvis came up behind him and laid a paw on his shoulder.

The dog barked with alarm and spun around.

"Purrvis! I asked you not to come up on my like that!" gruffed the dog.

"Keeps you on your toes, Flop. I want you to meet a new friend of mine – Ralph Phillips. He's from Earth too – a Hollywood writer, actually. Flop is an engineer from Alabama. Radio engineer. He's been doing some interesting work."

"Welcome to the hellhole," said Flop. "You must have just escaped from above, eh?"

"That's right. Purrvis tells me that you might have another sort of escape."

"He does, does he?" The beagle nodded and his long ears flopped up and down. "Well, maybe he's right, and maybe he's wrong." He pointed with his paw-hand to the assortment of radio guts on the worktable. "Damnedest business, the magic-electronics. Don't work like normal electronics. Physics is all-unpredictable here. Gotta use these weird spells to get the resistors and capacitors right. And when the transistors are actually little compact piles of pixie dust. . . . well, they're just unpredictable, that's what they are."

"Last time we talked, Flop, you were working on something that could cut the bond that kept a soul inside one of these animal bodies, allowing it fling back to it original home."

"True, but I don't think it'll work across the dimensions. Lots more work on that one before you can get back to Hollywood. Oh well – a Hollywood writer's brain doesn't really need a soul from what I hear."

"Too true," I said, "but you know, my real body is still in this world!"

"No kidding! Well, you know, *that* might just work. I've never tried it of course, and it could be awfully dangerous . . . But I'd love to test it if you're willing to make a go of it!"

"Yes!" I said without equivocation.

"You see! I *thought* old Flop might be able to help you out!" said Purrvis.

"Unfortunately there's one little problem." The beagle leaned over underneath the workbench and pulled out an assemblage of electronic parts on a piece of wood board. "I'm lacking a very vital part of the thing. It needs a special kind of crystal. A crystal that old Ricknow's got in *his* shops, but we haven't managed to steal yet."

"Do you know what it looks like and where it is?" I said without hesitation.

"Oh yes, certainly. But there are all kinds of vicious creatures guarding it when the workers themselves aren't doing their stuff."

"It doesn't make any difference," I said with a sigh. "I have to try."

Chapter Nineteen

After I'd assured them that I was rested, and after they insisted on feeding me something, 'for energy,' Purrvis and Flop led me up the winding corridor. We walked for a very long time, and took several turns in the tunnel, and one long set of stairs before Flop stopped, stuck his long snout near the wall, and snuffled.

"Here. We're close. Damned close."

"Right," said Purrvis. "The secret panel is just along here, Flop, dangle that lantern over here a ways." The cat reached out with its clawed fingers, scraping at the sides of the corridor walls. "Yeah!" He scrabbled at some controls, something clicked, and with a half-whispered hush of greased hinges, a small door much like the one that led into the study opened.

"Okay! Here we go!" I said, stepping through the door eagerly.

"No – wait!" said Purrvis.

I'd already stepped into the gloom, though, and as soon as I did, my feet gave way from under me. I slipped and fell into a lighter area.

Even as I was falling, though, I managed to turn around and scrabble for purchase. Being a monkey helped. I caught and I held, finding myself dangling over a precipice.

I hazarded a look downwards as I clung. Below me was a large room, dim now save for the occasional glow of a fire and of electronic bulbs. I could see worktables and groupings of equipment.

Doctor Ricknow's magic-electronic laboratory.

I sensed presences down there, but I saw nothing. The smell of burnt insulation and soldered wiring along with other, more organic smells hung over the place in a miasma.

In just a moment, I found a cat's claw and a dog's paw reaching down for me. "Up you go there," said Purrvis.

I grabbed hold and easily boosted myself up and back through the hole with a monkey's nimbleness. I took a deep breath and made sure my footing was solid. "Thank you."

"That's all right. Should have warned you," replied Purrvis. "Knew you were hot to get that crystal, but didn't realize you were *that* hot!"

"Didn't realize that the door was near the ceiling," said Flop. "And neither do the folks down there. Which is why we use it. A lot safer than down on the floor!"

"What's crawling around down there?" I asked.

"You saw something?" said Purrvis.

"Not so much *saw* as *felt*," I said, shuddering a bit.

"As I said, there's valuable stuff in this laboratory ... And odd forces are at work," said Flop. "Otherwise I'd just lope in one day and grab that crystal myself."

"Let's just say they're animals like ourselves, possessed of souls a little darker than ours ..." said Purrvis. "From a dark dimension? Botched experiments of soul transportation?"

"Nazi war criminals?" added Flop.

"Whatever they are, they're guards, I take it."

"Precisely. And to get to the crystal I need, I suspect you're going to have to meet up with one or two."

I nodded soberly. "Just tell me where it is."

"Oh damn," said Purrvis. "It's bloody suicide it is."

"Well, I don't know of any other choice."

"No, I mean it's a foolhardy mission on your own ... Flop, you'd be no good. You're a dog. But I think I can be of some help. And I brought a couple of weapons." He handed me a dagger. In his paws I could also see the gleam of a blade. "I've worked down there. I know my way around. Flop, just tell me where that crystal is, and we'll give a damned good try of getting a hold of it!"

So Flop did just that.

*W*hat they hadn't told me was upon opening that door was that you had to sidle along a piece of wood and then hop down upon the top of a large metal shelf to get down without jumping into the dark. Being in a monkey's body, I was able to accomplish this without a great deal of problem, and Purrvis did so as well, although it was clear even though he had a cat's agility, he was a bit out of training.

We crept along the top of the shelving, Purrvis leading. "There's a way down, believe it or not."

"We could just jump," I said. The floor was not that far away. I hadn't been in that much danger when I dangled above it; I wondered now if monkeys landed on their heads or on their feet in such circumstances.

"No. We need to take the way down so we can mark the way up. And *out*, I might remind you."

"A very good point."

With feline grace, he groped his way through the dark, finally coming up with an 'Ah!' and then taking advantage of it, swinging around and climbing down a makeshift ladder.

I descended into the gloom after him.

The smells became more intense as I lowered myself, and I thought I smelled blood and waste and harsh animal smells beneath the other more chemical ones. We bounced down on a hard wooden floor and Purrvis shushed me as I landed beside him noisily, ready to scramble back up the ladder at the first sign of danger.

"Right. This way, I believe."

We walked along a row of workstations, and from within clumps of equipment energies pulsed like ghosts struggling to release themselves from electronic graves. Here, that coppery blood and iron smell of magic was very strong indeed and it was mixed with the smell of technology. Somehow, the combined result had both a modern smell and an ancient taste. It gave me the creeps.

There were clickings and snicklings and snaps of electricity and the hum of amperage. I realized as I walked behind Purvis that not merely my hackles were rising, but the fur along my entire back was standing on end. I was in a keen state of readiness — I could feel the adrenaline pricking at my nerves, painting everything in the clarity of intense awareness.

Just *what* was out there, waiting for us?

I had the terrible feeling that I was going to find out sooner than I wanted to.

He strode down an aisle without being bothered. Purrvis was wrapped with intense concentration. He seemed to be sniffing out this crystal as much as he was remembering Flop's directions.

Finally, he stopped me. "Yes!" He pointed. "That cabinet there. Position and description fit perfectly. Let's have at it." By the dim light, I could see that underneath a work station, draped with wires and cables like mutant vines, was indeed a cabinet. It was unremarkable and plain, much I dare say like many another cabinet beneath the workstations here.

Fortunately it was not locked and so it swung open easily.

But as soon as that door opened, the seeming plainness of the cabinet disappeared immediately.

Something shone from within like the North Star inside of a box.

"The crystal!" I said.

"Yes," replied Purrvis.

It blazed in a lambent, encapsulated chevron of cool fire, and I was entranced. Amber and aquamarine highlights skipped and flittered within the white and yellow of it, hypnotic gestures of some invisible mesmerist. As I stared into it, it seemed as though my soul were already being tugged through my eyes and hurled into yet another dimension.

But a dimension that was adamantly *not* Earth.

Purrvis's claws dug into my forearm. "Here, chum. Don't go zombie on me."

I shook my head, releasing myself of the spell.

"Wow," I said, shaking. "Pretty potent!"

"Some sort of magical energy, all right," said the cat. "We'll just have to get it out of there though, averting our eyes slightly ... Unless ..." He cast his eyes around. "Ah!" Found what he was looking for.

It was a piece of cloth. Purrvis took this and draped it over the geometrically astounding hunk of crystal, then carefully detached it from its setting. He hefted it downward and handed it to me. "There you go. Have a care with that ... it's quite precious."

I'd expected it to be warm, but even as my hand touched the glassy surface felt only cool smoothness. I tucked the cloth fully over it, lest some of the magic seep out, and then held it tight.

"Okay," I said. "What now. Back to the ladder?"

"I think that would be appropriate," said Purrvis and together, him leading the way, we did just that, quietly as we could manage.

We almost made it, too.

Down at the end of the aisle, something stood in the dim light, bristling and twice as big as us. The smell of sour sweat and old blood drifted down toward us, and I could see pointed extrusions wobbling above it with deadly razor edged barbed. It hissed and it snarled like something unearthed from hell, hungry and angry.

"Go through it?" I said, bringing out my sword with hand while I clutched the crystal under the other. "Around it?"

"No," said Purrvis. "Cumbersome looking thing. We'll run." He pointed. "The other way!"

It was a wise thought, I realized, since were both were light and limber and could most likely sprint a great deal faster than this monster ahead of us. I turned and ran and we were at the opposite end of the corridor before I knew.

Purrvis pointed and I loped after him, slightly weighted down by the wrapped crystal and yet generally able to keep up with the cat. He skidded around a corner and I followed.

"Uh oh." He said, coming to a stop so quickly I almost piled into him.

Coming toward us was another pile of ugly trouble, pulsing excrescences wafting before it, limned by a faint light behind. I glimpsed the sharp white of gnashing teeth.

"Definitely not a through street," remarked Purrvis, turning and making speed the opposite direction. He did not have to implore me to follow. I was on his heels in a trice, assuming he knew where he was going. Presumably back to the ladder, I thought, but a growl ahead cut us off.

Another one! Damn! What, had the beasts waited to see what we were up to and then gone about their business of nailing us?

"We're cut off!" I said.

"This way!" cried Purrvis.

"But that's not toward the ladder . . ."

"Just do as I say! Trust me, I know what I'm doing. It's going to cost us quite a few more breaths, but we might just pull this off!"

I saved my breaths and followed.

At the end of the corridor was a door. Yards before this door Purrvis leaped and with an amazing aim and athleticism I had not realized was in him, struck the doorknob perfectly. There was the click of tumblers and with perfect timing, Purvis pushed against the doorjamb with his foot and with all of his might. The wooden door swung open hard.

"Run through! Quickly!" he cried.

I did so, hurling around the doorjamb and out into the hall, still dim but considerably better lit. I turned around to see if I could be of help, and immediately saw what he was up to.

Still it would be a close one.

I could see three monstrous shapes converging in the room beyond, converging and heading in our direction.

Meantime, Purrvis still hung on to the doorknob as it banged against the wall, almost knocking him off. However the force of the impact forced the door back, swinging.

The creatures of the techno-magic lab shambled and lurched toward me, snarling and slavering.

By using his weight expertly, Purrvis urged it on and the thing slammed and slammed hard, right in the faces of things.

The monsters ran smack into the door and there was silence afterward.

Purrvis jumped down nimbly. "Talk about things that go bump in the night!"

He then urged me onward down the hall.

I ran, hugging the crystal by my side. We ran down the darkened corridor, me following Purrvis as best I could. The hallway, I could see, looked like something in a large castle, with wood and stone walls and all kinds of strange material plastered on the wall, knightly, magical and otherwise. Banners and crests. Things like that. However, I only noticed it in passing — I was running far too hard to take notice.

We'd been running for about a minute when we heard voices and footsteps ahead of us. At first I thought that we were being followed, but there were no sounds of real pursuit. Just footsteps and voices.

All the same, we were out in the open and about to be discovered. I was about to make this comment when Purrvis pushed me into a darkened doorway. He tried the doorknob but it was locked. "Damn!" he whispered. "Okay, you're going to have to be as quiet as possible while these gentlemen pass by."

I did not have to be told twice. I pressed my back up against the doorway, into the darkest possible area and breathed as shallowly as possible.

The footsteps neared. Muttering voices echoed through the corridor. I recognized one. Dr. Martinus Ricknow's voice.

"I don't care how it's done, that monkey has *got* to be found!" Fury crackled in the baritone.

Another voice. "I wouldn't worry about it, Doc. Lots of those things have escaped before, and *they* haven't caused any trouble."

"Probably got eaten by the rats in the subcellars!" pronounced another voice with satisfaction.

The men broke into view and I somehow mashed myself further back against the wall. I recognized the other immediately. Dyrk Ryonne and Harfield Moregnash. Hopefully their companion wasn't dragging along behind them. Hopefully Shalbot Purseblossom had been de-animated from his zombie state. Nonetheless, the shivers at the base of my spine told me to be on my toes!

To my horror, they stopped right there in front of us.

All they had to do was turn and look hard and they'd spot us, and that would be that. Ryonne and Moregnash had swords and those would be slinging in a moment, slicing us into bits!

"Right! Then who caused all that ruckus just now in the workroom?" Dr. Ricknow said. "Something's happening on down there!"

"There are always bizarre things happening in this place, face it, Doc!" said Dyrk Ryonne. "Look, that monkey's not going to cause any trouble. He'll lay low for a while . . . Maybe he's even trying to escape the place."

"He certainly caused enough trouble for poor Purseblossom!" said Moregnash. "And if it hadn't been for the Doc here, we'd probably even be swinging from a beam by our necks with hot coals beneath our feet right now!"

"Too true. He's been nothing but trouble. Still, his body is being put to good use now . . . All we have to do is to find that monkey that's holding his soul! Well, onward — let's see what developments await us down at the workshop."

"How would the fellow even *know* of the importance of the workshop, anyway?" said Ryonne. "And what could he do there? No, I think you are tacking too much significance on this."

"How can we attach too much significance on the means by which the Dark University may come to control not only this world, but many others?"

I almost gasped aloud. Here was Doctor Ricknow confirming what Purrvis had told me!

"And a lot more at stake than just that," said Moregnash.

The trio hurried on down the corridor, Ricknow's robes swishing on the stone, the smell of stale magic trailing after him.

"Let's go!" said Purrvis.

I did not have to be told twice. Cautiously, we stole down the corridor in the opposite direction, creeping along the sides quietly as we could.

Finally, we came to a doorway into which Purrvis lead me. He found another panel, opened it, and beckoned me onward with a tug on my arm.

The darkness swallowed us whole.

Chapter Twenty

The device flickered and snickered. An arc of electricity stranger than I'd ever seen before whipped and shivered and sang from electrode to electrode. The air smelled of positive ions, like the smell you get before the coming of a huge thundershower.

In the center of this device was a chair, and this chair was where I was supposed to sit, holding a couple of electrodes, with my feet slotted into metallic stirrups.

All in all it looked to me more like a volunteer execution than the sort of soul transfer it was supposed to be.

"Verdict?" said Purrvis. I noticed the cat was standing well back. He'd also taken up an annoying habit of smoking black thick cigars, so that thick mists of bluish tobacco smoke hung everywhere, obtrusive with harsh fragrance.

"All systems go!" said Flop, happily surveying some dials and an oscillator on a makeshift control panel. He stood back and regarded his handiwork. It was a gaggle of wiring and odd talismanlike arrangements. It all buzzed and hummed with sub-vocal incantations of spells and shifting layers of magic vibrated amongst the electricity like visualized mantras. In the very center of it, like a star, shone the crystal that'd we'd stolen from the workshop. "Damnedest thing I've ever done, that's for sure — but I *do* believe it will work!"

"Shame we can't test it on anything first!" said Purrvis, blowing out another stream of smoke.

I coughed and sighed. "Yes. A shame."

"Nothing for it. Prepare for engagement," said the cat, looking at me with a it's-now-or-never kind of expression.

Several days had passed since the burglary, hardworking days — particularly for Flop. However, he'd put his shoulder to the wheel and had performed admirably.

Since there was nothing more that I could actually do with the device, (and also Purrvis had wanted to keep me out of trouble and away from the corridors above where no doubt we were all being searched for in earnest) I kept busy studying and memorizing maps and books and such with the information I needed to understand this world and some of the true situation in which I was involved.

Now, though, was the moment of truth.

"You ready, lad?" asked Flop.

"Yes, I suppose so," I said, bracing myself. In fact, even though I was quite nervous, I'd was more bored than anything else and eager to get back to the party, where I had more power over this situation.... And eventually confront Mr. Escutcheon concerning what I had learned.

"Well then, why don't you sit yourself down in here and we can begin!"

I turned to Purrvis who put out his hand. "I'm sure we'll meet again, Ralph."

"What will you do in the meantime?"

"Carry on our underground war against these folks above us, I suppose. Maybe with this crystal that we managed to retrieve, we'll even be able to develop something that will send us back to Earth . . . Although I for one want to stay here until we can make sure Earth is safe."

I shook the hand warmly. "Thank you for your help. I'd have been hopelessly trapped without you."

"And don't forget — Escutcheon's not the villain that Ricknow is, but make no mistake — he's in this for power of his own sort."

"I'll remember that. Thank you."

"God speed and we'll be thinking of you. And if you happen to gather an air force of dragons to raid this dark and dismal place, then all the better for us and for the universes!"

I grinned. "I'll do my best."

So saying, I took my place in the chair.

"Yes, yes, my thought exactly, but for the lack of straps the thing would be like something in a Texas prison," said Flop. "Sorry, but it's the best that I could come up with."

"That's okay. Just as long as it works," I replied, slipping my monkey feet in the slots, grabbing the electrodes with both hands. They were chill and a shiver shot through me, as though in anticipation of the charge of electricity I was about to receive.

Purrvis stepped up to me, stood straight, and wiped back his whiskers with the back of his paw. He then extended his hand out for me to shake. It had all the elements of a hokey anthropomorphized animal book — except that the sentiments that shone in his grey almond-shaped eyes were the same as what I was feeling.

"Well, old sport. It's been awfully good to have you around. Funny thing, but I'm actually going to miss you."

I gripped the paw and shook it firmly. "Thanks for everything, Purrvis. I'd still be up in that cage if it weren't for you. Now we might just have a chance."

"We just might!" squeaked Flop excitedly.

"Just remember what we talked about, my friend. I don't know if we shall ever meet again . . . But if we do, it shall be in victory, eh?"

"And if it's back on Earth? Shall we know each other?"

"What? Of course we shall! I just so happen to look exactly like this as there as well!" He winked jovially. "And you?"

"I've been known to eat a few bananas and swing from a few limbs."

"Excellent. Then there will be no problem. We shall know one another immediately. And we shall have a proper drink then, not this godawful tea we put up with here, eh?"

I agreed immediately.

Purrvis patted me on the shoulder, gave me a thumbs up sign (difficult for a cat to do, but he managed it) and then stepped back to safety.

"Ready when you are!" I said, feeling profoundly nervous but nonetheless profoundly excited as well.

Flop nodded and turned serious eyes toward his controls. They sprouted around him like a mechanical garden. Slowly, he twisted knob-bulbs and thumbed switch-blooms. Finally, he lifted a hand and pulled down upon a lever-stalk, and in a flash of gilded light, a different reality blossomed and shivered before me, and I simply wasn't there anymore.

*W*here I'd gone, exactly, though was very difficult to say.
Purrvis and Flop and the magi-electronic paraphernalia dropped away before me eyes, and I was boosted into what seemed an entirely different plane of existence. And suddenly I seemed to be without my seat belt as well.

I'd half-expected to suddenly be catapulted into that mass-unconsciousness of filmic images, however, it felt more like simply patterns and figments of light and pixellation, randomly strobing through my being. As though I were flying through some kind of mammoth television channel tuned to a dead channel.

However, brief ghost images flashed, too subliminal to exactly pinpoint identity — but there nonetheless, like the hypnogogic substance of the land between waking and unsleeping, immediate and haunting but beyond grasp and comprehension.

I seemed to sail through this half-lit, magisterial land of color and throbbing symphonic whispers, all time and space leeched of memory and meaning.

And then, suddenly, I felt caught hold of as though struck by some kind of superscientific tractor beam on *Star Wagon* and held in place.

Gradually I felt pulled . . . a hypermagnetic pull, and I began drifting with focus and direction through layer upon layer of frizzled static-clouds . . .

Lower and lower I descended. . . .

And suddenly, with a snap and a rush of stereophonic sound loud and strange as a Pink Floyd concert, I rushed down to an explosive landing into disorientation . . .

. . . behind closed eyes.

". . . Ralph. . . . Ralph . . . are you all right?"

The words caressed me with whispered sweetness and gentleness. A woman's words . . . A woman's voice I cherished. It seemed a struggle to open those closed eyes, but like a diver struggling up from the depths of a dark pool, I rose up, reaching for her voice.

My eyes opened and I saw Lucinda looking down, pure concern in her eyes.

"Hi," I said.

"Well hello to you. Glad you're still around."

"What happened?"

"You fainted. That's what happened!"

I stirred, but my muscles felt tight and cramped — and different. I felt heavier, much more agile — all of course, because I was no longer in the body of a lithe little monkey.

Still, it was a vast relief to be back in my own body. It was like coming home. And I couldn't have asked for a more pleasant welcomer.

No sooner had I accustomed myself to the difference in bodies, but I realized that I was in someplace far stranger than I'd expected. There was a coolness and moisture to the air, and a dimness of artificial night. Earthy smells, that scent of magic, and of mushrooms, of Hypernius magnified. As though we were enclosed in those leathery wings, grown huge. A hundred mingled new sensations and tinglings . . . they converged upon me, overwhelming me with their diversity and intensity.

"Where am I?"

Lucinda looked down at me oddly, hands on hips of her breeches, those green eye penetrating.

"You don't remember?"

"Not exactly . . . I have to explain . . ."

"Yeah, you do. Thought you'd been acting a little strangely lately. Put it down to culture shock finally overwhelming you."

"How was I acting?"

"Aloof."

"I didn't say much?"

"No indeed." She put a light hand on me shoulder, closer and overwhelming with her femininity. "And you just ignored me. And I thought you fancied me. Quite hurt my pride, you did."

I took a deep breath, struggling to stand up.

"Stay there for a second. Recover." Real concern was in her eyes now. "You've got a real problem, don't you?"

"Lucinda, we *all* do." I tried to calm my heart, get my breathing back in gear. I licked my lips, turned, and touched a sidewall. Slick with moisture, glistening . . . a sheen of some sort of chemical substance came off in my hand.

"We're in some sort of caverns, aren't we?"

"Yes . . . of course . . . you didn't know that?"

"Exactly where?"

She looked at me oddly. "The Mountains of our Destination, of course. The Dragon Horde. There's no recollection at all?"

"That's what I need to talk to you about. I wasn't around to absorb anything."

She looked at me oddly. "You've got some explaining to do I think. You might as well make it to Professor Escutcheon the same time as me. Save you some breath."

"I don't think that's a good idea."

"Why not?"

I tried, as best as I could and in as succinct a way possible to tell her. I had to go on my instinct here . . . I had to trust her. I told her everything from the beginning that I'd left out before . . . and I segued into the whole business of what my most recent contact with Hypernius had done and where it had sent me.

And what I'd learned there.

Finally, it was Lucinda who was sitting down stunned in the large cavern, me whispering her in urgent words.

As I spoke to someone I realized I could trust, I let my defenses down, and suddenly all the fear and insecurity broke through. I felt vulnerable and instinctively sought refuge. Without totally realizing what was happening, I suddenly found myself in her arms, our faces close and her lips warm and near.

"I missed you . . . a lot," I said, and suddenly we were kissing.

It was warm and it was sweet and tender and seemed to fill me up in places that were parched and empty. However, it ended all too abruptly with a heavy hand on my shoulder.

The hand wheeled me around and I found myself staring up into the glowering features of Brank Toplin.

"Hey, chum. What do you think you're doing with *my* lady!" he said.

His other big hand reached down and grabbed me by the throat.

Chapter Twenty-One

Before I could say a thing, I found myself being lifted up into the air, then hurled against a hard wall.

I meant to say, *"Your* lady?" but the words were blasted from my diaphragm with my body's contact with stone. The sound of my impact and the whooshing expulsion of my breath echoed through the cavern.

Even though this would normally have put me down for the count, either the last few weeks of my life had put some metal in my spine, or I was just extremely pissed off. Anyway, I got up, and started flailing away at Brank.

I don't think he expected it, either, because I got a couple of good blows into his big bushy face before he picked me up, shook me and slammed me against the wall again.

"Toplin, you big oaf! Stop that!" cried Lucinda, grabbing him by the arm and pulling him away.

For my own part, I felt as though I was on my way back to monkeydom. Things were spinning around, I felt woozy and dizzy, and when I tried to get up, I didn't stay up long.

I was vaguely aware of Lucinda bending over me and lifting me up and propping me against the wall, tending to a couple of scrapes on my face and generally fussing about me in an apologetic and concerned way.

"What the hell was going on with you two?" Brank insisted.

"A lot more than what's going to be going on between you and me in the *future!*" she spat back.

"Look, I'm sorry. A jealous rage just swept over me! I lost control!"

"Clearly. As though you ever had any!"

Through my bleary brain, a few connections were made. While I was off ambling under the Dark University in my monkey body, these guys had patched up whatever problems they'd had and then renewed their romance. Naturally, my Doctor Ricknow-controlled body didn't object, just as it never made a pass at her. It was too busy observing the progress of Mr. Escutcheon's film scouting party.

"Wait. Wait a minute," I mumbled. "Look, I'm sorry. I've been . . . away, Brank. I didn't know. There are much more important things we have to worry about that who gets to kiss the girl!"

"There are?" Lucinda said. Then she stamped her foot. "Yes, of course there are! Brank, you should listen to what Ralph has got to say! We've got *big* troubles!"

I hadn't planned on telling Brank, but he seemed a likely candidate to enlist in my cause. So once I choked down some ale that he offered me and regained some more of my senses, the story came out piecemeal.

After I coughed up the last bit, Brank slapped his knee. "Damn! Looks like we'd better have a talk to with Escutcheon. This is all news to me! Not that I understand all of it . . . But I thought this was all a matter of treasure and glory and saving our country. I didn't realize that we had power-grubbing mixed up into it on our side!"

As I'd told the story again, I'd had a few more thoughts. "No, we'd better hold back a bit and see what's going on . . . Besides, like I say, *I've* been away, for one thing. I don't know where you've been, what you'd done . . . or what's going on now. All I know is that somehow we've made it to the Dragon Horde . . ."

Brank nodded. "That's right. Look, chum. Sorry about those fisticuffs back there. Wasn't warranted. Don't know what came over me."

"We've *all* been under a lot of strain, guys," said Lucinda. "Let's just forget it and get on with the next phase."

"Which is?"

She looked at Brank and her face had paled. "Mr. Escutcheon was going to see about getting access to those old volumes today!"

"Yes," said Brank. "But he didn't think he'd be successful — The talks with the Dragons are quite tenuous."

"Sorry, but I'm missing something. What's been going on?" I said.

"What if he tries something desperate ... And if Ralph is right, then he'll use those volumes for his own good ... not for our countries ..."

"I'm sorry, this is all —"

"Come. Let's go," said Lucinda. "We'll tell you on the way. I hope it's just not too late already!"

She grabbed my arm and hurried me along the cavern. Brank loped along side of us.

"Yes, you know ... I wondered what was wrong with you," said Brank. "You did seem remote and removed."

"God knows I *was* that."

"Dark University, huh ... And you really think that Dr. Ricknow was behind your eyes all the time, watching us?"

"Absolutely."

"Which means he must have seen everything that we've seen," said Lucinda.

"Well, I hope not all ..."

"Lummox!" she smacked him on the arm. "Everything that Ralph has seen."

"Right!" I said, puffing along to keep up with them. "What have I seen?"

We were approaching the end of a tunnel. We weren't going out into day and we weren't going into night — beyond wasn't outside at all, but just a larger and definitely slightly better lit chamber.

We slowed down and we walked out into it and I looked around me.

No, I thought immediately. I *haven't* seen this before!

Before us stretched what could only be the gigantic hollowed-out inside of a mountain. It stretched well up to a dim, craggy peak, and dove well down to a misty mysterious bottom. Inset along the walls were shuddering torches that illuminated many levels connected by ascending and descending stone staircases. Each of these levels was studded with large round openings, most larger than the one we were exiting. There was the feeling of grandeur and immensity here — and the that taste of glorious magic in the air, covered with the cool of the drifting air currents rising up toward the ceiling.

"Wow!" I said, stepping back, feeling a strange combination of agoraphobia and acrophobia descend upon me.

"Oh . . . of course . . . this is new to you," said Lucinda. "It's the Dragon Horde."

They began to move down one of the ascending stairs. I followed along behind them, hugging the walls and trying not to look down or up.

"How — how did we get here?"

"Hypernius, of course," said Lucinda. "The trip after Mollop was fairly uneventful —"

"Alas, Hurbal's wife wouldn't let him come along. We certainly could use him now!" said Brank.

"You — I mean, whoever was behind your eyes — and Professor Escutcheon seemed to find plenty of spots for film backdrops," continued Lucinda. "And then when we reached the mountains, a dragon dropped down . . ."

"Damned thing seemed like it would just as soon gobble us up as look at us." Brank's face bore the residual of the fear he must have felt, staring up at a gigantic dragon. "I tell you, I had my sword out, ready to set to — but I didn't expect to win!"

"I don't know why you were worried," said Lucinda. "It was for just such a moment that we brought Hypernius."

We passed by a torch that illuminated a streak of silver ore in the moist rock along the rim. Although Brank and Lucinda walked along seemingly with no fear, I kept my eyes trained away from the depths and the heights surrounding us. "And I assume it worked."

"Better than I could have possibly *dreamed!*" said Lucinda. "Hypernius is even more intelligent that we thought! He communicated with that big beast . . . and the fire immediately went out of its eyes. It turned around and led us to a gigantic cave — and it brought us here!"

"I don't know . . . I still think it had something to do with what those magicians were cooking up all the while. *Some* kind of spell was in the works, that was for sure." He sniffed, as though he was remembering something bad he'd smelled.

"Whatever it was, it worked. We got the royal treatment, and Professor Escutcheon has been looking through these caverns for a couple of days now, talking and setting up possible shots."

"And also getting what he could in the way of information about those Volumes he wanted to look at so badly," added Brank.

"From who?" I asked.

"The Council of Elders," Lucinda said. "They seemed dead reluctant at first — Professor Escutcheon communicated the idea of a movie to them and they seemed amenable enough. Who knows, maybe dragons are all hams at heart. God knows that little scamp Hypernius seems to be. He seems to be absolutely aflutter at the idea of starring in a film. You and Escutcheon seemed to have figured out his role by now . . . But

I'm getting ahead of myself. Apparently the Professor convinced them that there was something about the Volumes they guarded that would make a film possible . . ."

"How was he able to do *that?*"

"Again, the magic, I think . . ." said Brank.

"Explains a lot. That's the *main* reason he brought Meistercrow and Quintabulous, then," I suggested.

"You really think that the Professor is just as villainous as Dr. Ricknow?"

I shook my head. "No, but I think he wants power and he's convinced himself that he has to achieve it this way, and it's important enough to be ruthless."

"Then again, power corrupts," said Brank.

"I don't think it would be a good idea for *either* Ricknow or Escutcheon to get a hold of those Volumes now," I said.

"Which means no movie . . . no salvation for my country," said Brank, scowling. "This whole trip for nothing?"

"I didn't say that. I think I *might* be able to convince Escutcheon of the danger of what he's doing . . . I certainly understand the situation a lot better than I had before — In any case, he's mislead us all as to his true intentions and we've got to reappraise our roles in this thing."

"Just as long as we don't get those dragons too riled, okay?" said Brank.

"I can't guarantee that . . . but if he's about to open those Volumes, I've got the feeling that Mister Escutcheon is about to turn the tap on a lot more trouble that dragons can."

"I shudder at the thought," said Brank.

They led me up two staircases and then, thankfully, through a large portal that again descended deep toward the bowels of the mountain. As we hurried along, I told them a little more of what I'd learned under the tutelage of Purrvis at the Dark University. It was as much to work it out in my own mind as it was to relay to them.

Finally, the tunnel opened out into another larger chamber room, only thankfully with a solid enough floor. However, in the center I *did* notice some kind opening, through which mists seeped up. Oh God, I thought. Another precipice. Still I didn't have to be near the edge.

The chamber was empty.

Lucinda put her hands on her hips. "Hmm. Well, this is the Elders' council chamber, all right. This is where they said they would be."

"Haven't got a clue as to where they've gone . . . And we sure don't know these tunnels," said Brank.

"Might as well cool our heels then," said Lucinda, pointing to a dais. I for one was happy to sit down and I walked over to this and settled, looking around at the room we were in. Again, it was of rough-hewn rock with torches illuminating it. However, it smelled more of the outside, of the sky and of a cool freshness, which indicated to me that one or more of the bright holes near the top where accesses to the outside world. Available, of course, only to winged creatures, but at least I didn't have the faintly claustrophobic feeling of being shut off totally.

We sat down, and I regained my breath and tried to regain my thoughts. As for feelings . . . well, I was just in such a state of adrenalized numbness that I didn't dwell on those. I had to concentrate on keeping the universes in one piece —

Feelings of jealousy, emotional devastation and all the subtle other mental problems could be dealt with then.

Whatever the new relationship between Lucinda and Brank was, it wasn't smooth. For him, clearly she was still 'Bash,' and that was some comfort I suppose. They didn't even sit together now — each sat to one side of me and I definitely felt a low level of tension.

"How did you know how to come here?" I asked. "And what were we doing down there?"

"We've been here for two days now, and down there's our quarters," explained Lucinda. "This is where the meetings with the dragons have taken place, so we've been here before . . ."

"Though not for Escutcheon's meetings concerning the Volumes?" I asked.

"No, but from the way they talked, I assumed those would be brought up here. . . ."

"I can't figure *how* those dragons could be talked into unearthing what they were guarding . . . even with the persuasion . . . unless . . ."

The gears of my mind twisted and gnashed with effort.

"We're listening . . ." prompted Lucinda.

"Look, there's so much power in those books, its unbelievable. The problem is that the Dragons probably never knew exactly what they were sitting on. Maybe that's Escutcheon's secret. Maybe he's convinced them that they can gain quite a bit by unearthing their cache."

"Like what?" said Brank.

"Haven't you been listening, dummy? Like maybe a whole *world* to themselves!"

"That's very possible. . . . I mean, the mind boggles!"

"All by controlling and manipulating the imaginations of movie goers on Earth. Sorry, but it's a bit hard to swallow!" said Brank.

"You just don't want to admit the possibility that maybe you're the product of some hack Hollywood Errol Flynn sensibility!" Lucinda snapped.

"Utter nonsense!" griped Brank. "You know, I don't doubt that old Escutcheon has got something up his sleeve, but I honestly think all *that* is a little too . . . well, imaginative, I suppose."

"Far too big a concept for your little pea brain to fit itself around, eh?"

"Look, I really think I don't need to hurl insults back and forth, Bash."

"What, did you run out of vocabulary?"

Sounds from one of the tunnels interrupted the lover's spat.

"That'll be them," said Brank, nervously getting up, his hand resting on the pommel of his sword.

I didn't even have time to ask 'Who' before the dragons came in.

Chapter Twenty-Two

Dragons.

Meeting Hypernius had been quite an experience, but Hypernius was a younger dragon, without the gigantic sense of awe-inspiring majesty and ancient mysticism that clung to the creatures that slunk and wafted through the tunnels.

There were four of them and they arrived almost as though involved in a ceremony of some sort. They came from upper openings and they jumped down, their wings ripping open like parachutes, filling with hair and flying their mammoth bodies down to thump against the stone so hard I almost fancied I felt the earth quake beneath me.

"Sentinels," whispered Lucinda.

"Guard dragons," added Brank. "Must mean that the Dragon King is on his way back up."

"Presumably along with Professor Escutcheon, the Magicians . . ."

"And that Cache —"

"Dragon King?" I said. "You've not mentioned . . ."

"Shhh. Stand up and when you see him, bow extremely deferentially," breathed Lucinda. "This is pretty shaky territory we're on now, Dragon land . . . And the Dragon King's a quirky character . . ."

"But why?"

"You'll see."

Distantly there was the sound of a gong, and the drone of a chant whispered as though through gauze and incense. From the mouth of one of tunnels, smoke seeped and light sprang out through it, like muted lasers through dry ice at a rock show. The tat tat tat of drums, the blow of trumpet, the tread of feet.

A procession marched from the tunnel, through the smoke and out into the chamber, like apparitions gradually collecting themselves into flesh.

First came Hypernius, scampering and flapping along like an excited dog. At the sight of Lucinda the little dragon made a noise and yipped up to her. He put his leathery head out to scratch and I did so. But as I gazed into those amazing eyes, although I discerned immense intelligence there, I could not feel a trace of the contact that had pulled me through into the Dark University.

I looked up and I saw the two magicians, Thelonius Meistercrow and Quenton Quintabulous, staggering along under the weight of a chest with two handles on it. The wooden chest was encrusted with jewels, which shown hard and bright in the light of the torches. The magicians looked tired but excited, and they positively grinned at us with victory.

Behind them walked Mister Escutcheon in some sort of white ceremonial robe, carrying a staff and some sort of censor pot dangling from a chain, from which a dark aromatic smoke dripped and pooled along the ground they trod.

Beside him was a most remarkable creature, who could be nothing else but the Dragon King.

He was about seven feet high, walked on two legs and sported two arms from a man-sized torso. Here his humanoid qualities ended, for otherwise he had the leathery skin of an alligator, a sharp-fanged face, and wings that spread out behind him like a fallen angel's.

"A hybrid," I said under my breath.

"Not exactly," said Lucinda, "but we can't explain now. Just remember — he's the royalty here."

I rather gathered that from his mien and his bearing. Magisterial, to say the least. His eyes shown like agates and he seemed to look upon everything around him as though it were his and his alone. There was the feral gleam of ambition and conquest in his eye, and I could well imagine now why he had ascended to the opening of this ancient volume.

The Dragon Realm was insufficient for this creature.

This guy wanted a whole *world*.

And Escutcheon was just the one to give it to him.

All they would need is a simple movie that would adjust the minds of human beings on Earth properly. Exactly what role the ancient volume would play, I was sure I was about to find out.

Mr. Escutcheon looked solemn but invigorated.

He looked unnatural in the white robes, like a schoolmaster assuming the wrong costume, but not truly aware that he looked like a fake.

He regarded us all, and it seemed that the way he looked at me, he knew that I'd discovered his secret. However, it must have only been my imagination, because his gaze did not dwell on me at all.

"It is done!" he said triumphantly, gesturing to the box. "You may set that down just over there, gentlemen!" He pointed toward the dais and the puffing magicians happily dropped the burden.

"Heavens!" said Meistercrow. "Heavier than it looks!"

"Too bad we didn't have an anti-gravity spell," said Quintabulous. "Would have helped a lot."

"It will all be one when the volume is opened and the secret uttered," said Escutcheon. "Yours aches will be rewarded, your pains shall blossom forth into plenty!"

"Had a good day, did you?" said Lucinda. "And I assume that you're going to be able read this?"

"I have with me my scholars . . . And Lanton here will be of great help." He bowed formally toward the Dragon King, who bowed back with great dignity and gravity.

The Dragon King then took a key upon a chain around his neck and walked toward the chest. "I shall now do the honors," he said in a hissing growl.

He leaned over to stick the key in it hole, but suddenly I found my voice rising up in objection. "Wait."

Astonished eyes turned my way, questioning

"What's going on here?" I said. "What does this have to do with making a movie?"

"Oh, of course," said Escutcheon. "We all have our priorities. The movie will be made, my friend. Be sure of that. However, the book inside could well give us the power we need to make it properly."

Lanton the Dragon King nodded and a snarling kind of laughter issued from his mouth. "Yes, this 'movie' will be made indeed. And I am to have a vital role, no?"

"Indeed, Lanton. Now please ignore my screen writer for the moment . . . They are a contentious lot, but not to be taken too seriously."

"Actually, Professor Escutcheon," said Lucinda, "Ralph has some very serious questions that he's brought up."

"Questions about the purpose of this movie!" continued Brank.

"Why, it is to save our country, of course!" said Escutcheon. "What other reason is it for . . ."

"Look, I don't mean to be rude or anything, Doc or Professor or whatever you truly are, Mr. Escutcheon. But I'm afraid you just didn't tell me the whole story, now did you?"

The Dragon King was watching all this curiously. A kind of lizardy smirk remained on his face. Quietly, he inserted the key. Unfortunately, the fierce bearing of the creature — along with the towering presence of the other dragons, made a little difficult to challenge him physically.

However, there were always words.

"What makes you think that, Ralph?"

"My mind was a prisoner in the Dark University, Escutcheon. I met another prisoner, and — well, he kind of clued me into the metaphysics of this world . . . And gave me the real reason why you're so interested in cinema."

"Oh? How could that be?" said Meistercrow, nervousness flickering behind his fatigue.

"Sounds as though you've been through some serious delusions, Ralph," said Quintabulous warily, his voice squeaking slightly.

"No, let him speak," said Escutcheon. "Just what do you mean, Ralph?"

"A popular film on Earth can *change* this world, Escutcheon, can't it? And if you make the film the way you want to . . . you can gain control of this world . . . And who knows . . . maybe *other* realities." I pointed to the book. "What I can't figure out, though, is what's so powerful in this book that you want so badly."

The Dragon King twisted the key and opened the top of the chest. Nestled inside on black velvet was the most beautiful book I have ever seen. It drew all the eyes in the room upon its beautiful leather binding, strange words inscribed in ornate silver embossed illuminations.

"Can it make any difference?" said Lanton. "The legends are whispered amongst our people as to the importance of this book, and yet we have not been able to truly unlock its secrets. We have only felt it necessary to guard it. However, thanks to the efforts of Professor Escutcheon and our dragon kin . . ."

Hypernius flapped around eagerly, irrepressible despite the presence of his elders.

". . . we realize that it is our best interests to cooperate for the enrichment of all," the Dragon King said. He gestured toward the book. "Please, be our guest, Professor."

"I don't know if that would be wise, Professor," said Lucinda, stepping forward. "It would seem that you've tricked us?"

"Nothing of the sort! The movie will be made — our country will be saved . . . And I have much to thank you for — especially you, Lucinda, who so thoughtfully provided the services of Hypernius — a dear creature who has made things so much easier."

"Apparently my trust was misplaced," said Brank, stepping forward alongside Lucinda.

The huge dragon took a half step forward and glowered down.

Brank and Lucinda halted.

"Please — you make too hasty a judgment," said Escutcheon. "You do not give me a chance to show you my integrity... What I am doing is in the best interests of all!"

"But mostly in the best interests of yourself!" I said.

"And what is wrong with that, Ralph? Is that not the code of your own nation? Certainly, it is the key to the Hollywood ethic, no? And besides, Ralph, you have only to continue working with me and you will have success beyond your wildest dreams. Relax and do not cause further trouble — Wait — See... Have a little patience. I was about to reveal all anyway..."

He started to pick up the book, gently and reverently.

"Wait!" I called. "While I was... away... transferred, Dr. Ricknow had control of my body... my eyes. Surely he accomplished something... Surely he knows where you are now and what you are doing... And he's got his own agenda. Before you do anything rash, we should discuss *that!*"

"I imagined as much," said Escutcheon. "But don't you see?" He lifted the book out reverently. "This book will give me the power to change all that. This is the key that I needed to make everything I desire possible.... With this, we can make that film.... With this we can defeat Ricknow. Come, magicians. Come and help me translate the wisdom and the secrets of the ancients...."

The two magicians approached, and I gave up all hope. We just had to wait and see what happened. There was no way that we could accomplish anything now that would do anything more than get us hurt.

However, just then things got worse.

Just as Meistercrow and Quintabulous were bending over the ancient script, squinting and puzzling out words and concepts, there was a tremendous explosion in the center of the chamber.

All eyes looked toward it and were half-blinded by a burst of dazzling illumination and the sheen of metal and energy.

The brilliance died, and standing there were a group of twenty men, armed with guns and swords. In the center of this group stood Dyrk Ryonne, Harfield Moregnash — and Dr. Martinus Ricknow.

The Dragon King cast off his astonishment the fastest of us all. "How dare you trespass on the sacred soil of the Dragon Realm!" he said.

"We would not have done so unless it were not utterly necessary, your Majesty," said Dr. Ricknow, walking out ahead of his party. "You must halt the actions of that man, for it will surely bring catastrophe to us all!"

"Pah!" said Escutcheon, gripping the volume tight to his chest. "You, the Professor of Anarchy... You thrive on catastrophe and would welcome it if that were what I meant to achieve. No . . . I mean to restore order! Learning and beauty and all good things . . ."

"Save for honor, it would seem," said Ricknow. "Where is your precious honor, Escutcheon? You've tricked and lied your way here . . . Surely invalidating everything you stand for!"

"And you stand for Goodness and Truth. Pah!" said Escutcheon.

"Whatever you stand for, Doctor Ricknow," spat the Dragon King. "You are no friend of ours. We know that. Now be gone or you will forfeit your lives!"

The huge dragons took another half a step forward, smoke streaming from their noses, the promise of incendiaries roaring at the back of their throat.

"You think we would be stupid enough to come here without some sort of sort of defense?" He snapped his fingers and one of the men behind him — a technician of some sort — pulled up some mechanical device bedecked with switches and dials and began playing his fingers over it.

The word came to me immediately: technomagic.

Faster than the thought, a throbbing, glimmering field of force buzzed out in a spherical pattern. It frizzed over us, zooming like a swarm of bees through my ears and dopplering into a dark pattern around us, halting just past the magicians and Escutcheon and then opaquing into a black wall, shutting out the Dragon King and his minions.

With furious roars, the creatures slammed themselves against the wall, rattling it and making a horrendous commotion but doing not one jot of effective damage and achieving nothing.

We were for all intents and purposes trapped inside, along with Dr. Ricknow and his highly armed cohorts.

"And by the way, gentlemen —" said the Doctor. "We've created a reality here where these guns deployed here work very well indeed." He gestured with his fingers. "So if you'll be so kind to hand over that book, Professor Escutcheon, nobody will get hurt."

A fluttering of unreadable emotions passed over Escutcheon's face, resolving finally into a grimacing smile. "Well. I wondered when that trump card was going to be played, Ricknow. I knew you were working on something peculiar."

"All the result of superior research and academics, my adversary. Soon to be seen at *all* universities. Maybe we'll have a post for you in bonehead English, Escutcheon — but certainly not tenure track. Now if you'll be so good, you'll speed that precious little book over."

"Don't do it!" I said, fury passing over me and my better judgment. "I'd rather see you have it, Mr. Escutcheon, than *this* scoundrel!"

Ricknow regarded me. "So — it's the little monkey, back into tail-less ape form. I don't know how you did it, but congratulations. Nonetheless, I don't think you'll want to get riddled with bullets after all the effort the whole thing was."

"Just what's *in* this book, folks?" asked Lucinda.

"Good point."

"That doesn't seem to be any of your business, does it, big fella!" said Moregnash menacingly.

"You speak quite rudely backed by many men with many weapons, jackal," said Brank. "Would you be quite so nasty sword to sword?"

"Don't think you can separate us, warrior," said Ricknow. "And we'll happily shoot you if we must."

"It won't do you any harm to tell us exactly what's in that book," I said.

"You might as well, Ricknow," said Escutcheon, clearly just as happy to keep the patter going. "Somehow he's discovered much of the truth."

"Has he, now . . . no doubt while skulking about my campus. Well, there's no harm really — once I have the book I'll have the power to erase all harmful knowledge in every mind on this plane. . . ."

"What is it, Ricknow?"

"Allow me —" said Escutcheon. "What we have here is nothing less than the control guide to human consciousness — the mass consciousness that sculpted this reality and many others." He grinned. "An Owner's Manual, if you will."

Chapter Twenty-Three

*B*rank and Lucinda just stared blankly at that one.

But then, they hadn't had Fantasy World Building 101 with Purrvis back in Dark University.

"Thus allowing you to create the film that will do exactly what you *wish* with this world," I said. "And perhaps others . . . and perhaps even create your own. The ultimate power!"

"What?" said Brank, incomprehensibly.

"That book no doubt maps out the buttons to push and the combinations to achieve the desired effect ... I explained some of it earlier —" I said. "Suffice it to say that it will allow either of these gentlemen to make the sort of movies that will affect the mass consciousness of sufficient people to change reality here and elsewhere."

"Reality sculpting on different dimensions through cinema!" said Lucinda softly. "Lord, the power of Human Imagination!"

"Don't you see, though!" said Escutcheon emphatically. "Ricknow already *has* some of the knowledge in this book. *That's* how he's achieved the power here that he has. And perhaps in other dimensions as well! That's why I needed this book! And why he cannot be allowed to take it away from here!"

"Sorry, but I'm still not getting it." Brank shook his head blankly.

"Ralph, why do you think the film and TV industry on Earth are so terrible and so manipulative —" Escutcheon pointed at the dark wizard. "The influence of the Dark University!"

"That's a bit hard to swallow," I said. "I always thought it was because of greed and fear!"

"Why do you think I had to be so careful in recruiting you — and to get someone who was not already directly or indirectly controlled by Dr. Ricknow? And most importantly — why do you think we met up with that creature at the gate? It was a Guardian! One of the Dark University's guardians!"

It all fit together properly, and my conclusions must have shown on my face.

"So we should continue to fight for Professor Escutcheon?" said Bash, almost hopefully.

"Well, we know that little good's going to happen if Ricknow gets a hold of that book," said Brank, "But I'm damned if I know how to keep him from it. I don't like the looks of those weapons at all!"

"Wise resolve," said Ricknow. "And please believe me, this reality bubble we've conjured makes them work quite well ... And it also prevents any magic from effecting us. Now Phineas — are you going to hand that book over now ... Or am I going to have to pry it from your bullet-riddled body?"

"You'd do that, wouldn't you?" said Escutcheon. "But what difference does it make whether I give it to you or not? You're probably going to kill me anyway." He nodded at us. "And my companions in the bargain."

"You still don't understand, do you? I don't want to kill you, I want to defeat you, Phineas. If your death results, well, that's too bad — but your ineffective life is *far* more valuable to my plans than your death would be. What a waste of an unworthy opponent *that* would be! Why, someone might come along to fill up your place who was actually *competent!*" Ricknow snickered nastily. "So hand it over. Who knows what's in the cards? Perhaps you'll have another shot at it one day. I'll certainly let you go back to your pitiful little college now that you've guided me to it. And who knows . . . Soon you may have the opportunity to make your own silly little films after all . . . And thus defeat me. However, if you don't give it to me. Well, you're finished here and now!"

Escutcheon blinked sadly. His chin drooped mournfully onto his chest. He made the smallest of shrugs, the least of nods and then sighed. "Very well. You've won again, Ricknow."

He started forward, lifting the book up in front of him.

"No, *wait!*" said Lucinda. "Professor Escutcheon, you can't do it!"

She stepped out toward him, and thus guns lifted and cocked.

I pulled her back. "Take it from me, you don't want to get shot."

"Wise, little monkey," said Ricknow. "Just allow what happens to happen — stay out of this, and you too may find your imagination back where it belongs on Earth, conjuring up realities at the flip of our controls."

"Wait a minute," I said, defiantly. "I just thought of something. If this world and its people are the result of the guided imagination generation by the energies of minds on Earth — then you, Ricknow, and you, Escutcheon don't really exist!"

Ricknow and Escutcheon looked at one another, stunned for a moment, then broke out in laughter.

"We are as real as any on Earth!" said Escutcheon.

"Do not take too much pride in being from that place! It is merely a conduit of spiritual energy — an anchor, if you will. Its projections are just as real in their own way as the principal reality itself. The shadows, indeed, are in some ways more real than the casters! Now don't trouble your heads with metaphysics. That's my job now. Come on, Phineas. Maybe I'm being too hard on you. We'll let you teach a seminar class in American Comedy Films, all right? Just be a good fellow and hand over that book and neither you nor your associates will be harmed."

Mister Escutcheon sighed, his shoulders seeming to collapse into his body. Gone was the fleeting moment of hilarity in his eyes at my charge. Instead, he seemed the picture of total defeat as he shuffled forward, slowly pulling the book out from him and presenting it before him.

"That's the rational fellow!" said Ricknow. "You'll come to see that it's all for the best, Escutcheon. It is always best to have superior intellect in control."

"As you say, Ricknow. I bow to your superior mind."

The professor of cinema held out the book and, with a smirk, Dr. Ricknow stepped out to take it. "Why thank you, Escutcheon. I promise you, you will not be sorry."

"No. I will not be the one who will be sorry."

Grinning, Ricknow clasped his hands around the book. But as soon as contact was made, the grin vanished, a grimace of shock and surprise replacing it.

Electrical arcs spasmed, gnashed and slashed through the air, crackling like lightning between thunderheads. Bright light shot up in shafting, frizzling like fast fire through the force field surrounding us.

Consuming it.

Air rushed in, and the sound of an implosion rocked us all.

I felt as though I were losing my footing, then rapidly regained my balance. As the shifting world around me reassembled itself, I saw that Escutcheon had pulled Ricknow down and they were rolling around on the floor, wrestling for control of the book.

The roar of dragons swept down upon us all.

The soldiers of the Dark University raised their guns. Two fired — however, their efforts were rewarded only by fruitless clicks.

The reality bubble had collapsed.

It didn't take long for Brank and Bash to note the change.

"Come on, folks!" called Brank, hauling his sword out of his belt. "Let's get the bastards!"

He charged in toward Dirk Ryonne and Harfield Moregnash, who were struggling to negotiate their way through this change. They dropped their guns and pulled their own swords out.

"Scoundrels, nothing!" cried Bash. "We've got to get that book. Neither of those guys should have it." She swung toward me. "Come on, Ralph. We've got to give it back to the Dragon King. He can't use it — and its been safely kept here for years. Why not a few years more?"

"Okay," I said. What she said made a lot of sense.

I dashed after her.

The melee closed in around us as the clang and clash of swords and curses took to the air.

The two professors were still rolling around, struggling mightily, pulling the ancient volume between them. Somehow it managed to stay intact — it must have been a strong book in more ways than one.

"Stop!" thundered a voice. "Stop this conflict or pay a heavy penalty."

I spun around and there, haloed by a background of shivering jewel-like luminescence, was the Dragon King.

Lined on either side were even more dragons than before dangling over the assembled conflict like vultures over almost dead carrion.

"Cease!" said the Dragon King again. "Or feel the jaws of my brethren!"

A fairly considerable threat when there are several sets of teeth dangling over you, bright and sharp, reptilian eyes gleaming above them, a drop or two of smelly saliva splashing into puddles near your feet and the leathery smell of angry dragon enfolding you. Gigantic leathery wings flapped, sending a cold chill wind of reality swirling about.

There was the clatter of guns as they dropped onto the floor. Hands were raised tentatively in the multi-universal signal of surrender.

Not Brank's hands nor Bash's, though. They kept hold of their swords — but the Dragon King did not seem to mind overmuch. His attention was on what was still going on down on the floor.

Escutcheon and Ricknow were still rolling around, struggling over possession of the book. They somehow had dirtied one another considerably, and their robes had ripped to rags. Every few moment, a fist flailed, pummeling down or up with a smacking sound. Shreds and zaps of electrical power flowed and flittered over them making a lovely fireworks display.

"Stop them," ordered the Dragon King, stepping forward.

"We'll try. Come on, Bash." Brank gestured and the two of them raced over to the thrashing men.

However, when they reached out to try and pull them apart, they were rewarded by zaps of power.

"Yow!" said Bash, her hair standing on as she stepped back away from the conflict.

"Holy cripes!" said Brank, stepping back and nearly dropping his hand. "Hang on too long to those two, you'll fry."

The Dragon King nodded. "Step aside, then!"

The two obeyed, and the Dragon King walked up to within ten feet of the battling professors. "I demand that you cease this foolishness and return the book at once!"

I hurried over to Quenton and Thelonius. "Anything you can do, guys?"

"Absolutely nothing," said Thelonius.

"It's that book generating the power," Quenton said, shaking his head. "And there's far more magic in that book than we have access to!"

Even as he finished speaking, there was a crackle and a gasp. The Dragon King stepped back with a singed and smoking robe as reward for his trouble.

"We can only wait and watch —" He said. "And hope that they will come to their senses!"

It was quite a spectacle, those academic professors going at it. Somehow, they both kept grips on the book. They rolled and shrieked and battered at one another, and began to look like a couple of cats locked in deadly clawed combat.

And no one could stop them because of the arcs of power that were zapping around them.

"You'd think they'd wear out!" said Brank.

"Something's giving them energy . . ." said Bash.

"That book, obviously," I added.

"Yes," said the Dragon King, nodding seriously. "There is more going on in that battle than meets the eye . . ."

"No!" cried Dyrk Ryonne. "Ricknow, watch out . . ."

I swiveled my head to see what was happening, and immediately saw that the flailing duo were teetering on the edge of that hole in ground.

Harfield Moregnash ran out to try and drag his master from the edge, but was rewarded by a stunning charge of power for his trouble. He was kicked up and over and slammed back onto the obsidian floor, sliding back almost to where he had started.

"Is there anything we can do?" I said.

"Talk to them. You must make them stop!" said the Dragon King. "Not even we know where that hole leads. . . . It is a Mystery. The Legends say it leads to the source of Energy itself — No one has dared explore it."

"Mister Escutcheon. Doctor Ricknow!" I said, going up as close to them as I dared. "You've got to stop. You've about to go over the edge."

However, the two were like creatures possessed. They ripped and tore and hollered at each other. But even as I watched, Dr. Ricknow managed to wrest the book away from Mister Escutcheon. He leaped up and backed to the very edge of the ledge. Mist rose up and wrapped around him as though whatever it was that was below was trying to pull him in.

"Ha ha! Fool! I have it. I have it now, and the secrets in it are *mine!*" cried Ricknow.

"Damned if they are!" gasped the ragged Escutcheon. "I'll see you in hell first!"

The professor leaped up and charged Dr. Ricknow.

"Professor Escutcheon!" cried Bash. *"No!"*

However Escutcheon, if he heard, did not take any notice. He plowed straight toward Ricknow, who held up the book as though it power would ward off the attack.

It did not.

Escutcheon rammed directly into Ricknow midsection, his shoulder's connecting with the out-thrust book, jamming it back and causing a flash of light to illuminate the stark reality of the scene.

"Idiot!" cried Ricknow, but it was too late.

Escutcheon's momentum pushed them both over the lip of the hole. They hung suspended for a moment, Ricknow's arms windmilling as Escutcheon relentlessly grabbed up the book.

And then they fell.

Ricknow screamed, and the sound of his scream sounded long and echoey and continued for what seemed an eternity, until it was finally reluctantly swallowed up by time and distance.

We all just stood there, aghast, for long moments.

"Well, so much for *that* quest," said Brank finally. "Peace anyone?"

"You will leave," spoke the Dragon King icily. "You will all leave... immediately. Or suffer the consequences!" With a roll of his cape, he spun around and stomped off.

"I take it this means that the book cannot be retrieved," said Dyrk Ryonne.

"Lost!" cried the Dragon Kind. "It and your leaders — lost forever. Now be gone!"

The dragons glowered down, underscoring his command with menace.

Chapter Twenty-Four

The exit of Doctor Ricknow and Professor Escutcheon had not only been spectacular, but climactic. It was the end of the road, the curtain to the quest, and certainly the finish of *my* mission. There would be no film shot here now — no work for me. Nonetheless, I didn't feel cheated.

As we trekked back through this marvelous, enchanted land — this time with a fuller, better knowledge of its true nature and meaning, I was not only able to understand it better, but enjoy it more.

And with Ricknow's presence less perceivable, and the Dark University's power less because of his presumed demise, things seemed — well, lighter, freer.

The journey went quickly without many adventures, and by the time we arrived back in their homeland, Brank and Lucinda had achieved somewhat of a peaceful co-existence, thus increasing the romance of their relationship.

As for this land as well, even as we walked through the fields, we could see green shoots and blooms. Ricknow indeed had been holding the controls of the curse on the land — and now it was gone. Escutcheon had been successful in the mission he'd originally presented to him. His other, secret agenda had of course not come to pass — there would be no motion picture utilizing Hypotropia as a backdrop, its peoples and beings as characters and extras. There would be no new manipulation of any earthly mass mind to change reality here. That had already been accomplished in a much more direct manner.

Thelonius and Quenton were extremely cooperative and deferential all the way back. They took pains to show that not only were their magical ways mended, but they promised that never, ever again would they allow an individual to bend them to his will the way Escutcheon had. As we had all been essentially fooled by the elf, there were no real charges made, although from time to time Brank would glower at the pair and whack his sword down significantly, grumbling about ridding troublesome magicians from the countryside. This appeared to be enough, and most of the conversation from the two during the journey seemed to be about the changes that would be made in their University now that Professor Escutcheon was gone.

Personally, I was very pleasant and understanding with the men. After all, it was them I depended upon to get me back to Los Angeles. Without them, I'd be stuck here, with no way to get back to Earth. I was quite glad they hadn't toppled into that hole with Escutcheon and Ricknow, or gobbled up by some dragon, and I kept a close watch to make sure that Brank's temper didn't dispatch them during the trip. I even cultivated their good will somewhat. By the time we got back, we'd even played a few games of cards by the campfire.

As for Hypernius — well, Lucinda was in a bit of a pickle about the young dragon. She'd promised to make certain that he'd be returned to the Cracked Cask, but the Dragon King had demanded that the Dragon stay. I missed him on the journey back. I'd felt no stirrings of my 'Dragon Bond' during my stay at Dragon Realm, except for with Hypernius and though it had certainly gotten me into trouble, it had felt true and natural, and I'd rather wanted to explore it. Almost all of my questions concerning it remained unanswered. I could only assume that it cause lay somewhere deep in the depth-psychology scenario that Purrvis had painted for me. Nonetheless, it felt as though there was something else going on, something even more subterranean in my psyche. Now I would probably never know the full truth. Except, perhaps, in my dreams.

"Oh well," said Lucinda. "I can live without the Cracked Cask. Who knows — in a couple of years Hypy may show up to take up his post again by that door."

"In a couple of years, Hypy will be *too big.*" Brank shrugged. "No problem. I'll just explain to the owner that Hypy will be back any day. And who knows — maybe that won't be a lie!"

Back at the College I was given my old room back and I slept quite well.

The next morning, after breakfast, Quenton Quintabulous came to me.

"I believe that we'll have the door ready for you this afternoon, Master Ralph. Would that be a convenient time for departure?"

"Sure," I said.

I had to say my good-byes first, and that would give me plenty of time.

I scheduled lunch for Brank and Lucinda and myself at the Cracked Cask. So far apparently the owner still thought that Hypernius was going to show up at any time.

We met there early and we were scheduled to head for the 'Door' late — I wanted it to be a long good-bye, and I didn't fancy much the notion of facing Los Angeles again without a bellyful of good beer.

"Look, Ralph," said Lucinda, buttering a hunk of coarse bread. "Why do you have to leave at all? Just this morning I was talking to the Dean at the University. He's absolutely ebullient with the changes that have happened, and he needs more teachers now. In fact, it looks as though I'm going to be one myself. Why not you too, hmm?"

"That's very nice of you," I said. "But this really isn't my world..."

"It is according to what you said before!" Brank pointed out already boisterous with the good beer and haunch of cold mutton with mint sauce we were dining upon. Heady fare for a once depressed town!

"On some deep level maybe I'm part of the creation. But let's not get into metaphysics here. There's a lot I miss about my world. After all, it is my home."

"You realize you'll probably never have the opportunity to come back again," said Lucinda looking at me in an odd way.

"Perhaps my decision might have different — if things had been different here." I told her.

She just looked away, sipping at her beer morosely. I'd noticed a cooling on her part toward Brank that he himself apparently had not, but I wasn't the sort who was going to stay around long to see if it came to anything.

Besides, there was stuff, I was sure, to take care of back at my North Hollywood apartment.

We spent a long and affable lunch, drinking and joking and generally feeling in good spirits. Brank bluffly refused to think that we'd never see each other again — or maybe, as usual, he just refused to think. When he left finally to relieve himself, Lucinda leaned over toward me and said simply, "I'm sorry things did not turn out as they might have... in many respects."

I just shrugged. "That's the way it goes, isn't it?"

I felt as though maybe I should have coughed up something more eloquent there, but I just couldn't manage it. I looked into her eyes and she smiled slightly and demurely and I thought, well, that's enough of that. No regrets. Who knows — she may have chewed me up alive and spit me out. At least now I feel as though this very strange adventure has left me a better man.

"Yes, yes, I suppose it is," and she looked away.

Brank came back, we resumed drinking, and finally I had to excuse myself.

"We really should be getting back to the University," I said. "The door's supposed to be ready for me . . . and I should be pushing off."

Brank shrugged. "I think you should stay longer, but it's your life. Why you don't want to stick around and drink and go off adventuring with me, I'll never know. Sounds like the way of life here — especially now that this damned curse has been lifted, is *far* more appealing."

"Oh yes, it really is — but for how long? Like I said, it's not my home — I have to go back and deal with things there, confront things — I have learned here. . . . It's like I've been rummaging around in my own brain."

"Oh truly? What have you learned?"

I shrugged. "If I've learned only that I should value my imagining more, and their power and importance in the universe. . . . Isn't that enough?"

Brank had to agree. "Well, good luck to you. If good things happen here, I'll know you've been a successful writer. Right, darling?" He gave her a slobbery smack on the cheek.

"Right, Brank," said Lucinda, making a face.

I didn't care to get involved in whatever was going on there, so I simply stepped through the door.

The smell of fire. The leathery flap of wings. A roar and an eager yip.

"Hypernius," I said.

The dragon squatted there in his old place affably, looking as though he'd like to lick my face but wisely deciding not to. Instead I walked up and rubbed his neck and patted him in the manner that I'd learned he'd liked.

"Hypy!" said Lucinda as she walked out. She ran out and threw her arms around his neck hugging him. "How'd you get away from that grumpy old — well, never mind. It's so good you came back. I thought maybe you might."

Brank was grinning. "Well! So much for your worries. And you made good on your promise, Bash. Hypernius is back, and you're square with the innkeeper. You won't be restricted from the Cracked Cask."

"That's not why I'm happy to see Hypy, you oaf. I'm just plain happy he's come back. I just hope everything is all right back at the Dragon Realm. Old Ricknow and Escutcheon haven't crawled up from the depths, have they?"

Hypernius wasn't talking, as usual, but I got no negative feelings from him.

Lucinda suggested that I might want to try a dragon-bond, but I demurred.

"I really have to get back . . . and beside, the last time I tried that I got just a trifle bit sidetracked."

I contented myself with another pat on the creature's head and then bid him farewell.

"Take care, pal. And be good!"

Hypernius looked at me with sad, confused eyes as though to say, "Hey — you're the reason I'm here!"

But I turned around and walked back toward the university, not looking back.

I wanted to get out of here while the getting was good — otherwise, I was afraid if I lingered even an extra fifteen minutes, I'd stay forever.

*T*here it was before me — the door.

An arid breeze wafted through it, redolent of the sage of Tree People Park. I had an excellent view of the canyon, and beyond it the smoggy graph of streets that was the San Fernando Valley.

"Well, that's it," said Thelonius, tumbling down into an overstuffed chair, knocking off a doily in the process. He wagged an exhausted hand toward the aperture between dimensions. "Better step on through. I don't know how long our spell is going to last."

Quenton Quintabulous looked up from the smoky dregs of their magic workings. "I'd listen to the fellow if I were you, Ralph."

I nodded acknowledgment. "Just one moment." I spun around and whipped out a hand, grasping up Brank's meaty hand and pressing it firmly. "Thank you, good friend."

"Awh, you'll be back, Ralph," said the red-cheeked man, beaming. He whacked me across the back. "You won't be able to get this place out of your head."

"All too true," said Lucinda. "Especially if this place is *from* his head — and the heads of other people from his world."

Brank shrugged. "I don't care where we come from. The beer is good here."

"'I drink, therefore I am,' — the philosopher!" laughed Lucinda. She turned a more thoughtful face my way. "Well then. Good-bye, Ralph."

"Good-bye, Lucinda."

She stepped up and put her arms around me and kissed me, long and deep.

It was wonderful. It felt delicious and ripe and right.

When she stepped away her eyes were a little glazed. From tears. I didn't know . . . I couldn't deal with the emotion.

"Take care," I said, and I walked toward the door.

"Dream of me, Ralph!" I heard Lucinda say, just as I stepped through the portal. I heard a rushing wind behind me, a crack of mending filaments of reality and when I turned around I saw one last whisper of her face and then the door shuddered and zipped up tight and seamless against the blue of the sky and the path to the Hypotropia was no more.

Epilogue

Fortunately, no rock creature awaited me there in the Santa Monica Mountains, and no hiker noticed my sudden return. The sun was just dipping into afternoon, and the trails were clear.

I sat down on a boulder and gazed of the brushy canyon for a moment collecting myself.

When I felt better, I began to hike back up to the parking lot.

My car was gone. I hadn't given it much thought, though I must say I wasn't surprised. I'd been gone for weeks and the park police probably had it towed. It would cost to get it out, but I'd worry about that when the time came.

Just as well anyway. I'd had a few beers at the Cask and really shouldn't drive anyway.

You don't hitchhike these days in LA Far too dangerous.

So I just set off on foot.

It took me about forty five minutes to get down to Ventura and then I caught a RTD bus (eventually) back along Ventura Boulevard, changing on Vineland to head up through the area where my apartment was.

I'd always heard of culture shock but never truly experienced it until then. And who would have thought I would have experienced it in my own country.

Then again, every day in LA was culture shock, so I shouldn't have been surprised.

It was past four when I finally dragged myself through the courtyard with its palm trees, its cracked swimming pool, its ruined deck chairs. I swayed up the steps, managed to get my keys from my jeans out (how I ever managed to hang onto those through all my adventures I'll never know) and opened my door.

There were all kinds of notifications from my landlord of coming eviction unless I pay my rent. I kicked these aside, got a drink of water from the container on drinking water (not tap) in my refrigerator and then collapsed in my bed.

I must say, that bed with its beloved down pillow, was the welcomest thing so far about LA.

I immediately fell asleep.

If I dreamed any dreams, I don't remember them. Certainly I dreamed nothing about the world I'd just come from. It was as though my brain were just trying to shut it all out.

When I awoke, it was dark.

I got up, used the bathroom, and got another glass of water. I cooked a frozen Budget Gourmet dinner in the microwave and ate it while I watched a *Cheers* repeat.

I'd left my answering machine off, so I didn't bother to check that.

I went down and retrieved my mail from my stuffed box.

Nothing from my agent. Only rejections on the publishing front.

Lots of bills and warnings, etc., etc.

I picked up my phone and found that it had been turned off. I hadn't paid for that, either. I was just happy the electricity still worked.

So I walked down to the local 7-Eleven, bought some comic books and a twelve pack of Coors, and walked back.

I popped a beer, turned the television back on, and settled in for a nice comfortable depression.

I couldn't read, though, and I couldn't watch TV. I ended up in front of my computer, writing notes for a fantasy screenplay about a guy who gets suckered into traveling to a fantasy world to write a screenplay.

Somehow it all seemed too far-fetched.

I was halfway through it when I took a break and watched the repeat of the Channel 5 news. Nothing much had changed in this world, it seemed. Wars, recessions, poverty, crime, and violence. The dreamings of mankind seemed so much more interesting than their grim realities.

Someone knocked on the door.

I looked at clock. Who could it be at past one thirty at night? Not my landlord to collect . . . surely.

Still, I used my peephole.

"Yes?"

"Ralph, you idiot. Open up, okay? I don't like it much out here!"

I opened up, shocked beyond words.

Lucinda stepped through me, striding into the living room, looking around with her hands on her hips with disapproval. "Hmm. This place needs some redecorating. And some books, too. I think I might be able to help you out."

"Bash . . . I mean, Lucinda. . . . What are you doing here?"

"Are you going to just stand there and hold that beer in your hand without giving me one?"

Wordless I went to the fridge, got her one, and handed it to her.

"How do you open this infernal thing?"

"Oh, sorry."

I popped it for her.

"Don't I get a glass or something?"

I got her a glass and poured for her too.

"Hmm. Too cold and far too thin."

"It's the popular style here, I guess."

She sipped for a moment, looking at me in a curious way. "Oh well, like you say, when in Rome —"

"We're in LA, not Rome . . ."

"So you think you can put me up for a while?" she asked, grinning.

"Sure . . . but how . . . why?"

She shrugged. "I figured I had a place to stay here . . . I'd always wanted to see it. Those magicians got the door open for me . . . I'd dug your address out of Escutcheon's papers — along with some very interesting other stuff, I might add." She indicated the bag on her back, then pulled it off and set it on the couch. "We'll have an curious time going through it, I think."

A moment of uneasy, charged silence stood between us, and then a slow flicker of a smile came on her face.

"And," she said with a short burst of breath, slapping her palms helplessly against her thighs, "I figure, for all we traveled together — maybe we didn't get to know each other well enough. Maybe we need a little more time."

I nodded. "I wasn't me for a good portion of that time."

"So what do you say, my friend?" She flopped down onto the couch and crossed her leg. "I get to bunk here for a while? See the sights?"

There was no other way I could tell her how happy I was to see her: I walked over, pulled her up, put my arms around her and kissed her.

"You can bunk where you like, Bash!"

She kissed me again. "Good."

We kissed long and hard, and when we came up for air, she said, "Oh, by the way. I brought along some manuscripts in that bag, too. I never told you, but I'm a writer too. Maybe we can collaborate on something."

"Sure." We collaborated on a kiss.

It was about all I could take, and I was about to drag her off into my bedroom, when she pulled away.

"Oh. One little problem."

"What?"

"Come here." She pulled me to the window by the courtyard, opened the drapes, and pointed down by the pool. "There."

I looked down into the darkness. At first I couldn't see anything, but then the shadows moved and I discerned the flap of a wing and a piece of a large reptilian head, the gleam of a curious eye cocked up toward me.

"Don't worry. I told him to be very quiet," she said. "He really did want to come along with me, though."

I shrugged and sighed.

Life was still to have its larger problems for me, it seemed. But then, dragons did seem to be my destiny.

Printed in the United States
1776